TWO OF A KIND

"Oh, my God!" Nora screamed.

Sam braked to a stop so suddenly, they would have hit the windshield if they hadn't had their seat belts buckled. He turned to Nora, who continued to scream.

"What is it? What's wrong?"

"That!" Nora yelled as she fought to release the catch on her seat belt. "That! That!"

"What!"

Still screaming, she pointed. Sam looked, and then he screamed too. A large black tarantula was perched exactly halfway between them. Throwing open the doors, they bailed out, ran around to the front of the car, and clutched each other.

"Spider!" cried Nora.

"Really big spider!" Sam agreed.

Nora threw her arms around Sam's neck and he drew her closer. Somehow the hug turned into a long, hot, breathless, oh-my-God, this-is-totally-fantastic kiss that left them both senseless. . . .

BOOK YOUR PLACE ON OUR WEBSITE AND MAKE THE READING CONNECTION!

We've created a customized website just for our very special readers, where you can get the inside scoop on everything that's going on with Zebra, Pinnacle and Kensington books.

When you come online, you'll have the exciting opportunity to:

- View covers of upcoming books
- Read sample chapters
- Learn about our future publishing schedule (listed by publication month *and author*)
- Find out when your favorite authors will be visiting a city near you
- Search for and order backlist books from our online catalog
- Check out author bios and background information
- Send e-mail to your favorite authors
- Meet the Kensington staff online
- Join us in weekly chats with authors, readers and other guests
- Get writing guidelines
- AND MUCH MORE!

Visit our website at
http://www.kensingtonbooks.com

Sweet
Revenge

KATE CLEMENS

KENSINGTON BOOKS
Kensington Publishing Corp.
http://www.kensingtonbooks.com

PROLOGUE

When Nora Wynn pulled up in front of her office on Wednesday, the reporters were waiting for her.

"Ms. Wynn, all of L.A. knows you as the Queen of Revenge. How do you feel about that title, given what happened yesterday?"

"No comment," said Nora.

"Do you have any regrets about starting a business called Payback Time?"

"No comment."

"Do you think your advice may have inspired your former client to murder her husband?"

"I'm not going to talk about the murder. There's an investigation going on. All I'm going to say is that I'm not being charged as an accessory either before or after the fact. Now if you'll excuse me . . ." She pushed past them and entered her building.

She paused in the lobby and braced herself for what was waiting for her upstairs.

Those reporters don't know the half of it, she thought.

What a fool she'd been. If she could jump into a time machine, she'd go back to last April and stop this whole mess before it started.

1

Sam Gallo finished off the last of the Red Bull and stood for a moment on the big, psychedelic letters that spelled out VENICE. Then he walked toward the beach. The surf was hitting the sand in long, slow rollers, nibbling at the feet of the lifeguard stand, which looked like an alien landing craft surrounded by seagulls. Behind him, Sam could hear the nonstop noise of the boardwalk: the scrape and whoosh of the skateboarders, the ringing of bicycle bells, the cries of the merchants who hawked T-shirts, tattoos, and incense. The low-rider cars parked on the concrete pad were silent, but he could feel them back there, clustered in a tight circle like a flock of gaudily colored metal birds.

Sam was doing research for a documentary film on low-riders, and he had to finish up before the drivers broke for lunch, so as soon as the caffeine from the Red Bull hit his brain, he turned around and tossed the empty can into one of the red and yellow trash barrels that lined the boardwalk. The barrels were so bright they could probably be seen by ships at sea. This one had big circles on it that looked like eyes, but Sam didn't waste any time admiring either the barrel or his own skill. His ability to sink every shot had been the stuff of legend when he was in high school. It had transformed him from a lonely social outcast to a minor hero his junior year and had been the only reason he'd made the varsity team even though he was two inches under the six-foot height limit. Now, at thirty, he still had perfect aim.

As he hurried back toward the cement pad where the low-riders were parked, several women gave him appraising glances. Sam wasn't by any means the best-looking guy on the beach this morning, but he had brown hair that curled lazily over his forehead, hazel eyes, a wedge-shaped face, and a neatly trimmed red beard that made him look a little devilish. Since he usually couldn't come up with enough cash to hire a grip, he had to lug around his own film equipment, which gave him great biceps. He was smart too; plus he really liked women, and women, with one notable exception, liked Sam.

The exception was Sam's ex-wife, Nora, whom Sam, to his surprise, now saw skating down the bike trail toward him. He knew a visit from her didn't mean good news, but he was so struck by how great she looked in the little blue and red spandex outfit she'd poured herself into that he temporarily forgot that the two of them couldn't occupy the same space for five minutes without squabbling like two-year-olds.

Sam watched as Nora swirled with liquid grace, avoiding fire eaters, tourists, and weight lifters: long blond hair blowing in the wind, all arms and legs like a newborn colt. Although he knew he was out of his mind to think of her as anything but a sparring partner, he found himself feeling the same old protective tenderness he'd always felt toward her.

He really hoped she wouldn't fall or collide with anyone. She'd only taking up roller-blading a year ago when she'd started dating that fitness nut, Jason; and despite all the twirls and flourishes, she was a little unsteady at times. Sam's mother, Lucia, who kept in touch, had told him that Nora and Jason did all sorts of adventurous things together: parasailing, hang-gliding, mountain climbing, deep-sea diving, even bungee jumping. Although Sam had never met Jason, he loathed him on principle. Clearly Nora thought Jason was more exciting than Sam had ever been.

The look on Nora's face as she approached was more wary than friendly. Sam snapped back to reality. She wasn't his problem. Sure he felt some affection for her, but it was the kind of sentimental nostalgia a guy feels for his high school girlfriend. Nora had actually been his girlfriend in high school, although not technically a "girlfriend." She was a popular senior in his prebasketball hero days when he had arrived as a geeky sophomore, armed with his first video camera and a thick New York accent that made him the butt of a lot of stupid practical jokes. He'd always been grateful to her for befriending him back then, but they should have left it at that.

Suddenly, he realized he'd been staring at her like a kid looking at candy. He gave himself a swift kick in the butt for stupidity, reminded himself that he'd been over her for years, and turned to look at the low-rider cars as if he hadn't seen her coming.

Low-riders had been part of Chicano culture for decades. The owners, who were mostly young men, bought classic cars and installed hydraulic lifts at each wheel so any corner could be raised and lowered at will. Then they gave the body a custom paint job. The 1967 Chevy Caprice directly in front of Sam had shiny chrome hubcaps and imitation leopard skin upholstery. Bright orange flames ran down both sides, making it look as if it were doing ninety even when it was parked. On the hood, Caesar Chavez shook hands with the Virgin of Guadalupe; on the trunk the owner had painted a postapocalyptic L.A. taken over by a jungle that featured monkeys, snakes, and Mayan pyramids. Sam loved low-rider cars and intended to make a film about them as soon as he could get together enough cash to start shooting. This one was a work of art. It should have been in the Louvre.

He felt Nora come up behind him and skate to a stop. The musky smell of her perfume enfolded him. She'd never used perfume when they were married. She'd been a no-makeup, unscented-soap, just-wash-your-hair-and-shake-it-out kind of girl.

"Hi, Sam," she said. "You're not an easy man to find."

Sam turned around slowly, his face carefully fixed in an expression that conveyed neither eagerness nor hostility, simply a vague friendliness. "Hi," he said. He wondered what had inspired her to seek him out this morning. They hadn't spoken in a long time. A year, maybe.

"Thinking of buying a new car?"

"No." Her question was probably totally innocent, but nearly everything Nora said to him always felt like an invitation to go ten rounds without a referee. When they broke up, she had made him take their old brown Toyota Corolla station wagon because she hated stick shifts. Since his career as a documentary film director hadn't yet taken off in a big way, he was still driving it. He reminded himself that, unless his mother had paid her a visit recently, there was no way Nora could know that he had about as much chance of buying a new car as becoming the first tourist on the upcoming Russian expedition to Mars. She probably thought he had finally recovered from that fiasco with the South American adventure tour company and was making films on interesting topics. At least he hoped she did.

In the last four years, he had made a pretty decent living directing commercial, industrial, and educational films, and even managed to shoot two serious short subjects—one about after-school recreation programs for at-risk teens and one about Mixtec farm workers—but he was saving everything he made to do the low-rider film, which meant he was hardly rolling in spare cash.

"So how have you been?" she asked.

"Fine," Sam said cautiously. He wished he could talk to her without feeling as if she'd jabbed him in the stomach with a cattle prod. Even when they'd been in love, they'd always rubbed each other the wrong way. Five minutes after they got married, they'd had an argument about whether or not to rent a motel room or save the money and go back to the campground.

He decided he was being childish. "I'm thinking about doing a documentary on low-riders." He smiled at her and she smiled back. Nora's smile was radiant. There was no other word for it. Sam felt warning bells go off in his head. He had always been a sucker for her smile.

"Paid gig?" she asked.

He came back to reality again with a jolt. "No. I'm still trying to raise the money to start shooting."

"Oh."

Sam hated that "oh." Money had never been important to Nora, so she probably didn't really care whether he was being paid or not. But he suspected that "oh" implied she believed he had failed to get his life together and was wasting his time dreaming about unrealistic projects.

He found himself wondering how she'd tracked him

down and why she'd gone to the trouble of ambushing him on the boardwalk this morning. But of course, Nora could track down anyone who hadn't gone into a witness protection program. She ran one of the hottest match-making services in L.A., which meant she knew the name, and probably the Social Security number, of every available bachelor from Camarillo to San Clemente. She'd started the business after they got divorced, and in his mellower moods, Sam had liked to think she'd done it because she'd couldn't find anyone to replace him. That was before she met Jason, who was scheduled to replace Sam permanently in a couple of weeks.

In Sam's opinion, Nora was making a big mistake marrying the guy, but, hey, it was her life and if she wanted to live it with a rich-boy real estate developer with a pretty face who liked to play "sensitive" while he reamed the environment, well, Sam sincerely hoped they'd be very happy together.

He wiped the sweat off his forehead, readjusted his baseball cap, and decided that, as much as he enjoyed looking at her in the skating outfit, it was time to get this encounter over with as fast as possible.

"So what brings you here this morning?" He had a pretty good suspicion she hadn't dropped by to hand him a wedding invitation.

"Remember that piece of land we bought near Borrego Springs with the money your grandmother left you?"

Sam remembered it only too well. During the only spring of their six-month marriage, they'd gone on a camping trip to Anza-Borrego. It had been a rainy year, and the desert had been in bloom with yellow dandelions from horizon to horizon. They'd both fallen in love with the desert—it was one of the few things they ever agreed on—so they'd pooled some cash Nora had saved and a small inheritance from Sam's grandmother and bought themselves a piece of land for next to nothing, only to discover that it rained hard enough to make the flowers bloom about once every ten years, if that. Purchasing the land had been a rash thing to do, particularly since they'd had so little money at the time. They'd never been able to sell it, and probably wouldn't be able to until the next deluge. Technically, it was the only thing they still owned together.

Nora took a little red pack off her back, opened it, and pulled out some official-looking papers. "Jason doesn't think I should have financial entanglements with you, particularly not real estate. And I agree."

Sam felt his suspicion meter peg at one hundred. If Jason wanted him to sign over that worthless hunk of desert to Nora, someone had probably struck oil on it. Not that Nora would know that. Sam had lived with her long enough to know that she was honest—too honest sometimes.

Was there anything to be gained by refusing to sign? Should he tell her he had to talk to a lawyer first? The thought of calling a lawyer made Sam shudder. Dealing with those guys was like tossing money in a shredder. Plus, he still cared enough about Nora not to want to drag her through legal hassles. Also, it would probably be impossible to figure out what Jason was up to. *What the heck?* he thought. *Let her have the property for old times' sake. A wedding present from husband number one.*

"This," Nora continued, "is a transfer of title."

"Where do I sign?"

"Here and here. Both copies." She handed him the papers and a pen. Sam signed.

She looked surprised. "Don't you want to read it first?"

"Why should I? Enjoy. Build that cabin we always talked about. I hear Jason's rich enough to afford air-conditioning."

"What are you talking about?

"The land: that 1.2 acres of rock, rattlesnakes, and creosote bushes I just signed over to you."

Nora smiled at him with the kind of tolerant affection a teenage kid might get from his mother when he told her he'd decided to be a poet instead of going to law school. This was not the smile that made Sam go mushy in the head. It was the same smile that had annoyed the hell out of him when he was a lonely sophomore and she was a popular senior. "You really should read legal documents before you sign them, Sam."

Sam bristled. "Why? What's the point?"

"The point is, you didn't just sign the title over to *me*. I signed it over to *you*. You own the Borrego Springs property free and clear now."

Sam suddenly felt ashamed of himself. He didn't know what to say. "Sorry," he murmured.

"Sorry for what?"

"Sorry for thinking Jason was trying to rip me off."

Nora frowned and gave an exasperated sigh. "You know, you might have found a more diplomatic way to express that thought. Oh, what the hell? Look, Sam, I have an idea: let's stop fighting."

"Great," Sam said. "How do you propose we manage that?"

"Simple: we part friends and agree never to speak to each other again."

"We've tried that before, and it hasn't worked."

"Well, let's try harder. You pretend I don't exist, and I'll pretend you don't exist. Okay?"

"Sounds like a plan." Sam paused and then grinned devilishly. "So, I take it this means that in the future I won't have to listen to you remind me that only hairy barbarians leave toilet seats up?"

"Don't start." Nora stuck out her hand. "Just say yes."

"Okay, yes, it's a deal." As Sam took her hand, he was

bushwhacked by an unexpected pang of regret. He and Nora were so incompatible that their brief marriage had been the matrimonial equivalent of being abducted by aliens, but still he felt saddened by the thought that this might be the last time he'd see her: even though she drove him crazy, even though he definitely wasn't still in love with her, and even though he knew at least half a dozen women who were just as pretty, just as smart, and a hell of a lot easier to get along with.

Maybe he was imprinted on her the way baby ducks were imprinted on their mothers. Or maybe Nora put out some kind of special pheromone that made him want to smack up against her like a moth hitting a porch light. If he ever made enough money to hire a therapist, he might try to figure out the attraction. Meanwhile, he decided, he'd take her advice and work on forgetting she existed.

Nora folded up her copy of the title transfer, stowed it in her backpack, and gave him one of her good smiles. "Bye," she said sweetly; and without another word, she turned and skated away.

2

Three weeks after she signed the Anza-Borrego property over to Sam, Nora walked through the wrought-iron gateway that led to her Santa Monica office with the confident stride of a general. She'd driven to Venice and spent her lunch hour shopping in the upscale stores on Main Street. In the bags she carried were four pairs of perfect shoes. Shoes were Nora's one weakness—well, the only one she was willing to admit in public. Emelda Marcos had nothing on her. If she kept buying sling-back heels and cute little suede pumps at her present rate, sometime in the near future she was going to have to convert her entire house into a shoe closet.

She paused in the courtyard for a moment to admire the flowers before she went inside. Nora was in the business of selling romance, and romantic buildings weren't that easy to find in L.A., but this was another of her successes. Formerly an old hotel constructed about the time movies started talking, it was built in the Spanish hacienda style, with a walled-in garden that she had personally filled with star jasmine, purple sage, scarlet dahlias, and plants that bloomed all year long; not because she was a great gardener, but because she hired a landscaping service whose job it was to ensure that her clients never caught sight of anything dead. In the center was a marble fountain composed of three basins ringed by lions' heads. Water was pouring out of the mouths of the lions, making a pleasant splashing sound.

Nora smiled at the lions, which had clearly been made by someone who had never seen a real lion since they looked more like a trio of Saint Bernards. "Hi, boys," she said. Logically, being in the matchmaking business, she should have had cupids, but some idiot had decided that all fountain cupids should represent little boys peeing, and Nora figured that wasn't the message she wanted to send.

After her divorce from Sam, she'd become very practical about romance. Day after day, she worked with people who pursued love with less common sense than rabbits. On more than one occasion, a high-powered female corporate lawyer had sat in her office weeping uncontrollably over some cute guy in tight white pants who had cleaned out her swimming pool and then gone on to clean out her bank account. Older men often demanded to be matched with women younger than their own daughters, only to reappear in Nora's office a week or two later sporting back braces after skiing accidents or salsa-dancing disasters. Left-wing Democrats seemed to have a fatal attraction to right-wing Republicans; Buddhists fell for Baptists; vegetarians lost their hearts to chain-smokers. In other words, there appeared to be no limit to the mistakes you could make if you followed your hormones instead of your head, which was where Nora's matchmaking service came in. If you wanted to avoid years of group therapy, date people who hadn't done time in prison, and find someone you were compatible with, you came to Love Finds a Way.

After she waved to the lions, Nora's day remained perfect while she crossed what had once been the lobby of the hotel and walked upstairs. Then, abruptly, it stopped being perfect, and became filled with the usual hassles.

Caroline and Felicity, her two assistants, were standing outside her office door with Amber, the new bookkeeper, lurking in the background like an underpaid extra. There was a sense of drama in the air, and Nora immediately knew that whatever they were about to tell her wasn't going to be welcome news.

Felicity and Caroline were currently not only Nora's employees but her two best friends. Nora always put the word "currently" in front of the "best friends" description, because people moved in and out of L.A. so fast that half the time, just when you were getting to like someone, you found yourself at the airport waving good-bye to her as she passed through security.

Nora's friendship with Caroline and Felicity was proving more durable. For several years, she had played poker with them on dateless Saturday nights, cheered them on when love loomed on the horizon, and shopped for stylish shoes with them when life seemed impossibly grim. They knew everything there was to know about Nora's search for the perfect man that had ended with her finding Jason; and she knew everything worth knowing about Caroline's relationship with her late husband, George, and Felicity's string of unhappy love affairs with married men.

"She's here, in your office, waiting for you," Caroline whispered as soon as Nora got within whispering range. Caroline, who had been widowed at a young age, was fifty-four with no children and two badly spoiled, overfed golden retrievers. Before Nora hired her to handle Love Finds a Way's older, more marriage-minded clients, she had read scripts at Paramount. Caroline had started working at the studio when disaster films like *Towering Inferno* were the craze, and she still retained a love for devastating surprises. She made her announcement as if it were a particularly entertaining disaster film that featured tidal waves, alien invasions, and lots of special effects.

Nora froze, then slowly placed her shopping bags on the nearest table next to a vase of long-stemmed yellow roses. "Who's here?" she asked. As if she didn't know.

Caroline played along. "Your mother-in-law."

"Oh," Amber said brightly, "how nice."

Nora gave Amber a stony glare and immediately regretted it. Amber was a milky-faced redhead with freckles and big eyes. She was young, quiet, shy, and rarely showed this much enthusiasm. She was a gem of a bookkeeper. Nora had only hired her two months ago, and she wanted to keep her.

"I thought Jason's mom and dad weren't flying in from Wyoming until next week," Amber continued, digging herself in deeper.

Felicity shot Amber a warning glance. "This isn't Jason's mother."

"Oh?" Amber looked at Felicity with wide-eyed confusion. "But I thought you said Nora's mother-in-law was in—"

"Technically," Nora interrupted, "I don't have a mother-in-law."

"Tell *her* that," Caroline said, gesturing toward the office door.

"Legally, morally, and personally I don't have a mother-in-law," Nora continued, "and I won't have one for another five days."

"That's not what *she* says." Felicity delivered this line with suitable drama. Pretty, but not quite pretty enough, she had spent several years trying to make it big in the movies before she gave up and got a real job at Love Finds a Way. She handled the twenty-somethings, with occasional forays into the early thirty-somethings. She had a real instinct for matchmaking, possibly because she was nearly delusionally romantic—a handicap in ordinary life, perhaps, but a real plus in the singles business. A walking romance novel, Felicity never tired of the drama of boy meets girl, or girl meets girl, or boy meets boy. Like many matchmaking services these days, Love Finds a Way didn't discriminate.

Nora gave an exasperated sigh and rolled her eyes. "God help me. What did I do to deserve to be stalked by a fifty-eight-year-old Italian mama, particularly one I like?" She turned to Amber. "Tell me the truth: do I look skinny? Do I look like a bag of bones?"

"No," Amber said timidly. "You look great. You always look great, Nora. You look like . . ." She fumbled for a comparison. "Cameron Diaz."

That was a whopper of a lie, but Nora was in no mood to argue. In L.A., whenever you asked someone how you looked, they always compared you to a movie star. Besides, Nora did look a little like Cameron Diaz, particularly if you had severely impaired vision. The only difference between Nora and Cameron was that Cameron was thirty with blue eyes and an elegant, aristocratic nose; and Nora was thirty-two with brown eyes and a hopelessly cute turned-up Irish button.

Nora looked toward her office door again, and tried to plot her next move. "She's going to want to feed me," she said. "I know she is." Caroline and Felicity nodded. They'd both been through this before. Amber looked blank.

"She's going to tell me I look like a skeleton; and then she's going to say that I'm wasting away. As if I'd spent one moment wasting away over that son of hers. Has she brought food?"

"Homemade cannoli," Caroline said. "Plus something that smells like lasagna."

"The classic Italian all-cholesterol diet. Why am I

not surprised?" And with that, Nora walked into her office to face the inevitable.

She found her ex-mother-in law sitting in one of the comfortable padded chairs clients usually sat in when Nora did custom matchmaking interviews. Lucia had short dark hair, plump arms, a round happy face, and hazel eyes that were exactly like Sam's. She was thumbing through a copy of *L.A. Single Life,* the one with Nora on the cover. When Nora entered the room, she put the magazine down and gave Nora a warm smile that made Nora feel like a cross between an ungrateful child and a trapped rat.

"Daughter," she said affectionately.

Nora raised her hand. "Please, Lucia. Don't call me that."

"Why not? In my heart, you'll always be my daughter."

"Lucia, isn't it time you gave this up? Sam and I got divorced four years ago."

"Marriage is forever. In the eyes of God you're still my daughter." Lucia, a devout Catholic, was one of the few people Nora had met who took "until death do us part" literally. Sam's father, Aldo, was a labor lawyer who specialized in defending immigrants who worked for minimum wage. The two had been married for a good forty years, and appeared so happy with each other that Nora was sometimes tempted to ask them to act in a Love Finds a Way commercial. In many ways Lucia and Aldo reminded Nora of her own parents: two professors who were so much in love that they never noticed that they lived in a house filled with musty books, where every faucet leaked and no meal ever appeared on time. Nora often suspected herself of marrying Sam in the hope of being as happy as her parents and his. This was just the kind of romantic delusion she was always warning her clients about. When it came to a happy marriage, men were no more likely to resemble their fathers than women were to resemble their mothers; a fact she had learned the hard way.

She sat down at her desk and shuffled some client files around, stalling for time. Amber had recently organized all the hard copies of their records into color-coded folders: pink for matchmaking, blue for written correspondence, green for publicity, and so forth. Nora put the pink files in one pile, the blue ones in another, the green in a third. She liked things orderly. Actually she liked things at perfect right angles, but ever since Caroline warned her that this might be a symptom of O.C.D., Nora had resisted the urge to line her papers up in rows like soldiers.

She took a deep breath and looked up. Lucia was waiting expectantly. These conversations with her always went nowhere. Still Nora had to try. The trying would have been a whole lot easier if she hadn't liked Lucia so much and hadn't been secretly touched that she kept dropping in once or twice a year.

"Lucia, explain something to me: when Sam and I got married, you wouldn't recognize that I was his wife because we didn't have a church wedding. Now you won't recognize that we're divorced. Why is that?"

Lucia was a master at not answering questions directly, and besides she'd heard this one before. "Sam misses you," she said.

"He does not miss me. In fact the last time I saw him, we agreed that it would be better if we never spoke to each other again."

Lucia chose to pretend she had not heard that last sentence. "He works all the time."

"That's nothing new. He worked all the time when we were married. I once figured we ate something like three dozen dinners together in six months. Anyway, I'm glad to hear he's getting work."

Lucia sighed. "Work maybe, but his career's not

going well. Ever since you left him, he's been wasting his talent. I'm not saying it's your fault, Nora, but we both know he should be doing serious documentaries. Instead he's directing industrial and commercial films like *Golf Turf Maintenance* and *Upper Respiratory Infections*. I run a catering business. I feed directors. I see the drivel they're shooting these days. Sam could be another Pasolini or Les Blank if—"

Nora knew exactly what was coming after that "if." She had to nip this in the bud. "Lucia, Sam doesn't want to be another Pasolini or another Les Blank. He wants to be himself. Also, I didn't leave him, and he didn't leave me. We were married for less than a year, and we fought constantly. When he got that offer to go off to South America to direct adventure tour promos, I was about to start graduate school to get an MSW so I could do couples counseling. Our career goals were totally incompatible."

Lucia opened her mouth to object to the idea that two independent careers could break up a marriage, but Nora, who had heard this particular argument before, was too fast for her.

"It was the 1990s, Lucia, not the 1950s. I didn't feel like I could put my life on hold like some heroine in an Eisenhower administration sitcom and go traipsing off to the jungle to trip over poisonous snakes and swat mosquitoes. Sam needed money so he could stop directing commercials, and he didn't feel like he could afford to stick around until I got my degree. In the end, we left each other by mutual agreement. It's called no-fault divorce, and it's been legal in California since at least the mid-seventies. More to the point, I'm about to get married again in five days. And"—Nora decided to twist the dagger a little— "this time I'm having a church wedding."

Lucia sat back and looked at Nora sadly. "Do you love him?"

Nora chose to take this as a reference to Jason, although she knew Lucia meant Sam. "Of course." She pointed to her own face, smiling happily back at her from the cover of *L.A. Single Life*. "I'm a professional matchmaker, remember? Love Finds a Way's computerized database is the envy of the profession. I had the pick of every eligible bachelor in town. Jason's the cream of the crop. He's stunningly handsome, smart, witty, attentive. Also, he happens to be completely crazy about me. For example, he actually remembers my birthday: something that Sam could never quite master."

Nora had fallen in love with Sam for his kindness, his intelligence, his sense of humor, his quick wit, and his sexy good looks, but they had had a terrible time communicating with each other—so terrible that, in the end, none of the rest had mattered. The fact that he had forgotten her birthday and Valentine's Day had been one of the reasons they were no longer together—one of the smaller reasons, but a reason nevertheless. This, coupled with the fact that he had given her a set of socket wrenches for their first and only Christmas together, had convinced Nora that he had no idea who she was and never would.

"So this new fiancé of yours is perfect?" Lucia asked with a gentle sadness that made Nora feel as if she'd just kicked one of Caroline's golden retrievers. Nora took another deep breath and counted to ten.

"Well, of course not," she admitted. "Jason has his flaws like anyone else, but they're flaws I can live with." For a moment she was tempted to add that Jason was awesome in bed, but there were some things you couldn't say to a woman who had once been your mother-in-law, so she just smiled the perfectly confident smile she always gave her female clients when they asked if there were any men available who weren't married or gay. "Jason is the best. He and I had the most perfectly matched profiles I've ever run through the computer. I've never been happier."

Lucia looked at her thoughtfully. "So you love him?"

"What part of this don't you understand, Lucia? I know you don't want to hear this, but I adore him."

To her surprise, Lucia didn't try to talk her out of adoring Jason. She just looked at Nora thoughtfully and then reached for the pan of lasagna. "So," she said, "are you hungry?"

"Sure." Nora relaxed. The hard part of the conversation was over. Lucia was a wonderful cook, a whole lot better than Nora, which wasn't hard since Nora never ate anything she couldn't microwave. Nora loved to eat, but she hated to cook. She always took Lucia's visits as a sign from the gods that she should indulge herself. Lucia's lasagna was the payoff for having to listen to her talk about Sam.

Nora wondered if Lucia would keep dropping in with lasagna after she married Jason. Probably not. In many ways that would be a relief; but it would also be a pity. She had known Lucia ever since she was eighteen and liked her a lot. Often, after they got over the mandatory conversation about the divorce, they had interesting chats. Lucia's catering business took her to most of the film locations in town, and she knew all the gossip worth knowing. She was an intelligent woman, kindhearted to a fault. In fact her only flaw seemed to be her inability to face the fact that Nora and her son were totally incompatible.

"Here." Lucia handed Nora a plastic fork. "Dig in. You're eating Russell Crowe's leftovers."

Nora thanked her, took the fork, and stabbed a generous bite of Lucia's famous vegetarian lasagna. She might not miss Sam, but she was definitely going to miss his mother's cooking.

* * *

The rest of Nora's day was less eventful. She spent the morning and the early afternoon cloistered in her office doing interviews with private clients, one of whom entered by the back door wearing a scarf and sunglasses. Nora didn't specialize in matching up people who worked in the movie industry, but since the article about her service appeared in *L.A. Single Life,* more of them had been coming her way. At first, she'd been surprised. After all, why should famous stars and directors need a matchmaking service when they had every opportunity to meet people, not to mention their own fan clubs? But it turned out that some of the big names in Hollywood either didn't have the opportunities everyone thought they had, because they worked too hard to socialize, or they just didn't like what was out there, or, more surprising, they were terribly shy.

In deference to them, Nora had recently put a brass plaque on the wall behind her desk. The plaque read EVERY NIGHT I MAKE LOVE TO 25,000 PEOPLE; THEN I GO HOME ALONE. JANIS JOPLIN. Under this quotation, Nora had added the words IF JANIS HAD COME TO LOVE FINDS A WAY, WE'D HAVE FOUND HER A MATCH. It was a cheap shot, but Nora's VIP clients loved it, particularly since Joplin's music was currently undergoing a revival among the twenty-somethings.

At three, Nora checked back in with Caroline and Felicity to see if anything needed to be attended to, but as usual they had everything in hand including Nora's wedding gown, which had arrived by messenger. Since she'd sent it out to have the skirt shortened, Nora needed to try it on; so she climbed in with some help from Felicity and paraded around the office while everyone made admiring comments.

Nora had married Sam wearing a Grateful Dead T-shirt and a pair of stone-washed blue jeans. This time

she had vowed to do things right. She had shopped for
weeks until she found a gown so spectacular that she
felt a romantic flutter every time she looked at it. A copy
of a Victorian wedding dress, it had a satin bodice,
thirty satin-covered buttons up the back, a full skirt,
and a keyhole neckline trimmed with delicate wisps of
Brussels lace. The dress had cost a fortune, but she didn't
give a damn. This time she was marrying the right man,
and she had a computer printout to prove it.

At three-thirty, she took off her wedding dress, selected a suit from the half dozen or so she kept in a
closet in her office, redid her hair and makeup, and
headed for Hollywood to host an afternoon express dating party composed of forty hopeful singles between the
ages of twenty-one and thirty-six, plus a few older men
looking for younger women, and one older professional
woman who had stated on her client profile that she
liked "young guys with the shrink wrap still on them."

Few women in L.A. wore suits to an afternoon social event, but Nora favored them because, in her opinion, if the jacket was well tailored and the skirt was
short enough, they gave off just the right combination
of sexiness and independence; plus, unfortunately for
the backs of women everywhere, most men were suck-
ers for high heels.

She pulled up in front of the Sunset Room just as the
caterers were arriving with the hors d'oeuvres. Nora
hadn't invented express dating, but she had refined it to
an art by subdividing her clients into specialty groups.
Today's batch had all checked the box marked *strong
interest in food*. In the next two hours, each of them
would meet and talk to at least ten prospective dates
while consuming shrimp on skewers, toast rounds smeared with French pâtés, and other tasty tidbits guaranteed
not to drip, stick in their teeth, or give them bad breath.

Nora checked out the inside and was pleased to see

that the tables had already been set up. There were fresh flowers and candles since the place was rather dark, and small bowls of gold-wrapped chocolates and bread sticks for nervous eaters who couldn't wait for the hors d'oeuvres to arrive.

The Sunset was the perfect place to hold an event like this since it was empty during the day and could be rented for a reasonable price. Also it had the added cachet of being a spot where famous movie stars hung out. Of course the movie stars wouldn't show up until late this evening, if they showed up at all; but there was nothing like being able to tell people they were planting their derrieres in the same seat where Drew Barrymore had planted hers only hours ago to make them feel special.

Nora had one of the caterers help her place a table and chair on the raised platform that bordered the VIP room so she could have a full view of the crowd at all times. Then she sat down and pulled a green silk bag out of her purse. The bag was embroidered with purple dragons. From it, she extracted a small bowl-shaped Tibetan bell. She positioned the bell so it was in easy reach, surveyed the room one last time, and sat back, satisfied.

With a little luck, things would be routine from here on out. The rules of express dating were simple. A man and a woman would be placed at each table. Every twelve minutes, Nora would strike the bell, and they would shift to an adjoining table: men to the right, women to the left, forming a new couple. They were not allowed to ask each other where they lived, how much they made, or what they did for a living; but other than that, any question was fair game.

While they were getting to know each other, Nora would quietly wander among them listening for mismatches. At the first sign of serious trouble, she would separate the pair as quickly and discreetly as possible. This personal, hands-on approach was exhausting. As far as she knew, no other matchmaker in town did it as thoroughly as she did. But then no other matchmaker had such a high a percentage of satisfied clients.

The singles appeared and took their places at the tables. At five sharp, Nora stood up, explained the rules, and rang the bell for the first time to signal the start of the event. There was a burst of nervous laughter, as there always was whenever the singles shifted partners, and everyone rotated to form the first new pairs. Nora settled back to observe the results. Soon she would have to go down and wander from table to table listening for potentially fatal mismatches, but right now she figured she deserved a glass of ice-cold seltzer water with a twist of lime (she never drank alcohol when she was working), and three minutes of totally self-indulgent woolgathering. In her experience, it took at least five minutes for two total strangers to start hating each other, but she liked to leave a wide margin of safety.

Her three minutes were soon up. At the tables, everyone appeared to be having a good time. They were nervous, of course, because express dating was a nerve-racking experience, but even the shyest seemed to be trying to make a good impression; and at least three couples were already staring at each other as if they'd just won the lottery.

She spent two more hours watching for trouble, but there wasn't any worth mentioning. At seven sharp, she rang the bell for the last time, collected the preference cards, and wished everyone a good night. When she examined the cards, she was pleased to see that thirty-six of the forty singles had checked a box that indicated they would like to see at least one of their partners again. *Am I the best matchmaker in L.A. or what?* she thought.

As she climbed into her car and drove out of the parking lot, she congratulated herself on another job well done.

3

After the express dating party, Nora had agreed to meet Jason for dinner at the Bangkok-Xocimilco, a high-end Mexican-Thai place not far from her office. Nora was particularly fond of the bananas flambé, which always made their way down the little stream that ran in front of the tables like a burning Viking ship being sent off to Valhalla. The bananas were a special-order item, and when she arrived, she was pleased to see Jason was already in the process of asking the waiter to launch them in their direction after they'd finished the main courses.

"Hi, pumpkin," he said when he caught sight of her.

"Hi, sweetie pie," she replied, blowing him a kiss. Using pet names in public was seriously uncool, but they both liked doing it. Besides, they were getting married in a few days, and if you couldn't display affection for each other just before your wedding, when could you?

Nora sat down beside the food stream and ignored a boat of chicken sate that was floating past accompanied by a small dish of Mexican mole sauce. She stretched out her hand to Jason, who took it, turned it over, and planted a kiss on her palm. Once again, she congratulated herself for managing to take such a handsome man out of circulation. Jason was broad-shouldered and well muscled with a square face; dark, closely cropped hair; and teeth so naturally white that people often assumed he used peroxide gel on them. Amber probably would have said he looked like Ben Affleck, but Jason's face was saved from Affleck's too perfect symmetry by a broken nose, the souvenir of a skydiving accident, and rather large ears, which Nora found cute.

The truth was she found everything about Jason attractive, including the wild streak that made him skydive. At one time his wildness hadn't been limited to extreme sports. When he and Nora first got together, he'd confessed that in his early twenties he'd been something of a Don Juan. Fortunately, by the time he met Nora his bed-hopping days were in the distant past; but Nora could easily see what had made women fall all over him; and although she knew it wasn't a good idea to go around comparing husbands, she couldn't help thinking that he was significantly better looking than Sam.

"Have a hard day?" Jason asked, unaware that he had just won the Best-Looking-Husband Contest.

"Not bad." Nora gave him another smile and thought about all the intimate little dinners they'd be having together in the years to come. "The express dating party went off with no major problems." She decided not to tell him about the visit from Lucia. There was something a little weird about having your ex-mother-in-law dropping in on you with homemade lasagna a week before your wedding to husband number two. Jason never seemed to mind that Nora had been married to Sam, but she liked to spare him the details.

They sat for a moment gazing into each other's eyes while boats filled with lemon grass chicken salad and cilantro-stuffed fish tacos bobbed by, sending wonderful scents wafting in their direction. They had so much in common that sometimes when they were together, Nora felt as if she were looking into a mirror, which was just the way she'd planned things when she selected him from her own database.

She and Jason were both thirty-two-year-old, single, physically fit nonsmokers with a good sense of humor, who exercised at least three times a week, were allergic to cats, liked lobster better than steak, green better than blue, and coffee better than tea. Their favorite wine was Montepulciano d'Abruzzo; their favorite dessert (on occasions when they couldn't order flaming bananas), cheesecake. They preferred Italy to France; and loved movies, long walks on the beach, and lazy Sunday brunches, although they didn't get many of those because they both ran very successful businesses. At the time they started dating, they had both been looking for a monogamous relationship leading to a marriage that would include two children: a boy and a girl; their own if possible. But if they had any problem conceiving, they were both fine with the idea of adoption.

Actually, Jason had agreed to adopt so readily that Nora had been a bit startled. It wasn't what he'd said, but how he said it. At the time, she couldn't help thinking he sounded as if he intended to order the kids like ink-jet cartridges and have them shipped FedEx. But then she had reminded herself what a good heart he had and how easy he was to get along with. Also, although Jason didn't know it, he had a PGF of 9, which was about as good as it got. The PGF was the Potentially Good Father scale. Nora had hired a psychologist from UCLA to create it for female clients whose biological clocks were ticking. No other matchmaking service in L.A. had it, and none of her male clients, including Jason, were supposed to know it existed. Jason also didn't know that Nora had hired a private detective agency to do a background check on him to make sure he had never gone bankrupt or done prison time, a precaution she started taking after a particularly bad, but mercifully brief, post-Sam affair with a bisexual belly dancer who didn't tell her about either the belly dancing or the bisexuality until they'd been together for over a month.

Sometimes she wondered if Jason had a few secrets of his own. Since they were so perfectly matched, it was likely he did. But that too was healthy. All the experts agreed that relationships thrived on a combination of togetherness and independence. As one of Nora's professors at Cal Poly had never tired of pointing out: even the most happily married couples needed a private life apart from their spouses.

They let go of each other's hands and picked up the menus simultaneously like a trained dance team. Flaming bananas were not the only thing you could special order at the Bangkok-Xoc, and both of them liked to look at their options before they started hauling boats out of the water.

"How was Riverside?" she asked as she pursed her lips and tried to decide between taking potluck or ordering the special shrimp *a mojo de ajo* in rice paper.

"Fine." Jason studied his menu. His eyes lingered on the specials. He also appeared tempted by the shrimp. Suddenly he looked up and gave her a triumphant smile. "Guess what bright young developer just might get his variance."

Nora lowered her menu. "Oh, honey, that's wonderful!" she said with every bit of enthusiasm she could muster. Jason had driven to Riverside to present a development plan to the Regional Water District and attend a meeting of the county planning commission. He was trying to get a variance in the zoning laws so he could build a high-end, luxury retirement community in the desert west of L.A. He and his partners had picked up the land for a song, but without water it was going to remain a wasteland with—as he was fond of pointing out—a tax base near zero.

Although Jason had been a very successful real estate agent since he was in his early twenties, Serenity Sands was his first stab at moving into large-scale land development. That's where the big money was, and although she secretly detested urban sprawl, Nora was doing her best to stand behind him 100 percent. He had only scored a 3 on "interest in conserving the environment," while she was a strong 8. It was one of the few places their client profiles hadn't matched, and she sure as hell didn't intend to let it lead to the kind of petty arguments that had wrecked her marriage with Sam.

At the first opportunity, she deftly changed the subject. Soon they were chatting happily about their upcoming honeymoon in the Virgin Islands. Jason had found them a spectacular rental on St. John's that featured a wraparound view of the Caribbean. Most of the island was a national park, which included an underwater snorkeling trail. Nora had never snorkeled and was looking forward to lazy mornings spent in bed with Jason and lazy afternoons floating in crystal-clear water observing tropical fish. She had always liked fish, which were low maintenance. She even had a nicely landscaped pond filled with koi in her backyard. But the fish of St. John's were reputed to be seriously awesome. According to Jason, who had been to St. John's several times, they had stripes, spots, and polka dots, and came in all colors including green, pink, bright yellow, orange, and electric blue.

They talked all during dinner, snagging one delicious dish after another from the passing stream. By the time the bananas flambé came floating their way, they had agreed to see if they could change their tickets to include three extra days on St. Thomas so they could spend a few evenings at the clubs. They both loved reggae and salsa, and Jason was one of the few men Nora knew who could tango as well she could.

Full of bananas and toasted coconut, Nora fell into a charitable mood. *I hope Lucia is wrong about Sam missing me,* she thought. To be honest, it didn't make her all that sad to think about Sam eating his heart out over her, particularly now that she'd found Jason. She and Jason communicated beautifully. They would rarely fight, and when they did they'd make up quickly. They were as perfectly paired as two people could be without being identical twins.

After dinner they drove to Jason's house in separate cars. They didn't live together, even though they took turns sleeping in each other's beds. Nora's parents, who had come of age during Woodstock, thought they were silly to spend so much time commuting, but privately Nora thought not living together gave their sex life extra zing. Also, after the whirlwind insanity of her relationship with Sam, she had decided that the old-fashioned idea that a girl shouldn't live with a man she wasn't married to wasn't such a bad idea after all. Jason—no surprise—felt the same. "Let's take things slowly," he'd told her. "Let's savor every step, sweetheart." And savor every step they did.

In a few days, however, she and Jason would be officially merging their resources, emotionally and legally. At her request, he was going to put her house on the market as soon as they got back from the Virgin Islands. The fact that Jason was handling the deal personally meant they wouldn't have to pay another real estate agent a commission. Still, Nora hated to see it go. The house in Pasadena had been the first she'd ever owned, and she'd miss her roses and her koi.

Jason lived near UCLA in a large, four-bedroom place his parents had had the foresight to buy in the early seventies before the real estate market went totally berserk. When his father retired, his mother decided she had had enough of city life. The two of them moved to a ranch near Jackson Hole, Wyoming, selling Jason the house for what they had paid for it plus as much interest as they would have made if they'd invested their money in government T-bills over the same period.

It was the kind of deal that would have made any good investment counselor pull his hair out by the roots, but Jason's parents could afford to practically give their only son a house in one of the nicest neighborhoods in L.A. if they wanted to. The Messiers were old California, or at least as old as California got. When half the world came west in 1849 to look for gold, Jason's many-times great-grandfather had owned the only bakery in Sacramento. Within weeks, bread was selling for its weight in gold dust, and the family fortune was ensured.

The Messiers had had their ups and downs since then, but if Jason wasn't born with a silver spoon in his mouth, he was certainly born with a well-diversified portfolio of blue-chip stocks. He was what Nora's friends sometimes disparagingly referred to as a "trustafarian." In other words, he didn't really have to work for a living, which made the fact that he did all the more admirable.

The drive took about half an hour. As usual they arrived within seconds of each other, and let themselves in the back door, pausing for a moment while Jason disabled the security system. His kitchen was large and pleasant with top-of-the-line appliances including a subzero freezer and a six-burner stove that wouldn't have been out of place in a medium-sized restaurant. It was also spotless because, like Nora, he never cooked anything that couldn't be microwaved; and, unlike Nora, he had a cleaning woman come in three days a week.

The first thing Nora spotted were two crystal wineglasses in the high-tech metal dish drainer. The glasses stood out because they were the only thing in the drainer. Nora had rarely seen anything parked there in all the months she had been walking in and out of Jason's kitchen. Jason was the kind of guy who liked to throw everything into the dishwasher and let the cleaning woman sort it out; but wineglasses were fragile and he wasn't into breaking expensive crystal.

"Been having company?" she asked.

Jason looked over at the drainer, saw the glasses, and smiled. "Ah," he said softly.

" 'Ah'?" Nora gave him a teasing smile. "Does that mean you've been having some starlet sex kitten in here for a bachelor romp?" Jason might have sowed a lot of wild oats in his twenties, but when he started searching for a life partner, he became a poster boy for monogamy. He was definitely the most trustworthy man Nora had ever met, except—to be fair—Sam. That's why she could joke about him having other women.

Jason grinned wickedly. "Not just one starlet. Dozens. Plus four or five strippers, all of whom were named Lola, as I recall."

Nora laughed. "Spare me the details."

Jason smiled, walked over to the drainer, and struck one of the glasses with his fingernail. It rang like a bell. "Seriously," he said, "I do have a confession to make. Last night, when I got back from Riverside, I got to missing you so much that I sat down at the kitchen table, poured two glasses of Montepulciano, and pretended we were having a drink together. I wanted to call, but it was too late."

"That," Nora said, "is incredibly sweet."

"That's not the end of the story. I have a surprise for you." He reached into his pocket and pulled out a small silver ring. "I made this for you. I've been secretly taking silver-working lessons."

Nora was struck speechless at the sight of the ring. It was such a thoughtful present, yet a little peculiar since he had already given her a diamond engagement ring, and in a few days he was going to give her a gold wedding band. Jason kissed her on the forehead and placed the ring in her hand. She saw that it was a wide silver band composed of two layers. Small flowers had been cut out of the top layer so the darker underlayer showed through.

"Thank you," she whispered. She was touched, although still mystified. She looked inside the band and saw a small squiggle that looked like an F.

"What's the F stand for?"

Jason followed her gaze. "Friendship, fidelity, and frisky fun," he said, giving her another smile. "Actually, it was supposed to be a J. I was going to engrave our initials inside the ring, but it turns out they don't teach you how to engrave until lesson number thirteen, and I was only on lesson seven, so I had to stop before I wrecked the whole thing. We can take it to a jeweler if you want and have our initials engraved inside the band by someone who knows what he's doing."

"It's beautiful," Nora said. "I love it just the way it is."

"Try it on."

She tried to slip the ring on the third finger of her ringless right hand, but it was too small.

"It's for your little finger. A very special private ring

just for you and me. Wedding rings and engagement rings are public. Everyone knows what they mean. But this one will be a secret between the two of us; and every time you look at it, I want you to remember how much I love you."

Nora slipped the ring on the little finger of her right hand. It fit perfectly.

There was only one thing that could happen after a moment like that, and after a while it did. They made love with special pleasure and special passion. Nora felt awash in love and trust and happiness. As Jason held her in his arms, she gave herself to him with a fierce abandon she hadn't felt so far in their relationship. Everything about him seemed different, and sweeter, and better now that he was practically her husband. He even smelled different.

She mentioned it to him afterward: that spicy, exotic scent that was such a turn-on and seemed to come off his hair and his skin in long, warm waves.

Jason ran the palm of his hand lightly over her bare rump and then gave her a playful swat. "I'll have to keep you away from Ben."

"Ben?"

"Ben White. That developer who specializes in fast food chains. Remember? I think I've mentioned him a couple of times. I ran out of soap at the athletic club today and had to borrow Ben's." He sniffed at his own arm. "I think it was sandalwood. Kind of an odd scent for a guy, but maybe his wife picked it out. Anyway, beggars can't be choosers."

He laughed and gave her a quick kiss. "Hey, I'm going to have to watch my step after we're married." He kissed her again and chucked her under the chin. "You have a nose like a bloodhound."

4

When Nora arrived at her office the next morning, she was in a great mood. As she passed the lions, she gave them a playful slap on their stone rumps. It was a fine day in May, there were orange and yellow poppies blooming on the hillsides, and the temperature was a balmy seventy-two.

But not everyone shared Nora's feeling that this was a perfect Tuesday. A middle-aged woman was waiting for her. She sat in the comfortable chair reserved for Nora's private clients, and she looked anything but comfortable.

Nora greeted her with a smile, apologized for being a few minutes late, sat down, and launched into the interview. "So why don't we just start off with you telling me a bit about yourself?" she suggested. She looked down and quickly read the client's name off the intake questionnaire. ". . . Rosalee."

The woman gave Nora a pained look.

"Or would you prefer I call you Ms. Lambert?" Nora added smoothly. Sometimes older clients preferred a formality that, as far as Nora's younger clients were concerned, had left the planet decades ago. Some still wanted to be called "Miss" or, if divorced or widowed, "Mrs." She'd even had professors who insisted on being addressed as "Dr.," which was always a mistake, since it inevitably led to questions about liposuction and face lifts.

"Rosalee will be just fine," the woman said. There was something abrupt and even a little hostile in her voice that set off an alarm in Nora's head.

Nora looked at her more closely, taking in every detail. Her body language: closed and defensive; her posture: depressed or possibly angry. Rosalee Lambert was probably somewhere in her late forties or early fifties, which given the gloomy first impression she made meant that she wasn't going to be easy to match. She had a normal, middle-aged body, a little thick in the arms and thighs; nice hair, auburn with red tints, which she wore pulled back from her face and done up in a ponytail as if she were in her twenties. Her eyes were pleasant, and even kind-looking, which was a plus: sea blue running to gray. Appropriate makeup. No fingernail polish, because no fingernails to speak of: a bad sign that spelled nervousness or anxiety.

Nora never told her private clients what to wear for the first interview, but it was always interesting to see what they chose. Rosalee had decided on the casual look. She wore a striped, short-sleeved, boat-necked T-shirt and white cotton pants, several gold chains, and rubber-soled canvas shoes with no socks. This outfit, plus silver earrings shaped like sails, suggested she might own a boat of some kind. It certainly wouldn't be a rowboat, because Rosalee had an unusually high credit rating: something Nora always had Amber check before a client came in for the first interview. Rosalee was also wearing a gold wedding ring on her left hand. Nora presumed there would be an explanation for the ring. The most likely was that she was recently widowed, which would account for the depression and anxiety, as well as for her desire to find a new mate. Widowed people, particularly those who had married young, often had a hard time living alone. It was part of Nora's job to keep them from latching on to the first person they dated out of sheer desperation.

Nora had no more information. Ordinarily she would have known what Rosalee did for fun, what she wanted out of life, what kind of men she wanted to meet, whether she'd rather drink Mandrins or piña coladas. But except for giving her name, address, and the required financial information, Rosalee had declined to fill out the intake questionnaire. Nora had had clients refuse to divulge anything about themselves before, but most of them had been high-profile movie people or politicians who were afraid the information they gave might come back to haunt them. Rosalee's reluctance was unusual. Perhaps she was hiding something; perhaps she was paranoid; or perhaps she was simply shy.

Nora smiled in an attempt to put her at her ease. "So?" she said.

The woman remained mute.

Nora tried again. "So, why don't you begin by giving me some idea what you're looking for? Are you interested in meeting a lot of new people and getting back into circulation, or are you looking for a long-term relationship and possibly marriage?"

"None of the above." There was something in Rosalee's voice that made Nora suspect that she might have underestimated her. Rosalee leaned forward. "What I want to do is ask *you* some questions."

Nora put down the questionnaire, which was totally useless anyway, and sat back. "Sure," she said. "Fire away."

Rosalee paused for a moment as if considering what to ask first. "So, what kind of services do you offer?"

Nora was relieved. This was a perfectly normal question. Of course, the answer was on her Web page and in the brochure she had sent to Rosalee when Rosalee first indicated an interest in coming in for a private interview; but no one read anything these days. At best, they just looked at the pictures.

"Well, we have several different plans. Our least expensive is on-line dating, totally cyberspace based, for people who want to post a photo and information about themselves. Love Finds a Way's system can only be accessed by a password. This means you will only be put in contact with people who have been thoroughly screened."

Nora could see Rosalee was getting bored, so she quickly finished describing the computer dating services and moved on to the social events: video dating, express dating, Singles Karoke Night, the monthly Dance Bash, Dinner for Six. Still Rosalee's face remained blank. It wasn't until Nora got around to explaining custom services like the personalized matching of client profiles that she sat up and began to show interest.

"The average is five to seven good matches and three excellent ones," Nora said. "We have a very high success rate on the first round. Great matching is our specialty and we're proud of the job we do. But if you don't find anyone you connect with on the first pass, you can come back for two more rounds at no extra charge. We can match you at almost any level. Most people simply fill out the questionnaire." Nora resisted a temptation to point out to Rosalee that hers was blank. "But if you want a more complete match, I can send you to a handwriting expert, a psychologist, and even an image consultant. Of course, the more time we spend matching you, the more it costs."

Rosalee nodded. So there would be no problem with

money. Good. In the course of her career as a match-maker, Nora had only had ten people go for the full package. Each of them had paid over five thousand dollars. Perhaps Rosalee would be number eleven.

There was a moment of silence. Nora sat back and waited. It didn't do to interrupt a client when she was thinking about service levels.

Finally Rosalee spoke. "So, tell me: do you match married people?"

"Of course not." Nora was disappointed and more than a little annoyed. Clearly Rosalee was wearing that wedding ring because she was married. Unhappily married, apparently. This entire interview had been a total waste of time. "It would be completely unethical," she said, a bit more primly than she had intended.

"Well, you're matching up Chuck at a pretty good clip."

"Chuck?"

"Chuck's his nickname. His given name is Dale. Dale Lambert. My husband. You've been matching him up with flat-stomached, big-breasted twenty-year-olds like there's no tomorrow."

Nora was appalled. "Please tell me you're kidding."

"I wish I were. I take it you didn't know Dale was married?"

"I had no idea."

"The bastard."

Nora couldn't help agreeing. "I'm sorry this happened. Matching married people is completely against our policy. I'll erase your husband from our database immediately." Nora leaned forward and pressed the intercom button. "Amber, could you please bring me a printout of Dale Lambert's profile?" She spelled the name Lambert. There was a little stutter of surprise from the other end, as if Amber had been caught napping.

"Wait," Rosalee said. "You don't get it. I don't want you to erase Dale from your database. In fact, I want you to go on matching him up with other women."

Oh, great. She was looking for a threesome. Nora decided that she'd had enough of Rosalee Lambert. "This isn't a sex service," she said firmly. "If you and your husband are looking for unusual combinations, I suggest you try the relationship ads in—"

"I'm not looking for kinky sex." Rosalee rose to her feet. "I'm not looking for sex at all. The hell with sex. I want revenge!"

"You want *what?*" Nora was so startled she nearly knocked the files off her desk.

"I want revenge, and I'll pay you whatever you want to get it! Dale's a currency trader for Bretano Global; he made a killing in the stock market when things were hot, and then shifted to cash just before it tanked. We have money to burn and I'm the one who writes the checks. I want to get even with the bastard, and I don't care what it takes!"

Rosalee lowered her head like a charging rottweiler. Her eyes had gone hard; her face was flushed. Her silver earrings swung back and forth; she drew back her lips so her teeth showed. "I want you to fix the low-life, adulterous son of a bitch up with the worst women possible," she snarled. "I want you to find him women who will make him sorry he was ever born; women who will scream and nag and *drool* on him."

Nora couldn't decide whether to be amused or alarmed. "All I can do," she repeated, "is take your husband out of our database. I can't intentionally mismatch a client."

Suddenly Rosalee went from rottweiler to sad middle-aged woman. "Please," she pleaded. Tears filled her eyes. "Dale and I have been married for over twenty years. I thought we were happy. I thought he loved me. Do you know how much it hurts to discover that you've spent the best years of your life with a man who's been cheating on you? Particularly when he's been cheating on you with women twenty years younger? I can't compete with those firm little butts and thighs. Those girls have skin like babies; they wear size twos. I might as well buy a ticket to Alaska and throw myself onto an ice floe."

"I'm sorry. I just can't do it." Nora pulled a tissue out of the box on her desk and passed it to Rosalee, who took it and blew her nose.

"Men like Dale should be branded." Rosalee sniffed, dabbing at her eyes. "They should have a big A for Adultery stamped on their foreheads."

She looked up at Nora and her eyes grew hard again. "Oh, I know what you're thinking. You're thinking I'm pathetic. You're thinking I should either forgive Dale or divorce him and make a new life for myself. But I'm a practicing Catholic and the Church won't give me a divorce. Plus, Dale talked me into signing a prenup from hell before we got married. If I leave him, I'll be penniless. It's not easy to be single at my age. And if you're single *and* poor *and* middle-aged *and* female, you might as well drive to the nearest recycling dump and volunteer to be composted."

Seizing her purse, she rose to her feet. "I don't know why I expected you to understand. You can't be much over thirty. Just you wait. Someday you'll be in my shoes. Nearly every woman is sooner or later if she lives long enough."

And with that, she strode out of Nora's office past Amber, who was just coming in with the printout of Dale Lambert's profile.

Nora stared down at her desk and tried to get her emotions under control. Rosalee had gotten a bit scary there toward the end. Also, Nora didn't appreciate being told that some day she'd be in Rosalee's shoes. What was that supposed to be? The curse of King Tut?

"Here's the printout you wanted." Nora looked up and realized that Amber also appeared upset. That wasn't surprising. Amber was so timid, she got semihysterical when the copy machine repair guy told her to buy more toner. The sound of Rosalee raging and pleading was more than enough to send her scuttling for cover.

"Don't worry," Nora said briskly. "Everything's okay." She pointed to the printout. "Never mind that. I don't need it. Just take Dale Lambert's name out of our database. He's been posing as single and using Love Finds a Way to meet other women. That was his wife in here."

"I heard. The whole office heard." Amber looked terrible. Even her lips were white. Nora hoped she wasn't going to faint. The floor was tiled, and she could knock herself out cold.

"Are you okay?"

Amber shook her head.

"Would you like to sit down?"

Amber shook her head again.

"Look, there's no need to get so upset. These things happen from time to time. They're not—"

"It's not that."

"What is it then? Are you sick?"

"No. It's my new boyfriend. He's not . . ."

"Not what?" Nora said, but all she got for an answer was sobs. She plucked another tissue from the box and handed it to Amber. It was good she bought tissue twelve boxes to a package. She was going through them faster than a therapist. Sometimes she wished people in this town didn't spend so much time getting in touch with their emotions.

". . . he's just not working out," Amber sobbed. "He seemed so nice. He was a couple of years younger than me and a lib . . . a lib . . ."

"A liberal?" Nora supplied helpfully. "A Libertarian?"

"No, a librarian!" Amber wailed. "He told me he spent so much time at his computer because he was doing research, but he was secretly having cyber . . . cyber . . ."

"Cybersex?"

This time Nora got it right. Amber gave a pathetic little nod and blew her nose. Nora walked over and patted her on the shoulder in a motherly fashion. "There, there," she murmured. She felt sorry for Amber. Apparently no couples in the world got along except for herself and Jason and her own parents, and . . . With a great effort of will, Nora stopped the ghosts of Lucia and Aldo from entering the room.

"Amber," she said gently, "cheer up. You have the best singles database in the greater L.A. area to chose from. So your current boyfriend didn't work out. Hey, honey, it's not the end of the world. You'll get over him, I promise. This town is full of men who'll adore you. And you know our motto?"

Amber looked up through her tears. "No," she said with a hiccup.

"Our motto is that falling apart because you can't have any particular guy is like starving to death because you can't find Brussels sprouts."

That might not have fixed up Amber's love life, but at least it made her smile a little.

Later that afternoon, Nora ran into Caroline and Felicity in the coffee room waiting for another pot to finish dripping.

"Amber's going through a hard time," she informed them.

"Tell us about it." Caroline helped herself to an oatmeal cookie and broke it in half. Breaking cookies in half was Caroline's usual method of weight control, which didn't work very well because she always gave in to temptation and ate both pieces. "The poor kid's been crying her eyes out all day. She told us she just broke up with some sex-crazed librarian."

"She's a total mess," Felicity agreed. "I tried to cheer her up by giving her a quick makeover, but it was a mistake. Her mascara's so smeared she looks like a raccoon. If I were you, Nora, I'd send her home and tell her to take two aspirins and go to bed until the first hysterical stage of the breakup is over. She's no good today, anyway. She's already crashed her computer twice, which is so unlike her."

"Good idea," Nora agreed. "I'll tell her she can take the rest of the day off."

Caroline sighed and nibbled at the rim of her half cookie. "You know, we should do something for Amber. Maybe we could make an effort to make her feel more like part of the team. She's the new girl on the block, which has got to be hard for her since I've never met a shyer person. She probably feels left out, not being in the wedding party and all. Not that you even knew her when you were planning your wedding, Nora; plus with that red hair, she'd look really terrible in green."

Caroline and Felicity were slated to be Nora's co-maids of honor, not a traditional combination, but Nora hadn't wanted to play favorites. They were wearing mint-green chiffon dresses designed to make them look as if they were floating down the aisle. Nora was paying for the dresses and also for the shoes, which she was having dyed to match. The rest of the bridesmaids, who were going to be outfitted in a paler shade of green chiffon, were only going to carry ivy and baby's breath, for a kind of simple Zen effect. A former client of Nora's had offered to Feng Shui the entire church for free, but unfortunately the minister who was performing the ceremony had nixed that plan before it got off the ground.

"I know!" Felicity said. "I'll take Amber shopping! She needs something to wear to your wedding, and I bet she hasn't found anything she likes yet. She doesn't seem very interested in clothes." That was an understatement if Nora had ever heard one. Amber dressed mostly in beige, as though trying to blend into the background or avoid predators.

"I'll go too," Caroline offered. She picked up the other half cookie, examined it, and popped it into her mouth. "There's nothing like a new dress to perk a girl up when she's in the middle of relationship hell. Felicity and I will hit the shops with her and do some serious retail damage. Amber deserves a treat. She's definitely the best bookkeeper we've ever had; plus her computer skills are off the charts. She tweaked the matchmaking program a little, and now we're getting a higher number of 'very compatibles.' I'd say they're up at least three percent."

"Why don't all three of you take the afternoon off?" Nora suggested. "We're in a lull at the moment. Rosalee Lambert was the last private client I had scheduled for this week. I've got to call caterers, meet with florists, and—"

"Have Jason take you back to his place and remind you why you're marrying him on Saturday?" Caroline suggested with a wicked grin.

Nora laughed. "That too," she admitted.

Four hours later, Amber had a new dress. It wasn't a dress that Caroline, Felicity, Nora, or perhaps any woman in her right mind would have picked to wear to a formal wedding, but it was what Amber had wanted: a fluffy pink peasant outfit trimmed in magenta ribbons that made her look like a wad of pink spun-sugar candy. In it, Amber definitely appeared fifteen pounds heavier and her red hair took on a flamingly unpleasant hue that made you want to throw a bucket of sand on her, but she was so clearly delighted with her choice that not even Felicity had the heart to order her to shorten the shirt so it didn't cut her off midcalf; and Caroline, who shared Nora's obsession with shoes, bit her tongue when it became clear that Amber was going to wear the outfit with white orthopedic sandals.

"Nora's the best boss in the whole world!" Amber said as she, Felicity, and Caroline sat at a café table having a post-shopping cup of coffee together.

"You can say that again," Caroline agreed.

"Absolutely," said Felicity.

Amber leaned forward. Her eyes became twice as big and all her freckles seemed to glow. "How did she get into the matchmaking business, anyway?"

"She inherited it," Caroline said. And then Caroline and Felicity told Amber the whole story: how Nora had been working for a small dating service; how the middle-aged woman who ran the service had matched herself with a very handsome, very young man and run off to Hawaii with him, leaving Nora the entire database; how Nora had turned that modest start into Love Finds a Way.

"So did the woman who ran of to Hawaii find happiness with her boyfriend?" Amber asked.

"Nope." Felicity sighed and took a sip of coffee. "It was a total mismatch. Marsha and the guy lived together for, what . . ." She looked at Caroline.

"A couple of months," Caroline supplied. "And then he broke up with her. Well, actually it was worse than that. Marsha's mother came to visit and he seduced her. Seems the women in Marsha's family had a thing for young guys. Anyway Marsha was so upset she went to a luau, started crying uncontrollably, and choked on the poi."

"How horrible," Amber murmured. Suddenly her eyes took on a dreamy expression. "But at least, for a little while, she *lived!*"

Nora was doing some living of her own that week and all of it in the fast lane. Although she was a professional party giver, putting on a formal wedding absorbed every minute of every remaining day before the ceremony. She and Jason had invited three hundred guests, including her former clients, his business associates, friends, and hoards of relatives who were flying in from all over the country and—in several cases—from all over the world. Her parents were driving down from Davis; his parents were flying in from Wyoming. Assorted aunts, uncles, and cousins, mostly on the Messier side, were coming from Paris, Rio, Montreal, and exotic little hideaways on the north coast.

In addition to Caroline and Felicity, Nora had four bridesmaids to whip into shape before Saturday, including Jason's two sisters, neither of whom liked the color of their dresses and who kept calling to ask if Nora might consider changing to violet, a color that made her actively nauseated. Nora had to make sure the caterers were bringing enough food and wine for the reception: a formal sit-down luncheon with ice sculptures, champagne, a live band, and dancing, which was to be held in a large canvas tent in Jason's backyard. The tent was going to be decorated with gardenias and stephanotis, fabulously expensive, but what the hell? The church was to be decked out with the same flowers, plus tuberoses because Nora adored the scent.

Of course she could have hired a professional wedding planner, but Nora wanted every bit of this wedding to be hers, right down to the pearl-encrusted satin slippers she was wearing with her wedding dress: imported from France and supposedly modeled on the slippers Marie Antoinette had worn when she married the future Louis XVI. The slippers had cost as much as the dress, but once again, what the hell? Sure, it would have been more sensible to opt for a simple ceremony and plow the money she saved back into Love Finds a Way. But she had no intention of letting her marriage to Jason come off as one of those modest, low-key events that screamed "second marriage."

She intended to walk down that aisle as if she'd never been married before.

On Friday, Caroline and Felicity took Nora out to celebrate her last night as a single woman. They'd offered her anything she wanted: a wild club scene, male strippers, a hunky guy jumping out of a cake, but Nora figured she'd be having all the naked, hunky guy time she wanted in the near future, so she asked them to take her to Jennifer Lopez's Cuban restaurant in Pasadena. The place was called Madre's, and on a good night you could find yourself sitting under a crystal chandelier sipping Cuban black bean soup in the company of Jay Leno, Brooke Shields, and Edward James Olmos. Nora was crazy about the Estafani salad, which contained, among other things, grilled chicken breast, machego cheese, and maple syrup.

On that particular night, there were no celebrities in sight except Lopez's ex-husband, Ojani Noa, who ran the place; but it didn't matter because the three of them were so busy laughing, reminiscing, and trading bites of food that they probably wouldn't have noticed if Nicole Kidman had walked in with Brad Pitt.

Madre's had a great wine list. Caroline, who had volunteered to be their designated driver, stuck to Pellegrino, but Nora and Felicity ordered two bottles of Dom Perignon, which meant by the time they got to the second half of the second bottle, they were both slightly tipsy.

"I'm so happy for you," Felicity kept telling Nora. "So damn happy."

"Thanks." Nora felt like crying with joy. How had she gotten so lucky? She had two wonderful friends, and in a few hours she would have a wonderful husband.

Felicity lifted her glass. "To the bride and groom. May you always be happy." Before they could clink with her, Felicity chugged half her champagne and spilled the other half down the front of her dress. "Ooops," she giggled. She put down the champagne flute, propped herself up unsteadily on her elbows, and leaned closer to Nora.

"Jason better treat you like a queen, or he's going to have to deal with me." There was a wild glint in Felicity's eyes that Nora had never seen before. She looked like she might grab one of the butter knives and go after Jason if he so much as looked at another woman. Or more likely, pitch forward and pass out face-first in the coconut flan.

Nora grinned. Felicity might have had way too much to drink, but this wasn't just the champagne talking. This was real loyalty. This was what friendship was all about.

"I second what Felicity said." Caroline raised her water glass. "One false move, and Jason is toast."

Nora seized their hands and gave them an affectionate squeeze. "You girls are the greatest," she said. "But you don't need to worry. Jason is going to make the best husband since . . ." She suddenly drew a blank. Were there any famous husbands? If so, she couldn't

5

On her wedding day, Nora woke to discover that even the weather had decided to cooperate. There wasn't a whiff of smog, only golden sunshine and blue skies, thanks to a stiff breeze that was sweeping the air clean from the San Gabriel Mountains to the sea. It was eight, and she was due at the church at ten, which gave her plenty of time to eat breakfast, drive to the motel where her parents were staying, and lead them through the maze of freeways so they wouldn't get lost and miss the ceremony. Nora had tried to convince them to stay in her guest bedroom, but they'd insisted she was going to have enough to worry about without looking after them.

Although she adored her mom and dad, she was secretly relieved not to have them around this morning. This was her last day in Pasadena and she wanted to say good-bye to her house in private. After she and Jason returned from their honeymoon, he'd be putting the place on the market. Real estate was a hot commodity these days, and houses in her neighborhood sometimes sold in hours for more than the asking price. Of course, during escrow, they'd be coming back to pack up her things. They might even sleep here a few more times. But today was the very last day her house would be totally hers, and she wanted to savor the moment.

She got up out of bed, strolled over to the window, and gazed fondly at her backyard. As much as she was looking forward to moving in with Jason, she'd miss her flowers, her swimming pool, and her little stone-rimmed pond full of white and gold koi. Jason had a swimming pool too and an even more elegant garden, but for two years all this had been hers.

She'd been willing to drive all the way from Pasadena to Santa Monica every day just to live here. Her house was a gem of California craftsman architecture, with an internal sunroom, a carved redwood fireplace mantel in the living room, a spacious, recently remodeled kitchen, two Mexican-tiled bathrooms, and four sunny bedrooms with closets ample enough to accommodate all the shoes she'd ever lusted after. She could walk to several good restaurants, a great deli, a supermarket, and a well-stocked natural foods store.

On hot nights, she could sometimes hear the steady roar of the freeway pulsing like a distant waterfall, but her street had virtually no traffic. Quiet and shady, it was lined with houses that looked like they actually belonged in California. This was an important feature, since several streets in Pasadena looked so midwestern that film crews were always using them as stand-ins for Ohio or Indiana.

Yes, Nora thought nostalgically. *I'll miss this place.*

She strolled over to the other side of the room to admire her front yard and realized with a start that there was one thing she definitely wouldn't miss: her neighbor, Mr. Jenkins, whose car was parked directly in front of her driveway!

Her nostalgic mood vanished. Throwing on a T-shirt

and blue jeans, she stomped out of the house, slamming the door behind her. She felt childishly angry that on today, of all days, he should have again chosen to make it impossible for her to back into the street. Had he no consideration for anyone! Didn't he know it was illegal to park there?

The man was impossible. A year ago, he had sneaked into her yard and drastically pruned a fig tree that he claimed was dropping fruit on his lawn and attracting wasps. Lately he'd been complaining that the rosebushes that lined her driveway were a foot over his property line. He'd lived in the same house for over fifteen years and suffered from the delusion that he owned the entire block, including the sidewalk and the street. When Nora threw a party, he called the cops if people parked in front of his place. He reported her guests' cars as abandoned, and on more than one occasion, he'd gotten them towed.

She hadn't wanted to carry on a feud with him. Time after time, she'd tried to make peace; but he seemed to thrive on making trouble for her. Well, this was the last straw. She was going to ring his doorbell and remind him firmly that he wasn't the only person on the planet.

She strode up his sidewalk past a horrible set of miniature plaster dwarfs, a wishing well, several gaudily painted Disney characters, and a shiny silver gazing ball mounted on a green plaster pedestal. No one else in the neighborhood had lawn ornaments, but Jenkins had so many he rotated them on a schedule that roughly corresponded to the seasons. The dwarfs and Disney characters were a staple. In the winter, he added a hideous plastic Santa Claus and a sled drawn by a team of equally hideous plastic reindeer; summer was Pooh and Piglet; fall was a flock of bright pink flamingos, which he was insane enough to deck out in little Hawaiian shirts that his ex-wife had whipped up on her Singer.

Spring brought on the wishing well and the gazing ball. Nora detested them all. They were tasteless and brought down property values.

She tried to ring his doorbell, but it was broken. That was another problem. He didn't keep his place up. It was probably riddled with termites that were going to eat away the foundations of her house when they got through with his.

Doubling up her fist, she knocked loudly. There was no response. She knocked again and then a third time. Finally, she heard the slapping sound of his footsteps. The man was retired. He wore nothing but shorts and flip-flops. She hoped that this morning he had at least opted to put on a shirt. She hadn't had her coffee yet and wasn't sure she could stand another look at the fishy white expanse of his paunch.

The slapping sound stopped, and she saw a blood-shot blue eye peering at her through the little glass spy hole in the door.

"What do you want?" an irritable voice demanded. No "hello," no "hi, neighbor." Did he even know how to greet someone in a civil fashion?

"I need to talk to you," Nora said.

"Start talking."

"Open the door."

"Why should I?"

"Because I can hardly hear you, that's why."

Apparently even he could see the logic in this. The door opened a crack, then completely, and Nora found herself being treated to the sight of a bare-chested, pot-bellied man dressed in pajama bottoms decorated with green and yellow ducks.

"What do you want?" he repeated.

"Do you know your car is blocking my driveway?"

"It's not my car," he said, and started to shut the door.

Nora grabbed the edge of the door and held it. He might be older, but she was stronger.

"It sure as hell is. It's your rusted wreck of a Chevy, and I want it moved *now.*"

"It's not my car."

"Well, then, whose is it?"

"My son's. I sold it to him yesterday."

"Is he living with you again?"

"Yeah. He broke up with that little tart he's been shacking up with, not that it's any of your business."

Oh, great. That was all Nora needed to hear. Ryan Jenkins was as bad as his father: a total slacker whose idea of a good time was repairing cars in the driveway, so he could then drive them around with the speakers blaring so loudly they knocked your fillings out.

"Tell Ryan to get out here immediately and move his car. I can't get out of my driveway."

"What's your big hurry?"

"I happen to be getting married today, and—call me silly—but I'd just like to show up at the church on time."

"Married, huh?"

"Yes, married." Nora was on the urge of screaming, but she managed to repress it.

"I thought you were already married to that guy who's always sleeping over at your place. The one with the weird-looking white teeth; 'the shark,' I call him."

"Well, you thought wrong." Nora was furious that he'd been spying on her; furious that he'd given Jason such an ugly nickname; and even more furious at herself for letting him put her in a foul mood on her wedding day.

"I'll kick Ryan out of bed and tell him to move his car," Jenkins said. "Wouldn't want the shark guy to cut and run just when he's offered to make an honest woman of you."

"Thanks," Nora said through gritted teeth.

"And another thing."

She braced herself.

"Congratulations."

Nora was so taken aback that she froze and stared at him in disbelief. Mr. Jenkins, first name unknown, had just said something pleasant to her.

"Uh, thanks," she stuttered.

"Usually it doesn't work out, though," he added dourly. "I suppose you know that."

"What doesn't work out?"

"Marriage. *Reader's Digest* says more than half of all marriages end in divorce these days."

"Thanks for sharing," Nora snarled. And turning on her heels, she stomped home to make herself a cup of extra-strong cappuccino.

Ryan, who as a rule never got up before noon, moved his car before Nora finished breakfast, and by the time she arrived at the motel to pick up her parents, she had forgotten about her ongoing feud with her neighbor. She was excited; she was happy. No, she was more than happy: she was ecstatic.

Everything was just as perfect as she'd imagined it would be. Her mother was wearing an expensive blue silk suit that Nora had helped her pick out—perhaps the first thing in years her mom hadn't ordered from Land's End. Nora's father was decked out in a rented tux that made him look positively elegant.

Nora was fairly sure that this was the first piece of formal clothing her dad had ever put on, since the family album indicated that, when her parents got married, her mother had worn a yellow miniskirt and a wreath of daisies around her head; while her father had worn white bell-bottoms, a tie-dyed shirt, and a beaded headband. They hadn't even had a proper minister. One of their friends who had paid twenty dollars to be ordained in some fly-by-night religious organization had performed the ceremony.

When Nora was thirteen she had checked out their marriage license to see if it was valid, on the theory that if you were illegitimate, it would be good to know it. But to her relief, everything had turned out to be completely legal. Her parents were as married as two people could be, and somehow they'd not only stayed together all these years, they'd stayed happy.

The traffic on the freeways was light on Saturday mornings, so they arrived at the church a good forty-five minutes ahead of schedule. Nora's parents stayed in the vestibule to talk to Jason's parents, while Nora made her way to the bride's dressing room where Caroline, Felicity, Jason's sisters, and two of Nora's former clients, whom she had matched with their own husbands, hovered around her in a fluttering circle of mint-green chiffon doing up the satin buttons on the back of Nora's gown, adjusting her veil, and securing her hair so it wouldn't come undone and tumble into her face while she was reciting her vows. Felicity even made sure Nora had something old, something new, something borrowed, something blue, and a silver dime in the toe of her shoe. Actually, the dime was one of the usual aluminum copper sandwich deals, but since Nora hadn't heard the final verse of the rhyme until five minutes before she was to scheduled to walk down the aisle, she figured that if copper and aluminum were good enough for the U.S. government, they were good enough for her.

It was amazing how many traditions and superstitions surrounded a formal wedding, but that was part of the thrill of doing things right. As Nora stood nervously in front of the door to the sanctuary, clinging to her father's arm, behind Caroline, Felicity, and the four bridesmaids, the thought occurred to her that today, for a brief moment in time, she was going to be part of a long line of brides stretching back hundreds, maybe even thousands of years.

The door to the sanctuary was closed. On the other side, she suddenly heard a soft rustling sound as if the entire congregation had breathed a collective sigh. Jason, his best man, and his groomsmen must have come out to stand in front of the altar. She imagined Jason standing there, waiting for her. Was he nervous? She doubted it. Jason was a rock of stability. Was she nervous? Yes. Did she have any second thoughts? Well, of course. A woman who didn't have second thoughts on her wedding day wouldn't be human. But there was nothing terrible; nothing that made her feel like sticking her head in the door and calling the whole thing off. She reminded herself once again that Jason was a 93 percent match with her on the client compatibility profile. Any closer, and they'd be clones.

And I do love him, she thought. *I really do.*

The organist paused and then launched into the processional music, not the traditional "Here Comes the Bride," but Purcell's "Triumphal March" to remind everyone that that Nora was walking down the aisle to celebrate a victory. The door to the sanctuary swung open, and one by one, the bridesmaids disappeared. When the last mint-green chiffon dress had left the vestibule, Nora's father squeezed her arm affectionately.

"Ready, honey?" he asked.

Nora nodded, too happy and excited to speak. Suddenly, her eyes filled with tears, and she felt weak-kneed and light-headed.

"Okay, sweetheart," her dad said. "Here we go."

The march up the aisle was a blur. Nora hardly saw the faces of the three hundred guests she'd invited. All she saw was Jason waiting for her, and behind him, the minister and the altar decked with white flowers and flickering candles.

As she drew nearer, Jason gave her a warm smile without a hint of nervousness. Nora smiled back tremulously and flashed her right hand so he could see she was wearing the little silver ring he'd given her. Jason's smile broadened, and he mouthed the words "I love you." Then he turned to stand beside her, and the ceremony began.

The minister beamed at them. He was an old family friend of the Messiers' who had known Jason since he was baptized. "Dearly beloved . . ." He spoke the traditional words in a rich, solemn baritone, reminding them that marriage was an honorable estate that should not be entered into lightly. Then he lifted his head, looked past them, and addressed the congregation. The words he spoke were the same words used to marry couples for generations. Nora and everyone else in the church had heard them dozens of times.

"If any man can show just cause why this man and this woman may not lawfully be joined together, let him now speak, or else hereafter forever—"

Suddenly, Nora heard loud sobbing to her left. Out of the corner of her eye, she saw that Felicity had broken into tears. Felicity's display of emotion was touching, but also a little irritating. This was Nora's wedding, and if anyone was supposed to cry, it was supposed to be Nora.

Felicity's sobbing grew even louder and more convulsive. She appeared to be losing it completely.

The minister seemed taken aback. He stumbled, lost his place, and began again. Nora was becoming increasingly annoyed. She turned and glared at Felicity, who was sobbing away, apparently oblivious to the fact that she was creating a scene. *Get a grip,* Nora thought. *I know you're one of my best friends, but this is way over the top.*

"If any man can show just cause why this man and this woman may not lawfully be joined together—"

"I'm pregnant!" Felicity cried.

Felicity's words bounced off the wooden pews and stone walls of the sanctuary like breaking glass. The minister gave a startled gasp and stopped in midsentence; and Nora and everyone else in the church stared at Felicity in disbelief. What an inappropriate time to make such an announcement. Was she out of her mind?

"Pregnant!" Felicity cried again. And then, to Nora's horror, she lifted her arm and pointed her index finger straight at Jason. "And it's your baby! Yours, damn it!"

"What!" Nora shrieked. She wheeled around to face Jason. "Jason, this isn't true, right? Felicity's having a breakdown. We have to get her out of here right now before she . . ."

But Jason wasn't listening. His mouth was slightly open, his face was pale, and he was staring at Felicity with the stunned expression of a man who has just had his life turned upside down. "Felicity," he murmured in a hoarse whisper, "shut up!"

"I'm not shutting up!" cried Felicity. "I called you dozens of times and left messages begging you to call me back, but you couldn't be bothered. I'm so mad at you for blowing me off that I don't give a damn who knows! You knocked me up, Jason Messier! Now you deal with it!" She took a few menacing steps toward him. Her face was white, her mascara smeared, her skin as green as her dress.

Jason clenched his fists. The tips of his ears had gone bright red and his mouth was drawn back in a grimace of anger. "Get out of here!" he hissed. "What the hell do you think you're doing!"

"What do I think I'm doing?" Felicity yelled. "I'm

giving you the good news! You're about to be a father, Jason! I wanted to use a condom. But noooo. You said it was like wearing galoshes!"

Galoshes! Nora's mind froze on the word and wouldn't move on. This was beyond horrible. She waited for Jason to deny that he had any part in Felicity's pathetic delusion. Jason had given up sleeping around years ago. He'd checked the *monogamy* blank on his client intake questionnaire. Sure, clients lied—but not Jason. Jason was all Nora's—Nora's kind, charming, honest, totally faithful husband-to-be who . . .

"The kid isn't mine."

Well, of course it wasn't! Nora experienced a jolt of pity, horror, anger, and relief that made her feel as if the floor were moving under her. Felicity was either totally crazy or else a hysterical liar. They had to get her out of the church immediately so the wedding could go on. She needed medical help, counseling, years of therapy, a good swift kick . . .

"Wanna bet this baby's not yours!" Felicity cried in that same terrible, echoing shriek. "You ever hear of paternity tests?"

"Shut up!"

"I'm not shutting up. I'm about to get louder!"

Jason suddenly pushed past Nora as if she didn't exist. Approaching Felicity, he seized her by the shoulders and drew her so close that her face almost touched his. "Listen," he hissed, "I've got clients out there, get it? You're wrecking everything!"

Nora stared at him in disbelief. Felicity was ruining their wedding, and he was worrying about his *clients!*

"You're not worming your way out of this like it's some sleazy real estate deal!" Felicity hissed. It was like overhearing a conversation between two snakes, but at least, Nora thought with mounting hysteria, they were whispering.

"Get out of here! We'll talk about this later!"

"Get out? Don't make me laugh. If I go now, you'll insist I get an abortion. Well, forget it. I've had enough guys bail on me. This time I've got witnesses, and you've got two choices: either your clients walk out of this church thinking of you as a fornicating, cheating weasel who abandons the woman he got pregnant, or they walk out of here thinking of you as a fornicating, cheating weasel who's honorable enough to marry her and be a dad to his kid. So which scenario is likely to get you the best land deals, huh? And, oh, yeah, my uncle sits on the Riverside County Planning Commission."

"This is blackmail!"

"You bet it is! Can you think of any better basis for a happy marriage?"

At the word "marriage" something inside Nora cracked and she saw the truth in all its spectacular cruelty. "You *are* the father of Felicity's child!" she cried. "Why, you lying, cheating, no-good—"

It was as if she'd been wiped off the face of the planet. Jason ignored her. Felicity didn't even pause for breath.

"Yes or no?" Felicity demanded.

"Yes," Jason said in a strangled voice.

Felicity grabbed Jason's hand, turned around, jerked him up beside her, and faced the minister with a smile of triumph that made Nora physically ill.

"Marry us!" she demanded.

The minister was aghast. "But, I couldn't possibly—"

"Oh, come on. I mean everything's set up, and you've already been paid. So how hard can it be?"

Nora didn't wait to hear any more. This was a public humiliation beyond her wildest nightmares. With a scream of misery and rage, she ripped off her veil, picked up the skirts of her wedding dress, and fled back down the aisle.

6

That afternoon Caroline called Nora half a dozen times and got nothing but her machine. By six, she was seriously worried, and by eight, close to frantic.

At eight-thirty, she decided to drive to Pasadena. It was a long trip thanks to a jackknifed big rig on the Santa Monica Freeway, but the moment she pulled up in front of Nora's house, her anxiety level went way down. Nora's car was parked crookedly in the driveway, passenger-side door open, turn signal flashing. Nora might have been too upset to park straight, but at least she wasn't wandering around in the dark.

Caroline sat for a moment, staring at the pale yellows and whites of Nora's roses and trying to figure out what to do next. Would Nora want company at a time like this? Probably not. On the other hand, if Nora had ever needed a friend, she needed one now. *I should have brought Goldie and Aurora with me,* Caroline thought. *There's nothing like a pair of warm dogs to comfort a woman who's been betrayed.*

Having not had the foresight to bring the golden retrievers, she was going to have to comfort Nora by herself. Well, so be it. Getting out of the car, she strode rapidly up to Nora's front door, and rang the bell.

No one answered.

Caroline rang the doorbell again. Still no answer.

"Nora? Nora, are you in there? Nora, come on. It's Caroline. I know you're home."

Silence.

"Nora, I'm worried about you. If you don't say something in about three seconds, I'm going to come in and get you."

"Go away," Nora snarled.

Caroline breathed a sigh of relief and removed her finger from the doorbell. "Well, good. You're still alive. I kept telling myself you were too smart to do anything stupid. Now come on. Be a good girl and open the door."

"Go away."

"Nora, honey, I know you're upset, but you can't just hide like this."

Silence.

"Nora?"

More silence.

"I mean it, Nora. Open this door. I'm really worried. This isn't like you." No answer. Caroline stared at the closed door grimly. "Okay, that does it: if you don't open up in the next ten seconds, I'm coming in whether you want me to or not."

Still silence.

Caroline folded her arms over her chest and began to count in a loud voice. On "ten" she tried the knob. The door was locked.

Caroline frowned and stood for a moment staring at the door. Then she shrugged. "Okay, be miserable then. I'm leaving. If you come to your senses and decide you need company, call me."

She walked back down the front steps making as

much noise as possible. Getting into her car, she started the engine with a roar and sped away. A block later, she pulled over, got out of her car, and returned to Nora's house. This time she didn't bother to ring the doorbell. Instead, she walked around back, stepped up on Nora's deck, and pushed open the sliding glass doors that led to the kitchen.

She found Nora sitting at her kitchen table eating M&Ms and drinking vodka straight from the bottle. Her eyes were red, and her hair was standing out in spikes all over her head as if she'd been pulling at it. She was still wearing her wedding dress.

"Go away," Nora said when she spotted Caroline. "I don't need your pity."

"I'm not offering you pity," Caroline said gently. "I'm offering you sympathy."

Nora crammed an entire handful of M&Ms in her mouth and washed them down with a swig of vodka. "Why bother? My life is ruined. Do me a favor, Caroline: get out of here, so I can see if it's possible for a woman to kill herself with chocolate."

"You're going to make yourself sick."

"Good," Nora said grimly, gobbling another handful of M&Ms.

"This isn't the end of the world, you know."

"Oh, yeah? Well, it will do."

Caroline strode over to the refrigerator and threw open the door.

Nora eyed her suspiciously. "What are you doing?"

"Like I said, you're going to make yourself sick eating chocolate and drinking straight vodka. I'm going to find you something else to drink."

"Sick would be fun. Sick would be a relief. What are you going to give me? Warm milk? You know, there's a reason people don't become milkaholics when their fiancé and their so-called best friend humiliate them in front of everyone they know. Milk doesn't work. It doesn't turn off the sound of the laughter."

"No one's laughing at you, Nora. Your mother was beside herself, and Amber was crying her eyes out. A lot of people were very upset."

"No laugher, huh? Well, think again." Nora gulped down another handful of M&Ms. "There were media people there, remember? I invited them because I thought the publicity would be good for business." She gave a bitter laugh, lifted the vodka bottle, and saluted Caroline with it. "Here's to the matchmaker who mismatched herself. That's what they called me on the evening news. Hey, guess what: I really did look great in this dress. And I shouldn't have bothered to hire a professional crew to make a video of the wedding, because KTTV got some killer footage of me running out of the church."

Caroline stared at her, appalled. "They didn't . . ."

"They did. I was featured in the segment where they put the human interest stuff, right after a guy who managed to get his cocker spaniel admitted to UCLA using fake SAT scores."

Caroline extracted a bottle of cranberry juice and a bottle of lime juice from the refrigerator and slapped them down on the table in front of Nora.

"What are those for?"

"I'm making us *both* a drink. Cosmopolitans—that is if you have any Cointreau."

Nora pointed to the cabinet above the sink where she kept her liquor. Then she dumped the remaining M&Ms out on the table and began to sort them into piles by color.

Caroline decided this was a bad sign. "Seriously, Nora, are you okay?"

"Oh, yeah. Never felt better in my life. Do you know what my parents wanted to do? They wanted to stay with me for a few days because they were afraid I'd 'do something,' as my mom put it. Yeah, I'm ready to do something. But I don't need to be put under a suicide watch. A homicide watch is more like it. That skunk! That little skunk!"

"Jason or Felicity?"

"I find myself alternating between skunks, but at the moment I was referring to Felicity. She was one of my best friends. Damn her! How could she have been having sex with Jason behind my back! I saw her every day. She was always smiling, always so helpful and sweet. I never suspected a thing."

Nora suddenly gave Caroline a sharp look. "I don't suppose you were also romping around in Jason's bed when it wasn't occupied by me?"

"I was never even tempted." Caroline opened the cranberry and lime juice bottles and went over to the cabinet to get the Cointreau. "I've gotten to the age where I don't even look at a man unless he's lost most of his hair. Besides, Felicity betrayed me too. She and Jason betrayed everyone."

"Like they care," Nora said bitterly, scooping up all the yellow M&Ms and popping them into her mouth.

Caroline said nothing, because it was clear that Nora was right. Jason and Felicity had left the church hand in hand, and although they hadn't looked blissfully happy, they were so caught up in their own messy situation that neither had appeared to give a damn about Nora or anyone else for that matter. Shaking up the drinks in Nora's stainless steel shaker, Caroline poured them into glasses, put the glasses on the table, and sat down.

Nora pushed the green M&Ms around in little spiral patterns, and then took a sip of her cosmopolitan. "So did the reception go on without me?"

"You don't want to know."

"Yes, I do. Did it?"

"Not really."

"What does that mean?"

"Well, I went over to Jason's to see if maybe the caterers would refund your money, but they wouldn't. In fact, they led me to believe that this groom-bolting-at-the-last-minute sort of thing isn't all that uncommon."

"How did my ice swans look?"

"I'm not sure. By the time I got there, their heads had melted off, and they were floating upside down in Jason's swimming pool. His nephews had been playing 'battleship' with them."

Nora made a choking sound somewhere between a sob and a growl. "Go on," she commanded. She picked up her cosmopolitan and took another swig. "Give me the rest of the gory details. I can take it."

Caroline picked up her own drink, stared at it for a moment, and then put it down without tasting it. "Okay. Since you insist, here goes: only about twenty people showed up, most of them Jason's relatives. They looked stunned. In fact everyone looked stunned. They wandered around like refugees. Your mother put in an appearance, glared at Jason's relatives as if they were scum, and insisted on saving the top layer of the wedding cake for you. She said she was going to freeze it."

Nora laughed bitterly. "Good old Mom."

"Also, I think you might be able to get a refund on the champagne, because the fountain stopped running early, and even at the rate Jason's relatives were guzzling, they couldn't drink enough for three hundred."

"I'm surprised they didn't use it to toast the happy bride and groom."

"What? Oh, you mean Jason and Felicity? No. That didn't happen. The minister refused to marry them. He told them he thought they needed extensive premarital counseling."

Nora made a choking sound and took another sip of her drink.

"Plus you can't just get married in California on the spur of the moment. You need to get a license."

"So don't tell me, let me guess: Felicity dragged Jason to Las Vegas, and as we speak they're being married in the Elvis Wedding Chapel by an impersonator in rhinestone pants."

"I don't think so. They were both looking pretty confused by the time they walked out of the church. Even Felicity looked like she'd realized that, even if you're pregnant and furious, you can't pull a bride switch at the last minute and expect the world to cooperate."

"Where are the two loathsome traitors now?"

There was a long pause. Caroline looked down and studied her drink intently. "I heard they left town."

"Where did they go?"

"I don't know."

"Yes, you do. I can tell."

Caroline continued to study her drink. Then she picked up her glass and took a long swig.

"They went to the Virgin Islands, didn't they?" Nora persisted.

"Yes," Caroline said reluctantly.

Nora gave a scream of rage and swept a pile of M&Ms off the table.

"Nora!" Caroline pleaded. "Calm down!"

"Don't tell me to calm down, Caroline! Felicity is sleeping in *my* bed. She's eating *my* mangos! She's looking at *my* fish!" Suddenly Nora gave a another screech that startled Caroline so much she almost knocked over her drink. Nora was staring at her right hand in horror. "The ring!" she yelled. "The ring!"

"What ring? What are you talking about?"

"This one!" Nora jerked a silver ring off her little finger and leaped to her feet with a wild look in her eyes. She ran to the kitchen counter, pulled the toaster out of the wall, flipped it over on its side, threw the ring on the table, and began to pound on it, cursing and screaming.

"Felicity!" she yelled. "Felicity! That was what he'd put on the inside! An F for Felicity!"

The toaster came down on the ring, smashing it flat. Carolyn backed away, taking the vodka bottle with her on the possibility that Nora might grab it next.

When Nora had reduced the ring to a hunk of flattened silver, she sat down, put her head on the table, and began to cry. "I thought Jason made that ring for me, but he made it for her," she sobbed. "And those two wineglasses in his dish drainer. He'd had Felicity over when he was supposed to be in Riverside, and when I spotted the evidence he gave me the ring to distract me. And the way he smelled! He'd used her soap! I bet they took showers together! What a fool I was! I should have known! He had a past. He'd cheated on women before I met him. But I was a sucker. I thought he'd reformed."

Caroline sat down beside her and watched her for a moment. Then she reached out and stroked her hair in a motherly way. "Oh, honey," she said softly.

"I thought I knew Jason," Nora wailed. "I thought since he was perfect for me, I was perfect for him. Oh, I knew he had some flaws, but not ones the size of the Grand Canyon. Did you know there was only seven percent of his profile that didn't match mine?"

"Seven percent lying, cheating snake," Caroline said.

Nora lifted her head and gave Caroline a grateful look. "Yeah." Then she began to sob again. "I thought Jason loved me! I thought we were happy! I thought . . ." Suddenly, she lifted her head again and a look of horror came over her face. "My God, just the other day I had a client in my office who said exactly those same words. And I thought she was pathetic. Maybe I deserve this. Maybe I brought it on myself by being so sure I was the world's greatest matchmaker. I bragged about how I studied men the way a duck hunter studies ducks. I thought I knew all about them. What was I thinking? Obviously, I don't have any better chance of finding myself a good mate than two people who meet randomly at a tractor pull."

Caroline gave Nora's head another consoling pat. "Nora, honey, let's get something straight right now: when a guy cheats on you, *you* aren't to blame; *he* is."

"Thanks for that," Nora said, and then she began to cry again. Caroline waited for the crying to stop, but it only got louder. Finally she couldn't take it any longer.

"Nora," she said gently, "you've got to stop crying. It's okay to grieve, but if you keep this up, you're going to make yourself sick."

"No," Nora said in that stubborn, slurred voice people use when they have had far too much to drink and aren't used to it. "I don't want to stop crying. Just go away and leave me to my misery. It's all I have left."

Caroline rose, took hold of Nora's hands, and pulled her to her feet. "March," she commanded.

"Let go of me!"

"No way. I said march. I'm taking you to the bathroom and putting you under a cold shower, and then I'm going to show you how to start getting over Jason."

"Therapy?" Nora said thickly. She stopped resisting and let Caroline guide her down the hall.

"No, not therapy. Pickle jars. You're angry. Hell, who wouldn't be? But instead of turning that anger on Jason, whom I shall from this day hence only refer to as 'the Rat,' you're beating yourself up. The only sure cure for torturing yourself over a man is to get a few empty pickle jars and smash them in the bathtub while screaming. Actually, you could smash them anywhere, but if you smash them in the bathtub, it's not as hard to clean up the broken glass."

"What am I supposed to scream?"

"Use your imagination," Caroline said grimly, as she stripped off Nora's wedding dress, pushed her into the shower, and turned on the cold water.

Ten minutes later a wet, cold, slightly more sober Nora was standing barefoot on the Mexican tiles dressed in a long-line bra and a sodden petticoat, throwing empty pickle jars into the bathtub and screaming at the top of her lungs. She told Jason everything she hated about him; and when she ran out, she started in on Felicity. It was a nice, satisfying, completely victimless tantrum; and when she was done she really did feel better.

"Great," Caroline said. "Next we're going to shred your wedding dress in your Cuisinart. No, wait. That might burn out the motor. We'll have to cut it up with scissors."

"Are you crazy? That dress cost me over a thousand dollars."

"Do you honestly think you're ever going to want to wear it again?"

Nora thought this over for a second. "Not even if hell freezes over." She bent down, picked up the discarded dress, tossed it to Caroline, and went off to find scissors.

By the time she returned, she'd begun to get into the spirit of things. "Can I bury the pieces in a shallow grave?" she asked Caroline as she handed her a pair of scissors.

"Sure."

"Or burn them?"

"Anything you want."

* * *

About a quarter of an hour later, Jenkins looked out of his kitchen window and was treated to the sight of two apparently insane females standing in his neighbor's backyard squirting charcoal lighter on a pile of white scraps. One of them was his neighbor, although at first he didn't recognize her because she looked like a wet dog, was wearing weird white underwear, and was obviously drunk.

The other woman took out a match, lit it, and threw it on the pile. There was a little pop like a balloon bursting, and the whole thing went up in flames.

"Hey, Ryan," Jenkins yelled. "Unplug yourself from the idiot box for a minute, come over to the window, and get a load of this."

Ryan muted the television, ambled over to the kitchen window, looked out, and made a low whistling sound. "What the hell are those ladies up to?"

Jenkins stripped the paper off a stick of gum and popped it into his mouth. "I figure the wedding went sour so they're doing a spell. Damn. I told her this morning that it wasn't going to work out, but this has got to be one for Guinness. Shortest honeymoon on record. She must have been the world's worst lay; and a witch to boot."

"A witch?"

"Yeah, there's a lot of them around these days practicing satanic rites. I saw a special about it on TV." Jenkins looked back at the bonfire, sucked the sweetness out of his gum, and shook his head. "Next thing you know, they'll be taking over the neighborhood."

In some ways, Jenkins's accusation of witchcraft wasn't so far off the mark. When Nora's wedding dress was reduced to a pile of smoldering rubble, she and Caroline went back inside and dropped a photo of Jason into a blender full of soapy water. Nora pressed the button marked *Liquefy,* and there was a satisfying brrrr as Jason's smiling face was blended into oblivion.

It might not be a voodoo doll, Nora thought. But it would do.

Yet, although Caroline's tricks for getting over Jason helped, they still weren't enough. By the time Caroline left, Nora had come to the realization that she was angrier than she'd ever been in her life. She went to bed an hour or so after midnight, but sleep was impossible. For the remainder of what was to have been her wedding night, she lay awake imagining ways to get even with Felicity and Jason. By dawn she had become a woman obsessed with revenge—not just revenge for herself, but revenge for every man or woman who had ever been humiliated, dumped, or betrayed.

At last, when the sun was peeking over the horizon and the damn birds were singing as if nothing had happened, she fell asleep, only to wake a few hours later with the worst hangover she'd had since college. Her eyes ached; her tongue was a wad of wet cotton; the place where she usually kept her brain felt as if it had been stuffed with wet Kleenex. The sight of the empty vodka bottle sitting on the kitchen table made her actively nauseated, and the thought of ever eating cranberries in any form made her gag. When she walked outside to inspect the remains of her wedding dress, the sunlight hurt her eyes so badly that she screamed and fled back into the house. Clearly drowning her sorrows in drink was not going to be an option.

She spent the rest of Sunday nursing herself back to health. By Monday morning she'd recovered. Technically, she wasn't due back in the office for two weeks because, hey, she was on her honeymoon, right? She and

Jason were lolling in bed right now, looking out at the blue Caribbean, and trying to decide whether to wind-surf, snorkel, or spend the day making love.

She spent five seconds imagining Jason and Felicity vacationing on St. John's. Then she put down her coffee cup, went to the refrigerator, took out a bottle of dill pickles, tossed them into the garbage disposal, strode into the bathroom, and threw the jar against the wall with a scream that would have prompted Jenkins to call 911 if he'd had his hearing aids in. Returning to the kitchen, she sat down at the table, and waited.

At nine-fifteen, she called the office. Amber answered on the second ring.

"Amber, this is Nora. Don't say anything. Particularly don't say how sorry you are for me. Just get me the phone number of a client named Rosalee Lambert. She was in last Tuesday for a private consultation. Also, find Dale Lambert's client profile. I know you took his name out of our database, but you have backups and hard copy, right?"

"Right," Amber said in a cowed voice.

"Reenter Dale Lambert's information in the database immediately and e-mail it to me as an attachment. I'm going to be working at home today. Is all that clear?"

"Yes," Amber repeated in a quivery little voice that made Nora want to slap her. Nora was suddenly ashamed of herself for being so abrupt.

"Look, I'm sorry if I sound out of it today, but I'm sure I don't have to explain how rotten I'm feeling. Put a 'please' in front of everything I just said, please. And just let me say again for the record: I really appreciate how well you do your job. You're the best bookkeeper I've ever had."

"Thanks," Amber said. But except for giving Nora Rosalee's phone number, she didn't say much else, and

Nora hung up with the impression that she'd frightened her half out of her wits.

Nora waited forty-five minutes to make sure Rosalee was out of bed and Dale had left for work. Since Rosalee had said Dale was a currency trader at Bretano Global, Nora figured any time after ten would be safe.

At ten-fifteen, she dialed Rosalee's number. "Rosalee?"

"Yes?"

"This is Nora Wynn from Love Finds a Way."

Rosalee said nothing.

"Look, I know we didn't part on good terms, but don't hang up on me. I'm calling to say that I've changed my mind about mismatching your husband, Dale. I've decided to start a small, very discreet service dedicated to helping deserving clients like yourself get revenge. I'm calling it 'Payback Time.' Are you interested?"

7

Fixing Dale up with dates from hell proved to be ridiculously easy. When clients filled out their intake questionnaires, they told Nora more about themselves than they suspected. Buried among ordinary questions like *Would you rather go to a movie or take a walk on the beach?* were questions that allowed her to draw up a psychological profile and screen out anyone who was dangerous, abusive, sociopathic, or just plain crazy.

There were always a few who fell right on the borderline: people who were sane enough to function, but hell to spend more than a few hours with. Nora called these her "Difficult Cases" or "DCs." Because they paid their money like everyone one else, and because she felt that, no matter how neurotic you were, you had a right to try to find happiness, she felt obliged to do her best for the DCs. Fortunately, the world seemed to be filled with ordinary people who were attracted to borderline personalities and often preferred them to saner, duller dates. When that failed, Nora just fixed the DCs up with each other and stood back.

Fifteen minutes after Rosalee Lambert became Payback Time's first paying customer, Nora had booted up her computer and opened the DC file. Although there were well over a hundred people in it, classified by their neuroses on a scale of one to ten, there were only half a dozen females who were completely intolerable. As far as Nora was concerned, all six had Dale Lambert's name on them.

The following morning, when Dale arrived at Bretano Global and turned on his computer, he found a message from Love Finds a Way in his mailbox. The dating service was happy to inform him that a match had been found that met his criteria. The woman in question had been contacted and had expressed strong interest. The service had given her Dale's phone number as per his request, and she should be calling him soon to arrange a date.

Dale deleted the e-mail and gave a silent yip of triumph. He'd have yelled out loud, but yelling in a bank was like yelling in church.

The restaurant Dale's date chose wouldn't have been out of place in Paris. Everywhere you looked, there were tables covered with heavy linen, candles, glossy white china, and waiters who moved so silently they seemed to glide across the floor on oiled wheels. But Dale only had eyes for her.

She picked up her napkin and spread it on her lap, leaned forward, and gave him a smile so slow and intimate that he felt like sweeping the dishes off the table and taking her for a ride she'd never forget.

"So," she said in a husky whisper, "before we order dinner, I just want you to know that I'm willing to have sex with you at any time."

Dale hadn't expected to meet a mind reader. He choked on his bread and went into a coughing fit. He'd only met this woman an hour ago, and he suddenly had gotten luckier than he had ever been in his entire life. She was dark, and small, and intense, with a tiny waist and huge breasts. Except for the mole on her cheek, she could have been a movie star; plus she was a good twenty years younger than he was. Had he died and gone to heaven? Apparently so. He grabbed for his glass, and took a gulp of water so cold it made his teeth ache.

"That's great," he stuttered. Damn it. He was actually flustered by her directness. *Calm down, man,* he told himself. *Stop acting like a horny teenager. Don't blow this.*

The woman, whose name was either Natalie or Jeanine—he was too excited to remember—leaned forward slightly so her breasts rose up over the rim of her dress like a pair of soft, white water balloons. "But first," she said in a husky whisper, "I have a question."

"Ask away." Dale gave a nervous laugh that made him want to kick himself.

"Are you fertile?"

"Fertile?"

"I mean, do you have a high sperm count?"

"I don't know." Dale stared at her in disbelief. "I, uh, that is, I've never counted."

She made a little cooing noise, reached across the table, and seized his hands. "I really hope you have a high sperm count," she said, "because I want to have your baby."

"My what!" Dale said so loudly that people at nearby tables turned to look at them.

"My biological clock is ticking," she said. "Tick, tick, tick. Can't you hear it, sweetheart?"

"No!" he cried.

She made a little purring sound. "And that's the alarm going off."

"Waiter!" Dale yelled. A waiter came scurrying over.

The Moulin Vert was the kind of restaurant that didn't believe in keeping customers waiting. "Check!" Dale said. There was panic in his voice.

"Oh, don't be silly," Natalie/Janine said. "We haven't ordered yet." She turned to the waiter and flashed him the same sexy smile she'd given Dale. Apparently she gave it to anything male that ventured too near her trap. "Just ignore my boyfriend here," she said, pointing at Dale. "He's only joking." She picked up the menu. "Now I'll have . . ." She paused and turned to Dale. "You're a currency trader, right?"

Dale nodded, unable to speak.

"Well, then, you should be able to afford anything on the menu."

"I thought we were going Dutch," Dale said in a strangled voice.

"Dutch?" His dinner companion laughed so wildly that even the waiter joined in. Again she pointed at Dale. "My boyfriend's quite the kidder, isn't he?" She studied the menu. "Let me see. For an appetizer we'll have a double order of the Beluga caviar with a bottle of the Veuve Clicquot La Grande Dame ninety."

Dale groaned. The Veuve Clicquot was $185 a bottle. He tried to protest, but there was no stopping her. By the time she finished ordering, he was in for $600.

A week later, Dale tried again. The next woman the dating service fixed him up with also asked him to meet her in restaurant. This time the place was Italian. Better yet, it was the last spot in California where you could publicly smoke and eat at the same time.

"It's like a speakeasy," Jackie had told him on the phone, "only instead of bootleg booze, you've got your bootleg smoke. It's a time warp. It's like totally illegal.

Completely fifties. You'll love it. Plus the food is great, and there's nothing on the menu over fifteen dollars."

A fifteen-dollar ceiling sounded perfect, and Dale had always had a soft spot in his heart for women who were willing to break rules. Besides, when he asked Jackie if she smoked a lot, she'd said, "No, only a little."

Unfortunately, this turned out to be either a monumental piece of self-delusion or a deliberate lie. All through dinner she sat across from him, chain-smoking one Camel after another and stamping the butts out in the butter dish. The smoke was so thick, he could hardly see her face. Everyone else in the restaurant was doing the same thing. There was so little oxygen, that even Dale, who sometimes smoked cigars, began to get slightly nauseated. Worse yet, Jackie talked nonstop about global warming.

"The ice caps in the Antarctic are breaking off," she said, flashing him a smile that displayed two rows of tobacco-stained teeth. "Did you know that?" She didn't wait to hear if he did.

"Where are the penguins going to live, I ask you? And the snow is melting off the top of Mt. Kilimanjaro. All the glaciers are melting. So why hasn't the U.S. been willing to sign the Kyoto treaty on greenhouse gas emissions? I'll tell you why. It's because the government has this secret agreement with the Canadians. Yeah, I know it sounds strange, but hear me out."

Dale didn't have any choice but to hear her out. Jackie never paused long enough for him say a word. In fact about half an hour into the date, he determined that she never even paused to inhale, unless you counted smoke. Maybe when she was a baby, the little hole in the top of her head had never closed, and somehow she had learned to suck air through it.

"It all has to do with this plan to remineralize the oceans," she continued relentlessly, tapping more ashes into the butter. "You see, you take iron filings and scatter them all over the surface of the ocean. The iron causes algae to grow, which absorb the greenhouse gasses. Are you following me here?"

Dale nodded. He was trapped, utterly, helplessly trapped.

"Great," she said. "Well, when the Canadians found out about this plan, which"—she took a long drag on her cigarette and stared at Dale as if daring him to try to say a word—"is totally brilliant if you ask me, there was this secret meeting between their prime minister and . . ."

For two more hours the monologue continued. By the time Dale took Jackie home, he was not only not in the mood to try to put the make on her; he never wanted to hear the words "greenhouse effect" again.

Dale was just beginning to wonder if he should try another dating service, when Love Finds a Way matched him with a woman who looked like a real winner. This time he put the nix on restaurants and made a date to meet her at El Floridita, a club in Hollywood that featured live music and dancing. When he arrived, he discovered to his dismay that the place also served Cuban food, but fortunately his date didn't seen interested in eating. She turned out to be sweet, sexy, and so beautiful it was all he could do not to drool. Her name was Bliss, and she was a blonde with a figure like those Playboy Bunnies he used to lust over as a teenager.

Bliss wore a low-cut red dress with tiny little straps that kept falling off her shoulders. The dress had a skirt so short Dale could see the tops of her stockings every time she crossed her legs. Real stockings held up by a real garter belt. Dale hadn't seen a woman wear a pair of those in years. And she was wearing high heels too, really high ones that made her butt sway when she walked.

Bliss not only insisted on paying for her drinks, she split the cover charge with him. El Floridita was filled with couples flailing around to Johnny Martinez and his Hollywood Salsa Machine, but Bliss insisted on dancing close and slow, smiling at him and rubbing up against him, and even nibbling his ear. She didn't give him lectures either. In fact, except for laughing and smiling and looking at him as if he were the most attractive man she'd ever met, she hardly made a sound.

That was fine with Dale. He'd decided after the Jackie disaster that he liked the quiet types. He and Bliss drank the club's signature rum cocktails flavored with fresh limes and mint leaves and slow-danced for hours, plastered together as if they'd been glued. By the time he took her back to her place, he was sure he was going to score. At the door, he didn't try to kiss her. He wanted to go slow and savor every moment.

Sure enough, she invited him in. Her place looked like it had been designed for seduction: low lights; big couches covered in crushed velvet; a soft wall-to-wall carpet of the kind that Dale knew for a fact wouldn't give you rug burns. Bliss put on some soft music and they danced some more. She was a little drunk, pliable, as ready to tumble into bed as any woman Dale had met in years.

When the time was right, he led her over to one of the couches, sat down, took her in his arms, and started to kiss her. That's when she began screaming. She screamed, and screamed, and screamed, and screamed, and nothing he could do or say could make her stop.

"Get away from me!" she shrieked. "Don't touch me! Get your dirty hands off me! What kind of person do you think I am!"

A totally crazy person, Dale thought.

Somehow he located his coat and tie. When he left, Bliss, the Princess of Mixed Messages, was still screaming.

Dale had struck out three times in a row and was getting desperate to have sex with a woman who didn't wear flannel nightgowns and bunny slippers, so against his better judgment he accepted a fourth date courtesy of Love Finds a Way. The woman's name was Ashley Clay. She was a photographer who told him on the phone that they would have to go someplace smoke-free because she was allergic to tobacco.

"My work developing film has made me sensitive to several hundred scents," she warned him. "But otherwise, I'm really easy to get along with."

Dale didn't like the sound of that, but Ashley did sound friendly and, other than the allergic bit, reasonably sane. Also, he liked the photo she'd e-mailed him. She was tall and thin and healthy-looking, with long brown hair (Dale had always liked long hair on women) and a winning smile. In the photo she wore tight blue jeans and a little cropped-off top that showed off her navel ring, which was a big plus.

Before they hung up, Ashley warned him not to wear any kind of perfume or use scented soaps or deodorant. Dale agreed reluctantly. For a while, he even thought about calling her back and canceling, but he decided his luck had to get better.

On the night of the date, he showed up at her apartment at 8:00 on the dot. Unfortunately, in the rush of getting ready, he had forgotten that aftershave lotion qualified as a perfume. Ashley answered the doorbell at 8:06, took one whiff of his Brute, and went into a coughing fit so terrible that within seconds she was doubled up on the hall rug gasping for breath and calling for her inhaler.

Somehow Dale managed to locate it, but every time he got close enough for her to smell him, she got worse. By the time he figured out he was going to have to toss the inhaler to her, she was turning blue.

Dale pulled out his cell phone and called 911. While he was waiting for the paramedics to arrive, he offered to give her CPR, which was as close as he ever got to kissing her, but she waved him away in panic.

The date ended with Ashley being loaded into an ambulance. Dale called the hospital a few hours later to make sure she'd survived, but other than that he never tried to contact her again. He had a strong feeling she wasn't going to be interested in a second date, and besides, he'd had enough. Philandering wasn't all it was cracked up to be.

After he called the hospital, he booted up his computer, canceled his account with Love Finds a Way, and wrote a nasty note demanding a refund. Then he drove home, where he found Rosalee waiting up for him.

Rosalee was wearing a ratty terry cloth bathrobe and curlers. She'd put on some weight lately and had cold cream smeared all over her face, but Dale didn't care. Taking her in his arms, he gave her the warmest kiss he'd given her in months.

8

Forcing Dale to come crawling back to his wife was one of the greatest successes of Nora's career, but she had known from the start that she couldn't go on intentionally mismatching clients if she wanted to stay in business. Besides the damage it would do to her reputation, there were just not enough Bliss Bronstads, Ashley Clays, Natalie Pickmans, and Jackie Weldons to go around. Nora had given Dale the cream of her DC file, and her only regret was that he hadn't hung around long enough to date Sorrel Taft, a wacked-out astronomy professor, who'd stated on her intake questionnaire that she was having a hard time getting "turned on sexually by earthlings" since her most recent alien abduction.

But even without the intentional mismatches, Payback Time was a success from the start. Nora soon thought up a number of other ingenious, discreet, wickedly comic ways for her clients to get revenge, and she didn't have to spend a penny on advertising. Rosalee told her friends, who told their friends, who told their friends. The number of clients coming in for private consultations grew geometrically, and by mid-July, thanks to word of mouth, Payback Time was threatening to become a bigger money maker than Love Finds a Way.

Nora quickly realized that she had struck gold. Revenge was an untapped market that attracted singles who had been dumped and betrayed, married people, long-term couples, and the newly divorced. People just couldn't seem to get enough of it.

"Send his underwear to the laundry marked 'Heavy Starch,' " she advised the clients who paid three hundred dollars apiece to sit in the comfortable chair in her office and sob into her Kleenex. Men, women: it didn't matter. They had all been hurt and humiliated; they were all suffering.

"Saw partway through the laces of her running shoes so they mysteriously break when she puts them on. 'Accidentally' wash a pair of red shorts with the whites, so all his underwear turns pink. Send a small contribution in her name to PETA or the Ku Klux Klan. Oversalt his soup, replace his coffee with decaf, change the password on his computer, uninstall all his printers. Flag down a pair of those Mormon missionaries who are always riding around on bicycles and tell them he wants them to come over to his house and tell him the good news. If he's already a Mormon, call up the Baptists and invite them to his place to help him understand the error of his ways."

Sometimes Nora went for technical solutions that were positively demonic. "Send her the 'fax of death,' " she would advise. "It's a classic. You just tape three or four sheets of blank paper together and put them in a fax machine. When the first sheet comes out, you loop it over and tape it to the free end. It goes round and round forever.

"Visit Web sites. You know: the ones that offer low-interest mortgages, Viagra by mail, and ways to make money at home in your spare time. Register in his name and then fill out every form you can find using his e-mail address. I guarantee that in less than a week you can increase his spam by three hundred percent. And don't forget to include his phone number, so he can get those great telemarketing calls at dinnertime. But don't do anything seriously illegal, immoral, or violent, or you're on your own. This isn't the mob. We're not talking about putting out contracts on people or even damaging property worth more than a few bucks. We're talking *petty* revenge. We're talking making their lives hell in *little* ways; we're talking about driving the rat-faced, lying, scum-sucking traitors crazy by inches."

That last point about not doing anything illegal or violent was particularly important because, ironically, Nora soon found herself in the revenge-control business. As she sat behind her desk dispensing advice, she heard things that made her shudder. The most mild-mannered people sometimes had fantasies that made the hair stand up on the back of her neck. She was still angry at Felicity and Jason, and might even have tried some of her tricks on them if she could have gotten away with it, but having gone public as a revenge consultant, she found herself in the position of not being able to take revenge on her own account. Still, angry as she was, she wasn't even in the same league with some of her clients.

Soft-spoken certified public accountants who had probably never had so much as an overdue library book spoke of wanting to plant heroin on ex-wives and frame them for drug trafficking. Sweet-faced older women with radiant smiles and blue hair asked her with all seriousness if she thought it might be okay for them to poison their neighbor's perpetually barking poodle and have it stuffed by a taxidermist.

"No, no, no," Nora told them. "Revenge is an art.

Plus it can rebound. Think. What's it worth to you to get even? Do you want to go to jail? Do you want to live the rest of your life knowing you've done something really terrible? I don't think so."

But just in case they didn't agree, she required them all to sign a contract. They would not, they swore, do anything "dangerous, illegal, or physically harmful." And if they did, well, then, Nora washed her hands of them. They would have to hold both her and Payback Time "blameless for any consequences." In other words, if they wanted to play around on the Dark Side, Nora wasn't going to take the rap.

Still, she sympathized with their anger. She knew what it was like to wake up at four A.M. grinding your teeth. She knew how it felt when someone made a fool of you in front of all your friends. She empathized with their humiliation, their surprise, their rage. And because she knew their pain from the inside, she was a genius at offering advice.

"Break empty pickle jars," she counseled abandoned girlfriends. "Cut up your negligee and give it a funeral. Play a Tibetan bell CD and imagine you're cutting the cords that bind you. And if none of that works, take an anger management class, because in the end you'll not only want to get even, you'll want to move on. Forgetting someone is the best revenge of all."

Nora could say that because she believed it. As time passed, she was gradually starting to forget how much Jason and Felicity had hurt her. Not entirely, of course. But the unbearable pain of her wedding day was becoming more of a sprained ankle than an amputated limb. Life was good. Both her businesses were booming; she was making a lot of money. Sometimes she was even happy for brief stretches before the memory of Jason pushing her aside at the altar came back to ambush her, destroying a night's sleep and leaving her feeling humiliated all over again.

There were even moments when she suspected that she'd been partly to blame for what had happened. Maybe she'd loved the idea of Jason more than she'd loved Jason himself. Perhaps that's why he'd cheated on her with Felicity. In any event, it didn't matter, because bit by bit, she was recovering her self-respect.

Then, one morning near the end of August, Caroline brought Nora news that sent her back to square one: Felicity and Jason had finally gotten married. Not only married: they'd had a formal church wedding followed by a tented reception in Jason's backyard that featured a sit-down luncheon, ice swans, a champagne fountain, a live band, and dancing. The tent had even been decorated with gardenias and stephanotis.

"No!" Nora cried. "Tell me it's not true! First Felicity takes my honeymoon; then she has my wedding!"

"Sorry," Caroline said. "But I thought you should know."

"What about her wedding dress? Did it have thirty satin-covered buttons?"

"I didn't see it personally, not being on the guest list; but I hear it wasn't anything like yours. It was a lacy thing; tentlike and frothy in a very expensive designer sort of way, because, of course—" Caroline came to an abrupt stop, but it was too late. Nora finished the sentence for her.

"Because Felicity's pregnant and it shows, right?"

"Right," Caroline admitted reluctantly.

"I don't care." Nora took a sip of coffee and managed a cold smile. "I don't give a damn about any of this. These two people mean absolutely nothing to me anymore. Jason who? Felicity who? Never heard of them."

And then, just to emphasize how very little she cared,

she put her head down on her desk and began to sob as if her heart had been broken all over again.

That night, Nora had a relapse. As she tried in vain to fall asleep, she found herself once again obsessed with revenge. Lying in bed, she went through scenario after scenario until she came to one that involved a perfect murder, one she might actually be able get away with. She named it "the Hollywood Death Diet."

The Hollywood Death Diet was an elegant, simple plan that involved liquid protein, poisonous mushrooms, and a watertight alibi. For hours, Nora turned it over in her mind, honing and refining every detail. If she carried out each step with the utmost attention, Jason and Felicity would almost certainly be wiped off the face of the earth, while Nora would go free. Best of all, they would do themselves in, which would mean that technically Nora would be innocent. She'd have the last laugh. In fact, she'd be the only one left alive, standing, and capable of laughter.

Yet even as she put the finishing touches on this beautiful murder scenario, she knew she'd never carry it out. She didn't have it in her to kill anyone no matter how badly they'd treated her. She hated guns and wouldn't have them in the house. She boycotted violent movies. When the evening news got too graphic, she switched channels. Nature specials that involved lions pouncing on gazelles made her scream and cover her eyes. When she found mice in her kitchen, she caught them in Have-A-Heart traps and drove them to a nearby park to set them free. She had to face facts: she couldn't even squash an ant without feeling guilty.

Still she went on refining the Hollywood Death Diet. Finally, when it was so perfect that not even Kinsey

Milhone could have cracked it, she gave a deep sigh, dismissed it from her mind, curled up around a pillow, and fell sound asleep.

She woke the next morning to the sound of sparrows singing gaily in the tree outside her window. Her body seemed lighter, the sunshine streaming into the room seemed brighter, and every flower in the garden seemed to have blossomed with particular beauty. While her coffee brewed, she impulsively dashed outside barefoot in her robe to throw bread crumbs to her koi and watched with pleasure as they flashed back and forth beneath the water like big gold and silver commas. What was with her? she wondered. Why was she in such a great mood? She hadn't felt this good in months.

As she sat at the breakfast table spreading orange marmalade on her toasted English muffins, she caught herself humming "Oh, What a Beautiful Morning." She stopped, knife poised over the marmalade jar. This was a nice change, but it was also weird. What was going on? Had someone dumped Prozac in the L.A. water supply?

Suddenly, she realized what was different: she was no longer angry at Jason and Felicity. Last night she had looked at the darkest part of herself, and discovered that it wasn't all that dark after all. Jason and Felicity were safe. She'd never harm them. Still, *in theory,* she could do them in at any time and never get caught, which meant that they lived at her pleasure. They were only going to grow old because Nora was a good person who was vastly superior to either of them.

Nora was the generous one, the moral one, the one who was capable of holding the lives of two people who had betrayed her in the palm of her hand and letting them go unharmed. She had all the power; Jason and Felicity had none.

Nora finished buttering her muffin and took a bite, savoring the crunchy texture. The orange marmalade tasted sweet and tangy, the coffee was perfect, the day was bright and full of promise; and she had just discovered the power of the imagination to heal.

9

On a warm evening in early October, about seven weeks after Felicity and Jason's wedding, twelve women and three men lolled on overstuffed cushions in a large, softly carpeted room in Nora's office building. In a corner, concealed behind a Chinese screen, an aromatherapy diffuser gurgled softly, sending out wafts of bitter orange and sandalwood. The drapes were drawn, and the only light came from several strategically placed candles which cast a golden glow over fifteen faces, making them look almost angelic. This was an illusion. The oldest was forty-six, the youngest only twenty; but they all had one thing in common: they had each paid $450 to take one of Nora Wynn's famous Revenge Fantasy Seminars.

"So, he's a lot bigger than I am, if you get the picture," a petite woman in white capri pants was saying. "Plus he gets totally wacked and starts yelling when I try to talk to him. So I'm going to wait until he's asleep, and then I'm going to tie him up with duct tape and force him to watch *Water World*."

Several members of her audience gasped audibly.

"For twelve hours straight," the petite woman added with a near-maniacal giggle. "Maybe if he's real sorry, maybe if he apologizes for sleeping with my therapist and trying to put the make on my sister, I'll let him watch some *Ishtar* too."

"Brilliant," said her nearest neighbor.

Nora was pleased. It *was* a good fantasy, but the woman in the capri pants hadn't thought it up. Caroline had. Caroline's years as a script reader had made her a genius at designing revenge scenarios for clients with no imagination. *Water World With Duct Tape* was one of the most popular, followed by *Ants in Their Pants* (which Nora personally found a bit predictable), and *Blue Screen of Death,* a fiendish computer-crashing fantasy that was guaranteed to provoke agonized screams, audible four rooms away.

Of course if you actually were going to carry out *Blue Screen of Death,* you would need some pretty serious computer skills, but that didn't matter. Want to imagine your ex-husband kidnapped by the insectlike aliens from *Independence Day?* No problem. Like to throw your former girlfriend in a time machine and send her back to the Middle Ages to catch bubonic plague or be beheaded for high treason? Go right ahead. In a revenge fantasy seminar, you could imagine anything. And the good part was, nobody got hurt.

Nora settled back on her pillow and listened to the rest of the woman's fantasy unwind. She preferred these canned scenarios to the ones her clients came up with by themselves. She and Caroline pored over them, checking and rechecking every detail to make sure they were either totally impossible to carry out or more or less harmless.

"You're playing with fire," Nora's lawyer had warned her when she asked him to draw up a contract for seminar participants. "You're asking people to understand the difference between fantasy and reality. Get a grip, Nora. You're living in L.A. where half the population thinks Spiderman is real and the other half thinks if they meditate long enough they'll be able to fly. I'm warning you: sooner or later some psycho is going to take one of those seminars of yours and go out and commit a serious crime."

Nora knew Matt was giving her excellent legal advice, but she told him to draw up the contract anyway. She had no intention of letting anyone unstable sign up for one of her seminars. Getting into one was going to be nearly as hard as getting into Harvard.

When the contract was complete, she had the psychologist at UCLA who had drawn up the original Love Finds a Way intake questionnaire create a new series of questions designed to weed out anyone unstable. The people who made it over the hurdles and into the seminars were as sane as astronauts. They were the kind of people who found a ten-dollar bill on the sidewalk and spent the next fifteen minutes trying to locate the person who dropped it; people who had never stolen a beer from a communal refrigerator; people who regularly paid the government more income tax than they owed because they were nervous about taking even legitimate deductions.

Time was confirming that Nora had been right to go ahead with the seminars. She'd been running them every weekend for more than six weeks now without a single incident. Far from going out and committing crimes, clients often dropped by her office afterward to thank her for helping them move on. She'd even managed to save a few marriages.

Unlikely as it might seem, revenge fantasies were the direct opposite of revenge. They made people more forgiving, not less. They were—as Nora never tired of explaining to new clients—a path to forgiveness, which

was why her seminars had become one of the hottest
tickets in town, why she now had her own radio talk
show once a week, and why her column "Bad Advice"
was currently appearing in the *Pasadena Star News*.

Sometimes Nora thought she should write Jason and
Felicity a thank-you note. *Nah, nah, nah,* she chanted
silently. *There's no revenge on earth as satisfying as
success.*

On the following Monday, it rained for the first time
in months. Water swept along the streets of Santa
Monica in quick, silvery sheets, stripping the petals off
the scarlet dahlias that surrounded the lion fountain
and knocking fronds off the palm trees.

"Buenos dias," Amber said brightly when Nora came
in to her office to collect a list of next weekend's seminar participants. Amber gestured at the storm. *"Soy
una tomate."*

"Are you saying you're a tomato?"

Amber blushed and dove for her dictionary. She had
recently developed a passion for learning Spanish thanks
to a new boyfriend who had replaced the cybersex-
crazed librarian who had given her so much grief last
May. Nora hadn't met the new guy yet, but from the
hints Amber dropped, he sounded like a much better
match: president of a corporation that made something
really boring like cardboard boxes, older, widowed, more
financially secure, more likely to read marketwatch.com
than surf over to some Web site that offered photos of
hot teenage chicks. Amber had been going sailing with
him on weekends. Nora had a hard time imagining
Amber getting up enough courage to climb into a boat,
but maybe the boyfriend had an electric motor and the
two of them only went out when there was no wind.

When Amber took her vacation time, the two lovebirds were going on a romantic trip somewhere south of the border—Mexico maybe. Wherever it was, Nora was sure it would have a first-class hotel since Amber's idea of adventure travel—like her own—involved hot water and room service. Meanwhile, Amber sat at her desk for hours at a time, toying with a corny little snow-storm paperweight, listening intently to a recorded language course, and muttering to herself, but so far she hadn't managed to master the vocabulary.

Amber flipped through the dictionary and pounced on a word. *"Tormenta,"* she said. "I meant to say *tormenta.* It means 'storm.' "

"Wonderful." Nora believed in encouraging Amber in every way possible. "We are indeed having a *tormenta* out there. So is the list ready?"

Amber took off her earphones, leaped to her feet, trotted over to one of the filing cabinets that lined her office, opened the top drawer, and pulled out a red folder, which she handed to Nora. Red was the color Amber had chosen for the Revenge Fantasy Seminars. Nora thought, not for the first time, that if Amber ever decided she didn't want to be a bookkeeper, she could step into interior decorating without missing a beat.

Nora opened the file, examined the list, and frowned. "Rosalee Lambert? What's she doing in here?"

Amber blinked and looked at Nora spacily. "Who?"

"Rosalee Lambert. You remember. The one whose husband we mismatched with all those DCs."

"Oh, yeah, of course."

Nora decided that she was definitely going to have to tell Amber to limit her time on the headphones. Learning Spanish was all well and good, but when it started making you momentarily forget the name of a client like Rosalee, it was time to take a break. On the other hand, maybe Amber was just addled with love for her new boyfriend. Nora had recently read that every time you had sex, your I.Q. went down ten points. She did a few quick calculations and grinned. Amber must have had a memorable weekend.

She looked back down at the list of names and her grin faded. "Dale must be cheating on Rosalee again." She looked up and saw that Amber had gone pale.

"How horrible," Amber whispered in that tiny little-girl voice that Nora always found more than a little annoying.

"Don't take Dale's cheating personally, Amber. It's not your fault, or mine either for that matter. We did our best for Rosalee." Ever since her bad experience with the librarian and the trauma of Nora's wedding, Amber had been hypersensitive about men who cheated on their wives and girlfriends. Sometimes having her around was like tending to a wounded kitten.

Nora pointed to the gaudy travel brochures that littered Amber's desk. "Think about your vacation. Beach, sand, sunshine."

And wild sex. But she didn't say that. With luck Amber would come back from her vacation with the I.Q. of pond scum. The kinks would go out of her shoulders. She'd loosen up. Brush the hair out of her eyes. Smile more. Lose the orthopedic sandals. Wear something that wasn't beige.

The following Saturday, Rosalee showed up for the revenge fantasy seminar promptly at seven P.M. and took her seat in the circle. When Nora asked who wanted to go first, her arm shot into the air.

"What fantasy would you like?" Nora asked her.

"My own," Rosalee announced. She got up, went over to the side of the room, and returned with a tennis racquet. "Blam!" she screamed. "Blam! blam!" With each "blam" she struck a cushion with the racquet. "Die, you low-life, cheating weasel!"

Rosalee paused, gulped in some oxygen, and explained to the startled ring of faces surrounding her that the tennis racquet was a bronze winch handle and the cushion was her husband Dale's head. With that, she took a firmer grip on the tennis racquet and began beating the cushion again. Within seconds, she wasn't in the seminar room. She was out on the ocean in a forty-foot yacht making sure Dale would never cheat on her again.

Nora forced herself to watch Rosalee's performance without flinching. She didn't like to see murder scenarios acted out so graphically, but people didn't need disapproval when they were in this state of pain and betrayal. They needed unconditional support.

As Rosalee went on killing the cushion, the other members of the seminar began to get nervous. There were discreet coughs. People on either side of her leaned away as if hoping to be out of reach if she decided to start smashing something else.

"Blam! blam!" Rosalee howled, hitting the cushion so hard it split, spewing stuffing all over the carpet. Throwing down the racquet, she hurled herself forward on the floor, and dissolved in tears.

"Perfect," Nora murmured as if she had been expecting it to come to this. "Absolutely perfect."

Rosalee kicked her feet and beat her fists on the carpet making soft divots. She cursed and screamed and told Dale exactly what she thought of him. She was having a temper tantrum, probably the first she'd had since she was two. After a while, her sobs became softer. Finally they stopped. She uncurled her fists and sat up looking dazed.

"I'm sorry," she said sheepishly. "I don't know what got into me."

"You're doing just fine." Nora gave her an encouraging smile.

Rosalee blinked and looked at Nora as if she hardly recognized her. "Really?"

"Yes, really. This is all part of the healing process."

"It is?"

"Absolutely." Nora turned to the other seminar participants. "So what do you think Rosalee should do now?"

"Check herself into a psych ward," Carl suggested. Carl was retired military and hadn't really gotten the picture. Nora glared at him.

"Continue with her fantasy," Julie said. Julie was a twenty-something film student at USC. Unlike Carl, she knew the difference between fact and fiction.

Nora gave Julie an approving nod. "Exactly." She turned to Rosalee. "So, what do you want to do to Dale now that you've killed him?"

Rosalee rubbed her wrists and looked thoughtful. "I don't know. I suppose I need to dispose of his body."

"Throw him over the side!" cried a woman who was going through a nasty divorce.

After that, suggestions came thick and fast.

"Tie some weights to his legs so he won't float."

"Wipe your fingerprints off that winch handle."

"Mop the blood off the deck. Then take off your clothes and throw them and the cleanup rags overboard. Don't leave hairs and fibers."

The "hairs and fibers" comment came from Carl. Nora was pleased to see he was finally getting into the spirit of the seminar.

Rosalee smiled and then began to chuckle wickedly. She had recovered from her crying fit and was clearly loving every minute of this. "I'll need an alibi," she said, looking around the circle.

Alibis weren't long in coming.

"Tell the cops your worthless husband hit his head and fell overboard."

"No, it's better not to tell them anything. Say you were asleep in the cabin, and when you came back up on deck, he was nowhere in sight."

Rosalee laughed and clapped her hands. "Great! If I say that, they can't even be sure Dale's dead! He might have accidentally drowned or decided to swim home, and since I've already cleaned up all the blood, they'll never be able to prove he didn't just leave me."

Carl waved his hand in the air furiously.

"Yes?" Nora said, bracing herself.

"This sounds like group therapy. Are you a licensed therapist?"

"No, but that's beside the point. This isn't therapy, Carl. It's fantasy. The difference was all spelled out in that contract you signed. It's what people do when they write poems or novels or film scripts or just daydream. In this room, anything is permitted: Rosalee can throw Dale to a mythical sea serpent; she can change him into a bat; she can even have him undergo a religious conversion and vow to remain faithful to her for the rest of his life."

"Not a chance in hell of that," Rosalee said with sudden bitterness.

Julie turned to Rosalee with all the wide-eyed innocence of someone who had never had a relationship that had lasted more than three months. "Why don't you just divorce him?"

"You don't have to answer that," Nora advised Rosalee.

"Heck, I don't mind." Rosalee shrugged and turned to Julie. "I can't divorce Dale. I'm middle-aged, I haven't held down a full-time job for twenty years, and I signed a prenuptial agreement that would leave me penniless. Also, I'm a practicing Catholic. Divorce is just not an option." She picked up the tennis racquet, twirled it between her palms, and then put it down on the carpet very gently. "It's a till-death-do-us-part kind of thing

between Dale and me. Besides, I think . . ." There was
a long silence. Rosalee continued to stare at the tennis
racquet.

"Think what?" Nora prompted. She suddenly found
herself remembering Lucia and Aldo, two Catholics
who were also married for the long run, but—unlike
Rosalee and Dale—happily.

"I think maybe I'm actually starting to forgive him,"
Rosalee said.

"Then this is working for you?" Nora was pleased.
Despite what she'd told Amber, she had felt a bit guilty
about not fixing Dale up with the entire DC list.

Rosalee looked up. There were tears in her eyes.
"Yes," she said softly. She looked around the circle.
"Thank you. Thank all of you. This has been . . ." She
stopped.

"Been what?" Julie asked.

"A fantastic experience," Rosalee said. "Absolutely
fantastic."

After Rosalee, Nora had one spectacular success
after another. For three weeks, Love Finds a Way hummed
along like a well-oiled machine, Payback Time continued to expand, the revenge fantasy seminars were packed,
and beautiful pairs of shoes went on sale all over town.
Every morning Nora woke up happy. Maybe not as
happy as she had been when she thought Jason loved
her, but happy enough to sing in the shower, admire her
koi, dance at her own karaoke bashes, roller-blade along
the Venice boardwalk, and even consider dating again.

Then, all at once, everything started to go wrong.
The first sign of impending trouble came in the form of
a letter notifying her that her car insurance had been
canceled due to six traffic violations. According to her
insurance company, she had made two illegal left turns,

racked up three speeding tickets, and gone the wrong way down a one-way street in Chula Vista.

Speeding tickets? Nora knew she hadn't had one in years. Illegal left turn? Absolutely not. Chula Vista? She tried to remember the last time she'd been there. Three years ago? Five years ago with Sam? The insurance company must have her confused with some other Nora Wynn. Clearly she needed to call them and explain that they'd made an error.

"I'm sorry," the pleasant-sounding woman on the other end of the line told her, "but all six of your violations are right here in our computer."

"Well, take them out. You've got the wrong person."

"I'm afraid not." The woman on the other end of the line read Nora her Social Security number. "That's you, right?"

"That's me, but I'm totally innocent."

"Wonderful," the woman said brightly. "Then I'm sure you won't have any trouble getting coverage from another insurance company. Good-bye and have a nice day."

"Wait a minute!" Nora cried. "You can't do this to me! Check with the police. They'll confirm that I never had those tickets!"

But it was too late. Once something was in their computer, the company never took it out. And no matter how often Nora kept calling back trying to explain, they wouldn't listen to her.

The next day brought yet another catastrophe. Her purse was stolen. Or maybe she left it somewhere. In any case, she couldn't find it. For over an hour, she and Amber and Caroline turned the office upside down, looking in every likely and unlikely place including the refrigerator in the coffee room, but all they found was dust, rubber bands, mineral water, and ice cubes.

"First I lose my insurance; then I lose my purse,"

Nora said. "This sounds like a perfect revenge fantasy scenario. So what do you think? Is someone turning the tables on me?"

Caroline helped herself to an Oreo, separated it into two halves, ate one, and nibbled at the other. "Possibly. But it could also be a coincidence."

"When did you last see it?" Amber helped herself to half a cup of decaf and carefully added hot water to make it weaker.

"I can't remember." Nora willed herself to be patient. She had already told Amber and Caroline that she couldn't remember when she'd last seen her purse, but Amber had obviously been too caught up in the search to listen. "I probably had it when I came in this morning, but that purse is so much a part of me, half the time I don't notice it."

Caroline popped the remains of the Oreo in her mouth and picked up another. "Sooner or later every woman loses her purse," she said with a philosophical shrug. "Maybe you'll discover you left it at a restaurant."

"Not likely. I always put it on the floor and wrap the strap around my foot so I won't forget it. Of course, sometimes I trip over the strap, but it's worth a few barked shins not to have to go through the hassle of canceling my credit cards, which I suppose I'm going to have to do immediately."

Caroline broke the second Oreo in half and began to nibble on the filling. "You might want to hold off on that," she advised. "In my experience, as soon as you cancel your credit cards, you find your purse. I'll call around for you and see what I can come up with."

That afternoon, while Nora interviewed new clients, Caroline and Amber called every place Nora had been in the last two days. Net result: no purse. Not even a possible purse sighting. Finally Nora gave up, canceled her credit cards, and took a taxi to the DMV to go through the hell of getting a new driver's license.

To her surprise, she failed the written test. Annoyed to the point of distraction, she grabbed a dog-eared copy of the instruction booklet and stood in a corner memorizing all the obscure facts that California drivers were supposed to know before they went out onto the freeways to shoot at each other. Then she took the test again, passed, and was given a temporary license. The only good thing about the experience—besides having a chance to meet a lot of interesting men with extensive tattoos and possibly prison records—was that the DMV had no record of her six supposed traffic violations, which was a good thing, because if they had, she wouldn't have been able to drive until she was too old to pass the eye test.

After her experience at the DMV, she was too tired to return to work. Instead, she drove home as carefully as someone transporting nitroglycerin. She intended to take a swim in her pool, make herself a cold glass of iced tea, put her feet up, and chill out. But when she pulled into her driveway, she saw that someone had been there before her. That morning when she left for work, she had had six rosebushes. Now she had . . . none.

She stared at the border of her driveway in disbelief. Every rosebush had been uprooted, put through a chipper, and carted away. In the gutter in front of her house, a few yellow and white petals and a handful of sawdust swirled in the breeze.

Okay, this proved it! Someone was clearly out to get her, and it didn't take a genius to figure out who that someone was. Nora parked her car beside the scar left by the missing bushes and strode over to Jenkins's house to demand an explanation, but when she knocked on his door, there was no response.

"Come out of there!" she called, pounding harder. "I know you thought my roses were over your property line, but they weren't! You can't simply chop down someone's flowers. It's vandalism and criminal trespass. And if I weren't an extremely decent person who has tried her hardest to be a good neighbor, I'd have you arrested!"

Jenkins opened the door so suddenly, she nearly fell into his living room. "What do you have your panties in a knot about this time?" he demanded.

"That!" Nora said through gritted teeth, pointing to the place where her roses had been.

"Your own guys did that." Jenkins chugged some beer and looked at her with relish. Apparently there was nothing he liked more than seeing her distraught.

"What guys?"

"Your yard guys."

"Liar."

"Ask 'em," Jenkins said, and slammed the door so hard he nearly took off her nose.

Nora stepped away from his door, pulled out her cell phone, and dialed her landscaping service.

"Did your workers take out my roses?" she demanded. "My neighbor insists they did."

"Why, sure, Ms. Wynn. You left them a note."

"What note? I didn't leave them any note."

There was a hurried conference. "Craig says he found a note on your front door. We got it right here. It says: 'Please chop out all the rosebushes along the driveway.' "

"It's a forgery. I can't believe this!" Nora glared at Jenkins's closed door. "Please save that note for evidence. I may contact my lawyers."

"I'm afraid the note won't do you much good, Ms. Wynn. It's not signed. Plus it was written on a computer."

Nora made a small choking sound.

"You okay?"

"My roses. My beautiful roses."

"Hey, we're really sorry about the mix-up, but how were we to know?" There was a pause. "You want the chips? You could use them for mulch."

"No, just give them a decent burial." Nora was sure Jenkins was behind this. He probably thought it was funny. She could just imagine him and his no-good son, Ryan, sitting in their living room laughing at her. Well, they better watch their step. The press didn't call her the Queen of Revenge for nothing.

Stowing away her cell phone, she strode past Jenkins's lawn dwarfs, resisting an urge to kick them. As she approached her own house, she saw the letter carrier was coming up the sidewalk whistling a happy tune like some kind of sunshine-drunk Disney character.

"Hi," he said cheerfully. "Great day, isn't it?"

"No," she replied sharply.

The letter carrier's smile faded. He examined Nora warily and fingered a small gas canister that dangled from his belt. *Great,* she thought, *that's all I need: maced in my own driveway by the United States Postal Service.*

"Just give me my mail, please."

The letter carrier held a handful of mail out to her. Nora accepted it and stood on the grave of her roses sorting through it. There were four catalogues, two credit card offers, a coupon for free pizza, a postcard from her parents, and an official-looking letter from the IRS.

Nora went inside, poured herself a glass of white wine, and sat for a while sipping it and staring at the letter. She had a strong suspicion that opening it wasn't going to be a happy experience.

10

Sam sat in the dark, drinking black coffee and brooding about the images that flickered across the screen in front of him. These were images he was responsible for, images he had been hired to create, and had sweated blood over. *And why?* he thought. *What's the point?*

This film, his latest industrial potboiler in an endless series of same, bore the thrilling title *Slurry Sealing of Secondary Roads in Low-Volume Residential Areas*.

What was "slurry"? Sam was glad you asked. Hey, he probably knew more about slurry than any other film-maker in Hollywood. Want to learn about fine aggregate mixtures, emulsions, water and mineral fillers, problems of oxidation, surface raveling, and curing periods? Then this was the movie for you: educational, accurate, boring beyond belief.

Sam watched in a kind of coma as large trucks moved back and forth sweeping streets and laying down a layer of what looked like black tar (But it wasn't tar. It was "slurry"!). He thought about the documentary films he wanted to make: films filled with action, adventure, social commentary, and beautiful cinematography offer-

ing award-winning material on some fascinating or important topic like art programs for homeless kids or the
origins of Cajun music instead of endless footage of
burly guys in undershirts putting out orange warning
cones.

The monster truck that laid down the slurry was
called "Top Gun." As it rolled across the screen, Sam
winced. The name seemed to mock him. He put his
hands over his eyes. He might make these turkeys, but
he didn't have to look at them: at least not at this stage.
It pays the rent, he thought. *And some day, if I just
hang in and keep going, I'll be able to afford to shoot
the low-rider film.*

There were so many great possibilities in L.A. for a
documentary filmmaker. Sam loved his adopted home-
town with a passion. He was a Lakers fan, a Dodgers
fan, an Angels fan. He loved the breathtaking sunsets,
the Hispanic flavor of the city, its theaters, its art muse-
ums, its symphony orchestras, the astounding array of
talented people who came from all over the world to
work in the film industry. It was frustrating not to be in
a position to catch more of this rich tapestry of daily
life on film. How long would he have to go on doing
projects he didn't want to do in order to be able to do
the films he . . .

"Sam?" a voice said. Sam removed his hands from
his eyes and saw a bureaucrat bending over him in a
motherly fashion. The guy's name was Arvie. He was
from the L.A. County Department of Public Works, he'd
hired Sam to make the film, and he absolutely loved
slurry. "Are you okay?"

"Fine." Sam forced himself to smile.

"Great film," Arvie said, gazing at the screen with
what appeared to be real pleasure.

"Thanks."

"We're pretty excited about it."

What kind of life did Arvie have? What kind of desperate misery drove a man to say he was "excited" by the sight of a road being repaved? Sam decided to take compliments where he could get them. "Thanks," he repeated.

"You had a phone call. I didn't want to interrupt you in the middle of the showing, but she said it was urgent. She said that, when she couldn't get you on your cell phone, she figured you'd turned it off. She left a number for you to call her back."

Sam felt a prickle of fear climb up his spine. Urgent phone calls were in short supply in his life. Were his mom and dad okay? "Did she leave a name?"

"Nora Wynn. You know her?"

Sam smiled and relaxed. It was flattering to have Nora phone him when they weren't supposed to be on speaking terms. Maybe she'd missed him. Of course, he told himself firmly, he hadn't missed her for a second. Still, it would be unfriendly not to call her back.

"Sam?"

"Yeah, I know her."

"Old girlfriend?"

"Ex-wife."

Arvie suddenly became intensely interested in what was happening the screen. "Did you know that the residual asphalt content of that slurry is a full twelve percent?" Arvie and Sam both stared at Top Gun as it spewed black goo out in a long, straight, steaming line.

Pathway to Hell, Sam thought; and then he got up and went outside to call Nora.

"I know we're not supposed to be speaking," Nora said, "but I need to ask you a question."

"Shoot." Sam wondered what this was all about.

Nora paused and cleared her throat. "Did you turn me into the IRS?"

"What!"

"I said, did you turn me into the IRS?"

All of the pleasure Sam had felt about getting a call from her instantly disappeared, and he had to resist an urge to throw his cell into one of the oversized aquariums that decorated the lobby. Why had he been stupid enough to think she might have missed him? "What kind of accusation is that?" he snarled.

On the other end of the line, Nora made a heroic attempt to keep her temper. She always hated it when Sam spoke in an irritable growl. Hadn't she just done her best to be brief and to the point? She decided to try again, but, as usual, their conversation was doomed before she opened her mouth.

"I'm not accusing you of anything. I'm sorry if it came across that way. I know it's a remote possibility, but a lot of bad things have been happening to me lately, and you're one of the few people who knows my Social Security number; so it's reasonable for me to ask if perhaps you turned me in for tax evasion."

"Reasonable, hell. Give me a break, Nora. Your Social Security number is all over the place. Any fourteen-year-old hacker could probably get it off the Net in two minutes."

Nora pressed her lips together and silently counted to ten. "So you're saying you didn't turn me in to the IRS?"

"No."

"Then why are they auditing me? Why are they asking for my back tax records?"

"How should I know?" Sam paused. He knew he should hang up, but he couldn't resist a parting shot. "Hey, wait. I just had an idea. Maybe you *were* cheating. Yeah, that's it. Maybe you were trying to write off your honeymoon as a business expense. Speaking of honeymoons, how's married life with Mr. Real Estate? Are the two of you still doing intellectually challenging things like bungee jumping?"

"That's a totally rotten thing to say!" Nora cried. "But I should have expected it. You always did go for the throat! You know perfectly well that I haven't seen Jason in months!"

Sam stared at the phone in confusion. "What?"

"You heard what I said!"

"Wait a minute: are you telling me you and Jason didn't get married?"

"Yes!" Nora yelled so loudly that Sam was forced to remove the phone from his ear. "And it's mean of you to rub my face in it. Like you didn't know. Like you didn't read it in the papers. Like you've been living in a cave or something. Like Lucia didn't tell you."

"She didn't as a matter of fact."

"You are such a bad liar, Sam Gallo!"

"I don't keep track of your life, Nora. The last I heard you were about to walk up the aisle and then head off to the Caribbean with Jason to snorkel with the sharks." Sam sat down on the nearest couch and tried to understand what she had just told him. Not married to Jason? How had that happened? He wanted to stop fighting with her and get the whole story, but once they started yelling at each other, it was almost impossible to make peace. "So what happened?" he said in what he hoped was a placating tone.

"None of your damn business!"

Sam suddenly became so angry that he felt as if the top of his head might fly off. "None of my business, huh? What happened, Nora? Did the groom wise up and make a run for it before you started nagging him to chew with his mouth closed?"

"Creep!" Nora cried. "You never fought fair!"

"Oh, yes, I did. It's just that 'fair' in your book always meant you got to have the last word."

"I bet you still leave toilet seats up," she snarled and rang off.

After she hung up, Nora sat at the kitchen table taking deep breaths. She was so angry she was shaking. Why had she given into the impulse to call him? What difference did it make? The tax audit was going to happen whether or not Sam admitted he'd had a hand in it.

She needed to adopt a more positive attitude. After all, she was innocent, so she had nothing to fear. Sure, the sight of that envelope with the IRS return address had almost given her heart failure. But her financial records were in great shape; she had reported every cent of income; she only took legal deductions; she'd never knowingly cheated the government out of a dime. This was probably just a random exploration of her finances triggered by a computer. The IRS did this sort of fishing all the time. It meant nothing.

Nothing, ha! a voice inside her head kept saying. *Nothing except hassle. Nothing except worry. Nothing except months of wondering when the ax is going to fall.*

Nora picked up her wine and took a cautious sip. Outside the kitchen window, a hummingbird was hovering beside the feeder, flashing the iridescent green feathers on his tail and sucking away at sugar water like there was no tomorrow. Nora experienced a moment of intense envy. She wished she was a bird. Preferably a migrating bird that could cross international borders, no questions asked.

Had Sam really not known anything about the audit? At first, he'd sounded surprised enough to be innocent. But then he'd gotten so angry. If he still harbored that much resentment toward her, wouldn't this be a perfect way for him to take revenge? A lot of the people who called her radio show claimed that nothing would give them greater pleasure than turning in an ex-spouse for tax evasion. In fact revenge via the IRS was so popular that Caroline was in the process of creating a new fantasy scenario called "the Audit From Hell."

She had to face facts: she was in the revenge business. That meant it was always possible that someone other than Sam—some disgruntled client or some random nutcase—had turned her in to the IRS to give her a taste of her own medicine. She should have asked Sam more questions, but there hadn't been time before they started to argue. Maybe he'd been innocent; maybe not. Now she'd never know. She'd thought her communication skills had improved over the years. Maybe they had, but not with Sam.

That was the trouble with having any contact with him. Every time they talked, she ended up more confused than ever. Why couldn't they get along? She didn't want to fight with him; she really didn't. They'd had a lot of good times together.

Yeah, and a lot of bad times too, the voice in her head said wearily. Nora took another sip of wine and reminded herself that, during the six months of their marriage, she and Sam had fought about every conceivable topic: money, work, politics, whose turn it was to do the laundry, whether or not beds should be made as soon as you got up or allowed to air—nothing had been too trivial.

Sometimes she thought they'd argued so much because they had married too quickly, didn't know what they wanted to do with their lives, and didn't know how to talk to each other about it. Their apartment had been another source of stress: a crummy one-bedroom unit with cardboard-thin walls and neighbors who liked to run the garbage disposal at four A.M., which had meant

Nora and Sam hardly ever got a good night's sleep. Nora had been neat; Sam littered every surface like a dying oak tree: leaving his film gear all over the place and burying the kitchen table elbow deep in vital scraps of paper that Nora was forbidden to move, or—God forbid—throw away.

In fact, the surface of that table had been so far beneath Sam's paper pile that they'd never used it for meals. Not that that mattered, because except for a few fancy breakfasts, which were Sam's specialty, they'd eaten on the run, bolting down microwaved Mexican dinners and waving to each other in passing as they rushed off to the low-paying jobs they'd been forced to take while they tried to get their careers up and running: Nora as a waitress, Sam as an assistant to a small-time producer who was filming a series of instructional films on industrial safety.

Near the end, their arguments had become so ridiculous that Nora hadn't known whether to laugh or cry. But they'd loved each other, and even when they were fighting, they'd always clung to the belief that they'd work out their problems and stay together. Then the final blow fell: Nora was accepted into graduate school at Cal Poly to begin studying for her MSW. Less than a week later, Sam got an offer to go to South America for a year to direct travel promos for an adventure company. For days, they fought over who would go and who would stay. *It's taken me years to figure out what I want to do with my life,* Nora had cried. *I'm supposed to start grad school this fall and I'm not sacrificing that to go off to live in the jungle!*

Sam had shut down emotionally, lowered his head like a charging bull, and stubbornly repeated two sentences over and over until Nora wanted to scream with frustration. *I need to take this job, Nora. It's the only way*

I'll ever make enough money to direct a film I care about.

In the end, neither of them had been willing to give in, and, although the paperwork for their no-fault divorce had taken the better part of a year to complete, that had been the end of their marriage. Nora had packed her bags and moved out. Not long afterward, Sam left for South America.

A few years later when she started doing match-making profiles, Nora filled out intake questionnaires for herself and Sam and ran them through the computer. The results were impressive: Sam Gallo and Nora Wynn were so incompatible that it was impossible to imagine they could ever have loved each other. But they had of course. That was the mystery and the pity of it: all that love wasted on the wrong person.

I'll never call Sam again, Nora promised herself. *Never.*

She put down her wineglass, got up from the table, walked into her study, booted up her computer, clicked on her address book, and deleted Sam's name. Then she sat staring at the place where it had been. It gave her a hollow feeling not to have any trace of him in her life.

For a few seconds, she dragged the pointer across the tool bar aimlessly, then restored the entry. There was no use going overboard.

She clicked on *Games* and started to play Mine Sweeper, but after two moves, she found herself unable to continue because she became convinced there was a mine under every square. Shutting down the computer, she went back to the kitchen to finish her wine.

Someone's out to get me, she thought. *If it's not Sam, who the hell is it?* Maybe the answer was "no one." Perhaps it was merely a coincidence that in less than forty-eight hours she'd lost her purse and her roses, had her car insurance canceled, and gotten that letter from the IRS.

She finished off the last of the wine and sat for a moment staring at the empty glass. *Do I really have an enemy?* she wondered. *Or is specializing in revenge starting to make me paranoid?*

11

The next morning Nora was sitting on the Santa Monica Freeway when her cell phone rang. Since she had been at a full stop for over five minutes, she had resorted to reapplying her mascara to pass the time. Around her, other commuters were involved in similar tasks. To her right a woman in a red Camaro was putting a coat of green lacquer on her fingernails; to her left a man in a Jeep Cherokee was eating a hamburger and reading a newspaper. The teenager behind her in the white pickup was bouncing up and down like a crazed squirrel, which probably meant he was listening to loud music, although mercifully he had his windows rolled up.

Nora put down the mascara wand and picked up the phone. She really should get a hands-free system, but given how much time she sat in traffic jams, it hadn't been a high priority. Out of the corner of her eye, she saw the woman who had been painting her nails stick her fingers out the window and wave them around to dry the polish. The man on the other side finished his hamburger and started in on a bag of fries.

"Nora Wynn speaking," Nora said in her best, up-beat, professional matchmaking voice.

"Nora." It was Caroline. "Turn on your radio *now.*"

There was something in Caroline's voice that filled Nora with foreboding. She reached out with her free hand and punched the little triangular *On* button on the radio, wondering what terrible disaster had happened.

The sound of a Mozart sonata flooded the car, and Nora relaxed. At least whatever had gone wrong wasn't serious enough to preempt regular programming.

"The radio's on," she told Caroline, "and all I'm getting is that soothing music the classical stations always play at rush hour to prevent road rage. So, what's this about?"

"Turn to the AM news."

"Why? Have I won the lottery?"

"Just turn to the news, Nora. Please. I didn't want to be the one to tell you this, but everyone else is out of the office."

Nora didn't like the sound of that. She jabbed the AM button and then hit a preset that took her to the right frequency. "Sunny with coastal fog in some areas . . ." the announcer was saying.

"They're just giving the weather."

"Wait."

Nora waited. The weather went on for a few more seconds, and then the regular news anchors came on. Their names were Sean and Lynda, and over the past six months Nora had developed a reluctant fondness for them. No matter what unspeakable event occurred, Sean and Lynda bantered away like two second-rate stand-up comics who had lost the house. There was something noble and doomed about their relentless good cheer that always made her want to send them a sympathy card and a fruit basket.

"Sean and Lynda are doing the usual happy talk,"

she told Caroline. "Sean's telling Lynda that she looks great in her new haircut. Standard operating procedure. He tells her that at least once a day. So what gives? The suspense is killing me."

"You don't want to know," Caroline said. "But that doesn't mean you don't have to. Just keep listening."

"And now," said Lynda, "for our top story: Bretano Global currency trader Dale Lambert disappeared last night while sailing his yacht from Catalina to Marina Del Rey . . ."

"No!" Nora screamed.

". . . Dale Lambert's wife, Rosalee Lambert, told police she was napping in the cabin at the time of her husband's disappearance and only discovered he was missing when she came up on deck to see why their boat had stopped moving. 'My husband must have fallen overboard and drowned,' Mrs. Lambert is alleged to have stated.

"Mrs. Lambert claims that when she discovered her husband was nowhere in sight, she panicked and radioed the coast guard. When coast guard officers boarded the Lambert yacht with Mrs. Lambert's permission, they found her in a dazed condition, holding a heavy bronze winch handle that showed traces of blood. An unnamed source has told this station that DNA tests are currently being conducted at the L.A. County Crime Lab to determine if the blood on the winch handle matches Dale Lambert's."

"Oh, my God!" Nora cried again. "Tell me it isn't true!"

"It gets worse," Caroline said grimly.

"The Lambert yacht was towed to Marina Del Rey, where it was met by L.A. County Sheriff's deputies who took Mrs. Lambert into custody on suspicion of murder. A warrant was obtained granting the sheriff's department the power to search the Lambert home, where deputies found a ticket to Paraguay issued in the name of Rosalee Lambert and Mrs. Lambert's diary concealed in a can of flour. According to our sources, the diary contained references to a Revenge Fantasy Seminar led by well-known matchmaker Nora Wynn, owner of the dating service Love Finds a Way. Wynn's latest business venture, Payback Time, has recently earned her the title of L.A.'s Queen of Revenge—"

"Say, Lynda," Sean interrupted, "is that the same Nora Wynn who got left at the altar a few months ago?"

"The very same, Sean. It appears that in Wynn's seminar—which, by the way, has been one of the hottest tickets in town—Rosalee Lambert described a plan to murder her husband by luring him onto their yacht, knocking him out with a winch handle, and throwing him overboard. Our source reports that in her diary, Mrs. Lambert also wrote about mopping up the bloodstains, but it seems she may have forgotten that part of her plan."

"So can we expect a first-degree murder charge to be filed against Mrs. Lambert, Lynda?"

"It already has been, Sean. Right now, Mrs. Lambert is looking at twenty-five years to life for premeditated murder."

"Any chance she'll be released on bail?"

"No, besides the murder charge, that ticket to Paraguay makes her a flight risk. The investigation of Dale Lambert's disappearance has just begun, but if his DNA matches the DNA on that winch handle, I'd say Mrs. Lambert had better call up OJ and ask him for advice."

"So I bet our listeners out there are wondering what a 'winch handle' is."

"They're very common on sailboats, Sean. They're used to raise and lower the sails. A bronze winch handle could be a very effective murder weapon since it weighs over . . ."

Nora punched the *Off* button and put her head down on the steering wheel. She tried to think, but her mind had frozen on the words "murder weapon" and wouldn't move. Surely Rosalee couldn't have been stupid enough to carry out her fantasy. *Please, God,* no.

"Nora? Are you still there?"

Nora picked up the cell phone and opened her mouth, but nothing came out. On the other end of the line, she could hear the office phones ringing. Reporters were about to descend on Love Finds a Way like vultures.

She was instantly ashamed of herself for thinking about business at a time like this. Poor Dale was dead. Okay, so he wasn't a nice guy. But murder? No. Surely not. Rosalee would never . . . or would she?

Nora remembered the ugly expression of hatred on Roaslee's face as she had beat the stuffing out of the cushion. What did it take to make an apparently sane woman mad enough to feed her husband to the sharks? Did Rosalee have it in her to kill Dale? She thought about Rosalee yelling *Blam!* and shuddered.

"Nora?"

"Do you think Rosalee did it, Caroline?"

"It sure looks like it, but what do I know? Anyway, she's innocent until they prove her guilty."

"She really might be innocent."

"Yeah, Nora, and pigs might fly. Seriously, this doesn't look good. Rosalee hated Dale's cheating so much she hired us to fix him up with losers. I wasn't there when she beat the pillow, but Amber was in the next office, and she said Rosalee's screaming scared her so much she had to take a tranquilizer. From what Amber told me, if that pillow had been Dale's head, Dale would have been history. And you have to take probability into account."

"Probability?" Nora said numbly.

"I just Googled the homicide statistics. Did you

know that women who murder kill their husbands or ex-boyfriends 45 percent of the time? Men only do in their wives and ex-girlfriends at 14.7 percent. Of course on the upside, a lot fewer women than men get the death penalty."

"Poor Rosalee. She must have been out of her mind."

"Quit thinking about Rosalee and start thinking about yourself. This is a mega-scandal. Your name's all over the news."

"So, what do you suggest I do? Clean out the bank account and run for the border?"

"You're kidding about running, right?"

"Right," Nora said, although at the moment it seemed like an appealing option.

"Good. Well, then, as far as I can see, our only choice is to sit tight the way the studios do when some big star gets arrested for drug possession. We're entering a no-comment zone here. We'd be nuts to make any public statements. We have to screen all phone calls and cancel the revenge fantasy seminars immediately before another client tries to send her husband to heaven. Unless demand drops for the singles events, they should be no problem. I'd say the chances of us accidentally fixing anyone up with a murderer are low."

"Don't say 'low'; say 'nonexistent.' "

"Nonexistent. Off the charts. Relax."

Nora and Caroline spent a few more minutes reassuring each other and trying to sort things out. Then Nora hung up and called her lawyer.

"It's not likely that you'll be charged with aiding and abetting Rosalee Lambert's plan to murder her husband," Matt said. "But deputies from the L.A. County Sheriff's Department will interview you, and they'll expect answers."

"What should I do? Take the Fifth?"

"No, you're innocent, so cooperate. The sheriff's department isn't going to like the fact that you were running those revenge seminars, but you have a contract with Rosalee's signature on it that says she knew it was all a fantasy."

"What if they do decide to charge me?"

"Relax. They won't."

"But if they do?"

"Then you'll have to hire yourself a good lawyer."

"I thought *you* were a good lawyer."

"I only do civil law. You'd need to get yourself a criminal attorney. I can come up with a list of names if it will make you happy."

"No, thanks. From what you just told me, I guess I don't need one right now." Nora rested her forehead against the steering wheel again and stared glumly at the odometer. "And thanks for not saying 'I told you so.' "

"Seriously, Nora: try not to borrow trouble. There's no body. If the blood on that winch handle doesn't match Dale's, the D.A. may decide to classify it as an accidental drowning. Even if it does match, there's always the possibility Dale hit his head when he fell overboard."

"What about Rosalee's diary? What about that ticket to Paraguay?"

"Oh, right. I forgot about those. Well, now you see why I'm not a criminal attorney."

"And if they do decide to charge me with helping her plan Dale's murder? Level with me, Matt. Given the fact that Rosalee took my seminar, what's the worst that could happen?"

"The worst? Well, to start with, you can cross the death penalty off your list. Since you have a clean record, your lawyer probably would be able to convince the jury you had no idea Rosalee was doing anything but blowing off steam. But let's say he's a lousy lawyer and the jury decides to throw the book at you for aiding and abetting. Maybe, absolute worst-case scenario: you'd get twenty-five years to life. You'd probably be a model prisoner, so sooner or later you'd get out on parole. Even Charles Manson gets regular parole hearings."

"Thanks, Matt. I can't tell you what a comfort it is to hear that I could be in prison until I'm fifty-seven." Nora broke the connection, tossed her cell phone on the floor, and put her head back down on the steering wheel. She felt dizzy and sick.

Gradually she realized that horns were honking all around her. Traffic had begun to move again. If she didn't want to get lynched before she could be arrested for helping plan a murder, she had to get going.

As she started the engine, she remembered that she had no insurance and only a temporary driver's license. What if she got into an accident? Would they tack ten more years onto her sentence? She was seized by a wild urge to laugh. Even the slightest possibility of being arrested as an accessory to murder really helped you not to sweat the small stuff.

By the time she pulled up in front of her office, a crowd of reporters and photographers was already lying in wait for her. Nora plowed through them, saying, "No comment," and fled upstairs to discover two deputies from the L.A. County Sheriff's Department sitting in the reception area leafing through back issues of *Single Life*. Their names were Johnson and Rodriguez, and they were nothing like the detectives on TV. Middle-aged, tired, and dressed in wrinkled sports coats, slacks, scuffed brown shoes, and open-collared shirts, they could have been unsuccessful car salesmen. But looks were deceiving. They proved to be sharp, quick, and intelligent.

For over two hours, they questioned Nora about Rosalee, Dale, and the revenge fantasy seminars.

Nora decided that, since she was innocent and since they hadn't said a word about charging her as an accessory, the only thing to do was follow Matt's advice and cooperate. But the fact that Rosalee had been Payback Time's first paying customer didn't go down well. Although Rodriguez and Johnson were polite, they obviously believed Nora had been running a school for criminals; and she had the feeling that if there'd been a shred of incriminating evidence, they would have been happy to see her spending the next twenty-five years as Rosalee's cellmate.

"Are you saying you never suspected Mrs. Lambert might actually harm her husband?" Rodriguez kept asking.

"At the end of the seminar, Rosalee told everyone in the room that she was starting to forgive Dale," Nora insisted. "I knew she was upset that he'd been cheating on her, and she certainly wasn't beyond a little petty revenge. But she claimed to be deeply religious and totally committed to her marriage. She left us all with the impression that she still loved Dale, despite everything. And she seemed like a smart woman. It never occurred to me that she would be dumb enough to tell her fantasy to fifteen people and then actually carry it out."

She wanted the deputies to tell her that anyone might have made the same mistake, but Johnson and Rodriguez said nothing. They just sat there interviewing her, taking notes, and drinking coffee. When they were finished, they thanked Nora for being so cooperative, and then asked her not to leave the L.A. area while the investigation was in progress.

Shaken by what she took to be a veiled threat, Nora canceled the karaoke bash she was supposed to host that evening and drove home. As she approached Pasadena, she turned on the radio. Again she heard Sean and Lynda tell the story of Dale Lambert's death, but this time with a new twist. Dale, it seemed, had been doing illegal currency trading. Millions of dollars were missing. Worst yet, he had left behind a two-million-dollar life insurance policy that named Rosalee as beneficiary. The charge against Rosalee was now premeditated murder for financial gain, which, as Sean cheerfully pointed out, made her eligible for the death penalty or life without the possibility of parole.

In all fairness, that should have been the end of the worst day of Nora's life, but there was more to come. As soon as she got home, she slipped into her swimming suit and went outside to do some laps in her pool. The first thing she saw as she stepped off the back deck was all six of her koi floating belly up in the koi pond.

Nora ran over to the pond, fished one of the dead koi out of the water, and placed it on the grass next to a pot of basil. The koi's golden scales glittered in the late afternoon sunlight. The grass was soft and freckled with shadows. No dogs barked; no leaf blowers whirred in nearby yards. Everything seemed so peaceful that Nora could almost imagine that both Dale and her koi were still alive.

For a long time she knelt there, staring at the fish. Gradually, she began to feel frightened. The pond was full of oleander leaves. Oleanders were famously poisonous. Did oleander sap kill fish, or was there some other deadly substance in the water? And if the oleander leaves had killed her koi, how had they gotten into the pond? The Santa Anna winds were fierce, but these were *green* leaves. It would have taken a lot of force to strip them off the oleander bushes across the street and blow them over her house and into her koi pond. Could this possibly be the work of a dog? A raccoon?

She wanted to believe her fish had died by accident, but too much had gone wrong in too short a time. Someone was definitely trying to take revenge on her. But who was it? How far was all this going to go? Would her unknown enemy stop at vandalism, or was he out to kill her the way Rosalee had killed Dale?

Calm down, she told herself. *No one wants to murder you. You're not in any physical danger.* But the harder she tried to believe she was safe, the more frightened she became.

Picking up the dead koi, she quickly slid it back into the pond, hurried to her house, locked all the doors, and activated the security system. For a good twenty minutes, she sat in the living room with the drapes drawn and her cell phone in her hand, prepared to dial 911. Then, bit by bit, she got a grip on her fear.

All her life she had faced things head-on. If she had an enemy who was out to get her, there wasn't much she could do about it except go on living her life as normally as possible. So what was normal these days? Well, she might not be able to escape the Rosalee/Dale scandal, find her purse, convince her insurance company that she didn't have any traffic tickets, get the IRS off her back, resurrect her roses, or bring her koi back from the dead; but maybe she could still save the rest of her flowers from disappearing into a wood chipper.

She rose to her feet, put her cell phone in her pocket, unlocked her front door, made sure the coast was clear, and swiftly walked across her yard, stepping over the scar where her rosebushes had been and sweeping past Jenkins's lawn ornaments. When she reached his front door, she raised her fist to knock and noticed that he had installed a new doorbell. She paused, then rang it. The thing actually worked, but Jenkins either didn't hear the chimes or didn't intend to respond. She could hear him moving around inside, so she rang again.

The door opened suddenly and he stood before her clad in baggy plaid shorts and a sleeveless T-shirt. "What the hell do you want this time?" he snarled.

Nora took a deep breath and looked him straight in the eye. "Peace."

Jenkins glared at her suspiciously. "A piece of what, girlie?"

"I want to make peace with you. We're neighbors. We shouldn't fight." She gestured at her driveway. "My roses are gone, so they aren't over your property line anymore—if they ever were. So what do we have left to fight about?"

"Are you drunk?"

"No, I'm cold sober. Seriously, I want to hire Ryan."

"To do what?"

"Watch my place. Be a kind of security guard."

"No way in hell."

"Pardon?"

Jenkins took a step forward so his body filled the entire doorway. "I been hearing about you on the TV. 'Queen of Revenge,' huh? Well, looks like your chickens just came home to roost, didn't they, Queenie?"

"Mr. Jenkins, can't we just—"

"Can't we just get along?" he said, mocking her. "Oh, so now the Revenge Queen wants to pull a Rodney King, does she? You know what I think? I think you're getting exactly what you deserve."

As angry as she was, Nora had to admit that he might be right. She bit her tongue and tried again.

"I don't think you understand. I don't want to fight with you, and I want to pay Ryan a decent salary to guard my property. Say fifteen dollars an hour."

Jenkins laughed so hard he began to choke. "Ryan? You want to hire that no-good slacker? You really are crazy." His smile suddenly disappeared. "Go away."

"Mr. Jenkins—"

"Get off my property. I wouldn't let Ryan throw you a life preserver if you were drowning in your own damn pool." And with that, he stepped back and slammed the door in her face.

Defeated, Nora went home to call the Pasadena police and file a vandalism report. Halfway through punching in the numbers, she changed her mind and hung up. No one was going to do an autopsy on a school of koi. The police would probably dismiss the whole incident as an accidental poisoning; and even if they didn't, the last thing she needed right now was to report something that might suggest that another one of Payback Time's clients didn't know the difference between fantasy and reality.

12

The morning after Rosalee's arrest, Nora drove to Santa Monica as usual, which proved to be a mistake. The reporters and video crews were still camped in front of her building. Once again, she swept past them saying, "No comment" and made it to the safety of her office. She had just taken off her jacket, kicked off her shoes, and sat down at her desk to go through a pile of phone messages, when she heard a timid cough.

Looking up, she saw Amber standing in the doorway. Amber appeared to be upset. Well, at least that was nothing new. Amber had looked upset on a daily basis well before Rosalee pushed Dale off the yacht. Nora wondered what had happened now. Jammed copy machine? No cheese and peanut butter crackers in the snack room? It would be nice to have something insignificant to think about for a change.

She gave Amber a warm smile. "Come on in." Amber walked into the room, paused in front of Nora's desk, and looked around nervously as if fearing a serial killer might jump out from behind the potted Ficus.

"Sit down. Make yourself comfortable."

"I'd rather not, thanks."

So what was this about? Amber had always tumbled into a chair the second Nora invited her to take a seat. There was a long silence. Amber stared at Nora with an unfathomable expression on her face. Nora stared back, thinking that despite everything, Amber was looking better than she had in weeks.

This morning, instead of wearing beige, she had on a greenish blue linen blouse that matched her eye color. She also wore a reasonably short skirt and sandals that didn't look orthopedic. It seemed strange to think of Amber thriving on scandal, but some people did. Nora, unfortunately was not one of them.

Amber continued to say nothing. At last, Nora grew tired of waiting. "So what's up?" she prompted.

Amber blinked. "It's all those phone calls, the ones from the reporters."

"You don't have to answer the phones, Amber. That's what we have Miriam for." Miriam was their new temp, a replacement for Vicki, who had been a replacement for Jeff, who had been a replacement for the traitorous Felicity. There had been too much turnover in recent months, but at least all the temps had been competent people who had their feet on the ground. Not one of them had ever shown the slightest interest in being in the movies; and all were married—or in Jeff's case permanently partnered. Hiring partnered temps was Nora's new preference. Felicity's betrayal had taught her that a matchmaking service needed to employ people who weren't inclined to sample the stock.

Amber blushed to the roots of her hair and looked at Nora anxiously. "I've been covering the phones for Miriam. She had to leave early a couple of times this week. Her kid's been sick."

Well, that was interesting. Nora wished Miriam had

come to her. She was always willing to give people time off to take care of sick children.

"The reporters . . ."

"Don't tell me you've been talking to them!"

"Oh, no. But I have to listen. They say there's some sort of ethical problem with Payback Time."

"Ethical problem? Are you telling me that a pack of tabloid news hounds is questioning *my* ethics?"

"Oh, no, Nora. Not you. Not you personally. But they say Payback Time was a . . ." Again Amber froze.

"A what, Amber?" Nora prompted impatiently.

"A-disaster-waiting-to-happen-just-like-an-earthquake-which-is-why-well-why-I-just-have-to-re-sign-because-I-can't-listen-to-such-terrible-accusations-and—"

Amber was speaking so fast Nora could hardly understand her. Nora held up her hand. "Please stop." Amber stopped. "Did I just hear you say you were quitting?"

Amber nodded.

Nora suddenly became suspicious. So Amber was bailing on them, was she? Did this mean Amber was the mystery person fouling up her life? Nora stared at her, trying to find some trace of guilt or hostility in her face, but there was nothing but a timid sadness mixed with sincere regret.

I'm getting totally paranoid, she thought. *Amber's not the fish-killing type, and she doesn't have the hacking skills to get those fake traffic tickets into my insurance company's computer. Also, I'm not firing her; she's quitting of her own free will—and reluctantly too, from the look of things. It's logical that she'd be the first to crack under the pressure. She's never been a fighter.*

Amber blinked nervously and Nora realized that she'd been staring much too intently. She cleared her throat. "So," she said, "you're telling me I'm losing my bookkeeper?"

Amber nodded again.

"This isn't the greatest time for you to quit."

"I know. I'm sorry. But I am." Amber took a couple of scurrying steps toward Nora, stuck a piece of paper in her hand, and then hastily retreated. "There it is. My resignation. In hard copy. I've left all the accounts in order. The person who replaces me shouldn't have any trouble."

Nora felt a sinking sensation that was becoming all too familiar. She put Amber's letter of resignation down on her desk without looking at it. "Amber," she said in a super-calm voice designed not to startle Amber into flight, "are you sure you want to do this? You've been a wonderful employee. Isn't there anything I can do to persuade you to go on doing our books? Raise your salary? Give you extra vacation days?"

"No! I couldn't. Thank you. I've loved working here. You've been a great boss, Nora. But no!" And with a small squeak, Amber turned and fled.

After Amber left, Nora went into Amber's office and checked her computer, but there was nothing on it that indicated Amber had been up to dirty tricks. Her browser cache was full of cookies from Spanish-language Web sites. Her old e-mail was either perfectly appropriate for the bookkeeper of a matchmaking service or boring beyond belief. As far as Nora could tell without doing a formal audit, every spreadsheet was perfect down to the last cent.

Nora sighed and turned off Amber's computer. All she had managed to do by snooping was prove beyond a doubt that Amber had been working hard and leading a life almost totally devoid of imagination. She wished Amber happiness. Maybe now that she was no longer working for Nora, she'd find more time to have fun with her boyfriend. Maybe she'd even manage to get married and have those three kids she was always talking about.

Nora rolled Amber's mouse back to the exact center of her Mona Lisa mouse pad. Then she went off to locate Caroline and tell her they were going to need to hire a new bookkeeper.

Amber resigned on Thursday. Friday brought a fresh series of disasters, so many that Nora seriously considered having her horoscope done to see if the planets had turned against her.

Actually, the day started out on a hopeful note. When Nora pulled up in front of her office, she found that the reporters and video crews had moved on to new scandals, and the Dale Lambert murder was—to some extent at least—yesterday's news. But her relief was short-lived.

At noon, Caroline walked into Nora's office and found Nora sitting at her desk staring at her mail. A lot of bad things seemed to be coming in hard copy these days, including Amber's letter of resignation, which Nora still hadn't bothered to read.

"Good news," Caroline said cheerfully. "I just found us a new bookkeeper. How's that for speed?"

"Great," Nora said without enthusiasm. "Did you make sure he or she hasn't done prison time for embezzling?"

"I'm amazed how well you're managing to keep your sense of humor. Yes, I did a thorough background check."

"You'd be even more amazed if you'd read my mail, not to mention my e-mail." Nora pointed to her computer. "The *Pasadena Star News* has canceled my column. No surprise there. With Rosalee under arrest, the revenge advice I've been handing out is way too controversial. Also, the radio station just e-mailed me and said that this week my segment was going to be pre-empted by a special on keeping squirrels out of bird feeders. They were too cowardly to admit they never intended to let me get near a microphone again, but it doesn't take much to read between the lines. Plus—"

"Don't tell me there's more?"

"Oh, definitely."

"Ever read the Book of Job?"

"I read it when I was a kid but my memory for the details is vague. Does it feature a former matchmaker whose love life is nonexistent and whose business is on the skids?"

"No, just dead cattle, boils . . ."

"Sounds like exactly what I need to cheer me up. Seriously, I've got another problem: it appears that whoever stole my purse stole my identity."

"Oh, no!" Caroline tumbled down into a chair and stared at Nora in disbelief. "Are you sure?"

"Positive. I just got my credit card statements." Nora picked up one of the statements and examined it glumly. "I don't suppose you know where I could hire a good exorcist?"

"I thought you canceled your credit cards as soon as you figured out your purse was missing."

"I did. These are bills for *new* accounts. Apparently the thief used my Social Security number to get a Visa card and a Mastercard, plus a charge card for some high-end patio furniture store called—and I'm not making this up—Barbie Q's."

"Who did it?"

"I haven't a clue. Whoever it was bought gear from a surf shop, men's and women's clothing, china, linens, perfume, CDs, patio furniture, and a fancy gas grill. Fortunately they showed restraint. There can't be more than seven thousand dollars' worth of charges here."

"Seven thousand dollars!"

"Seven thousand one hundred dollars and eighty-five cents to be exact. I just called the credit card companies, explained that I was a victim of identity theft, and put a fraud alert on all my credit records; but do you have any idea what a hassle it's going to be to straighten this mess out?"

Caroline stretched out her hand. "Give me those statements. I'm going to run the items they bought against our client profiles and see if we've been matching up any surfing couples who love music and baby back ribs. Maybe we can figure out who has it in for you."

"Everyone has it in for me."

"Don't say that."

"Seriously. I've specialized in attracting people who want revenge. There are going to be hundreds of possibilities."

"Granted, but I bet not all of them surf." Caroline would have said more, except the phone rang.

Nora glared at the phone and then poked it with a pencil. "I'm not answering that. It's bound to be bad news. I'm sorry I ever gave in to the temptation to get even with Jason and Felicity. It's brought me nothing but trouble."

"You never tried to get even with them. You just *thought* about it."

"The gods don't care. Seriously, don't pick up the receiver. I'm cursed. I'm going to sell Payback Time and Love Finds a Way for whatever I can get for them, shave my head, join a Zen monastery, and spend the rest of my life trying to retool my karma."

"Don't be silly." Caroline reached out and picked up the receiver.

"Hello," she said cheerfully. "Love Finds a Way. Caroline Adams speaking." Someone on the other end of the line said something, and Caroline's face went white.

"No, Ms. Wynn just stepped out of the office for a moment. Yes. Yes, I'll give her the message." Caroline hung up, looked at Nora, and gave an apologetic shrug. "You were right. I shouldn't have answered."

"Don't tell me. Let me guess: my house burned down? No, that's not bad enough. I'm insured for fire. On the other hand, I don't have earthquake insurance, so probably there was a 7.1 quake centered under my living room that affected no one else in L.A. Or maybe a comet strike. Five pounds of red-hot rubble from Arcturus. Nothing left of my grandmother's china but a pit of green glass and maybe a chance to sell the story to *The National Enquirer.*"

"It was Deputy Rodriguez. He'd like you to answer some more questions. He says there's been a new development in the Dale Lambert case."

"Well, go on. Don't stop there. What is it? Come on. I can take it. What happened? Did Rosalee confess?"

"I don't know. Rodriguez didn't say. He called on his cell. He and his partner are out investigating another case, so they'd like to meet you in about an hour at Krispy Kreme."

"What do you suppose would happen if I didn't show up?"

"I suppose they'd make you come in for an interview and you'd end up in one of those rooms you see on TV. You know—metal table, bright lights, no windows, bad coffee."

Norah smiled grimly. "Well, at least the hot doughnuts at Krispy Kreme are awesome. Who knows, they may be the last thing I eat that isn't served on a tin tray."

Krispy Kreme specialized in cheer. It had cheery orange and green tiles outside, cheerful green awnings, and a super-cheerful neon sign that lit up in red and green when the doughnuts were hot from the oven. Inside, the tiles were green and white and the chairs were silver. There were old-fashioned photos of the original Krispy Kreme factory on the walls, and if you got bored with those, you could sit at the little greenish blue tables and look through a big plate-glass window. On the other side of the window, doughnuts in various stages of completion rolled by on a stainless steel conveyor belt, passing through vats of hot fat and other contraptions until they emerged puffed, piping hot, and ready to eat. In short, it was a strange place for a police interrogation, but seconds after she sat down, Nora knew that was what Johnson and Rodriguez had invited her there for.

Rodriguez took a sip of coffee and frowned at Nora as if trying to decide whether or not to glue lie detector cables to her chest. "What do you know about Sam Gallo's activities during the last several months?" he asked.

For a moment Nora thought she'd heard him wrong. "Sam? My ex-husband? What does Sam have to do with this?"

"That's what we're trying to determine."

Nora put down her blueberry-filled doughnut without tasting it. Rodriguez and Johnson had both ordered the Krispy Kreme signature Hot Glazed, which had struck her as a lack of imagination on their part. Evidently, she'd underestimated them.

Rodriguez took a neat bite out of his doughnut and returned it to the precise center of the square of waxed paper that Krispy Kreme passed out in lieu of plates. "For example, when was the last time you spoke to your former husband?"

"About three weeks ago."

"Before Dale Lambert disappeared?"

"Definitely."

"What did you and Mr. Gallo talk about?"

"The IRS. I called Sam to ask him if—" Nora paused. She didn't want to tell them about the tax audit, but it looked as if she wasn't going to have a choice. They probably knew about it anyway. In fact, they probably knew everything about her including that she had once been caught running with scissors in the second grade. "I'm being audited by the IRS. I didn't think it was likely that Sam had turned me in to the feds for tax evasion, but I wanted to ask him because he's one of the few people who knows my Social Security Number. I'm not evading my taxes," she added hastily. "I've paid every dime I owed, state and federal."

"That's not under our jurisdiction." Johnson picked off a flake of sugar glaze and put it on his tongue like a pill. "That's between you and the IRS."

"Seriously," she insisted. "This audit is a mistake. It's either some kind of computer error, or else someone's trying to get even with me."

Johnson and Rodriguez exchanged a look that indicated they weren't surprised to hear someone was trying to get even with Nora.

"What did Mr. Gallo say when you asked him if he could provide information about your tax audit?" Rodriguez asked.

"Sam claimed he'd had nothing to do with it. Then we fought—he and I always fight. And then I got mad and hung up on him."

"What did you fight about?"

Nora felt her face going red. "He said I used to nag him about chewing with his mouth closed. I accused him of leaving toilet seats up."

"How often do you talk to him?"

"That was the first time since last April. To tell the truth, I've seen Sam's mother more than Sam since the divorce. She brings me lasagna."

Rodriguez took out his Palm Pilot. "What's her name?"

"Lucia Gallo."

"Could you please spell that?" Nora spelled Lucia's name as Rodriguez entered it. When he finished, he snapped the Palm closed and took another bite of doughnut. Nora felt completely confused. Who were they going to ask her about next?

Rodriguez swallowed and cleared his throat. "So, were you aware that Sam Gallo was having an affair with Rosalee Lambert?"

"What!" Nora was so startled she knocked over her coffee. Fortunately for Krispy Kreme's liability situation, the hot river didn't flow into Johnson's lap, but it was a near miss. Everyone scrambled for napkins. Nora mopped up the spill on the table while the two deputies took swipes at the floor.

"I'm really sorry," she said.

"No problem." Johnson straightened up and examined his doughnut, which had been reduced to a soggy brown mass. Nora wondered if she should offer to buy him another one. No, he might think she was trying to bribe him. She stared at the wet napkin in her hand as if she'd never seen one before. The words "Sam," "Rosalee," and "affair" had taken up residence in her mind. As she put down the napkin, they began to rotate like a merry-go-round.

Rodriguez retrieved his Palm Pilot and repeated his question.

"I had no idea Sam even knew Rosalee," Nora said. "It's totally impossible. Rosalee's not even Sam's type. There has to be some mistake."

"I'm afraid there's no mistake, Ms. Wynn. Yesterday, we received a letter from an anonymous source. It claimed Sam Gallo and Rosalee Lambert were . . ." Rodriguez turned to Johnson. "How did they put it, Carl?"

"The letter alleged Lambert and Gallo were 'going at it hot and heavy.' "

"Hot and heavy," Nora repeated numbly. "Oh, great. Just what I needed to hear. I'm really trying not to imagine this. Not that I care, you understand."

"Ordinarily we'd figure the letter came from some nut. There are a lot of disturbed people who like to get in on high-profile crimes. But the letter about Lambert and Gallo also contained this." Rodriguez took a snapshot out of his pocket and slid it across the table. "Take a look."

Nora picked up the snapshot and stared at it. Then she stared at it again because she couldn't believe what she was seeing: a man and a woman sat in a sidewalk café under a large white umbrella, leaning toward each other like lovers. The woman was Rosalee Lambert, red ponytail and all. The man was definitely Sam.

"Can you confirm that this is a photograph of Sam Gallo and Rosalee Lambert?"

"Yes."

"Does it look doctored to you in any way?"

"Doctored?"

"Faked? Photo-shopped?"

"No."

"The crime lab is checking that possibility out. Meanwhile, if you look close, you can see they're playing footsie."

Nora looked, winced, and slid the snapshot back to him.

"You know nothing about this?"

"Absolutely nothing."

"Do you know where Mr. Gallo was at the time Dale Lambert disappeared?"

"No."

"He and Rosalee Lambert deny knowing each other. Can you confirm that?"

"No. But I can't imagine why they'd know each other. As you know, Rosalee was my client, but there's no reason Sam would have met her."

"Mr. Gallo doesn't have an alibi for the time of Dale Lambert's disappearance."

"I'm sorry to hear that. Sam and I might not get along, but I can't believe he'd murder anyone. That's what you're implying, isn't it? That Sam and Rosalee conspired to kill Dale?"

"We don't imply, Ms. Wynn. We just investigate. Still, your ex-husband is in financial trouble. His last two independent documentaries didn't turn a profit. Did you know that?"

"No, but Sam never was very concerned about making money. He does his documentaries for love, not profit. I always respected him for that, although I have to admit that when we were together the instability and unpredictability of his life sometimes drove me crazy."

The deputies exchanged unreadable glances.

"Did you know Dale Lambert had a two-million-dollar life insurance policy plus at least another million in assets, all of which he left to his wife?" Rodriguez asked.

"Only when I heard it on the radio like everyone else."

"Did you know he'd been doing illegal currency trading and that millions of dollars are missing?"

"Only when I heard it on the radio."

"Is there anything more you can tell us about Sam Gallo's relationship with Rosalee Lambert?"

"No. I'm as surprised as you are."

Nora braced herself for more questions, but it seemed they had come to the end of their list. Rising to their feet, Johnson and Rodriguez thanked her politely for her time and again warned her not to leave town.

After they left, Nora sat for a long time lost in thought.

As she pushed the uneaten doughnut around on the waxed paper and sipped cold coffee, she was seized by the horrible fear that Sam actually might have plotted with Rosalee to murder Dale. If he had, then he wasn't the Sam she'd known. He was some other Sam: a Sam who might also steal credit cards, kill fish, and . . .

She didn't want to go there. She didn't want to believe a man she'd once loved was capable of such things. But people changed, and a lot of time had gone by since she and Sam had shared a life.

13

The night was warm, scented with eucalyptus and the exhaust of millions of cars. Back East people were already up to their waists in snow, and ice storms had brought down electric wires, but outside Nora's office window, bats were flitting past the street lamps gobbling up moths, and the insurance agents who occupied the building across the street were out on their roof barbecuing salmon fillets and drinking cold Pacifico.

Usually on a Friday night, Nora would have been hosting an express dating event or singing at a karaoke party; but after her run-in with Rodriguez and Johnson this afternoon, all she wanted to do was bunker in and do paperwork, so she had sent Caroline off to tango at a singles dance bash while she went over her tax returns and tried to figure out what might have flagged an audit.

Examining her old returns was a lot like reading a badly written diary: boring but strangely fascinating. She was just looking wistfully at the income from her stock dividends and kicking herself for not having sold before the market plunged, when she heard the outside door to the building slam shut.

She started, then froze, held her breath, and listened for more sounds. How could she have forgotten to lock the front door! She was completely alone up here. What if the person who had stolen her identity and killed her koi had decided to pay her a visit?

To her dismay, she heard heavy footsteps coming up the stairs. This was definitely not good. Her office door had no lock, there was nowhere to hide, and whoever it was had already entered the reception area. She cast around frantically for something to use as a weapon. The only thing in sight was a red glass paperweight shaped like a heart. Seizing it, she prepared to hurl it. She'd played on a church baseball team when she was a girl, and she used to throw a pretty wicked fastball. Maybe she could stun her attacker with the paperweight before he jumped her.

The door burst open. "Nora!" said the intruder. "What the hell is going on here!"

Nora lowered her arm. "Sam?"

"Damn right it's Sam." He strode toward her desk. His face was pale with anger and his beard bristled like a set of porcupine quills. "I've had enough of this! It's time you did some explaining!"

She was so relieved he wasn't a psycho-killer, she could have hugged him. It was an impulse that quickly passed. She put the paperweight back down on her desk and tried to gather her wits. Only a few hours ago she'd been wondering if he'd helped Rosalee murder Dale. Was he dangerous? He didn't look dangerous. He just looked the way he always looked when he got angry.

"Explain what?" she said. If anyone had explaining to do, it was he.

"You know perfectly well what. Two deputies from

the L.A. County Sheriff's Department have been questioning me all afternoon about that wacko client of yours."

"I assume you're referring to Rosalee Lambert."

"No, Carmela Soprano. Seriously, Nora, what is this? Some crazy plan on your part to frame me? I've never met Ms. Lambert, and, given her expertise with winch handles, I'm not planning to ask you to fix us up."

Sam glared at Nora with a stubborn, self-righteous expression she had always hated. "You know," he continued, "I never would have thought you were capable of a dirty trick like this. You were always hot-tempered, but you used to be a pretty decent person before you started telling all the women in L.A. to dump itching powder in their boyfriends' boxer shorts."

Nora forced herself to take several deep breaths before she answered. This was definitely a new record: from an impulse to hug Sam to a desire to yell at him in under ten seconds. "I have plenty of male clients," she said with near-surreal calm. "I've never once advised anyone to use itching powder, and I have absolutely no motive for framing you."

"How about your crazy, totally paranoid idea that I turned you in to the IRS?"

"Well, did you?"

"I told you I didn't!" Sam paced from her desk to the window and back again. "You know what I think? I think you've never forgiven me for leaving you and going to South America to direct those travel promos."

Nora felt her face going hot with anger. "Wait a minute! *I* was the one who didn't want to come along, which means, technically, *I* left *you*!"

"Technically, yes. But if I'd known you were going to leave me, I'd have left you first."

"So your theory is that I'm taking revenge on you for

the failure of our marriage?" Nora clenched her fists until her nails dug into her palms. "Is that what you're saying?"

"Right."

"In your dreams, Sam. The day our divorce was final, I threw myself a party. My girlfriends gave me a new blender to replace the one you walked off with."

"What do you mean 'walked off with'? You didn't drink daiquiris. How was I supposed to know you wanted it?"

"I might not have drunk daiquiris, but I snacked on protein powder sometimes when I was in too much of a hurry to microwave something. You have to *mix* protein powder, Sam. You can't just stir it with a spoon. It gets all lumpy."

They glared at each other. It was just like old times. There was a long, tense silence. Finally Sam spoke.

"Okay, let's move on. If you didn't send that letter to the cops, who did?"

"I have no idea."

"I'm supposed to believe that?"

"Yes. Just like I'm supposed to believe you didn't turn me in to the IRS. You believe me; I believe you. It's called compromise."

"Don't try to do couples counseling with me, Nora. I'm not in the mood for half-baked psychotherapy." He started pacing again. "Do you know how bad this kind of publicity is for a man who wants to raise money to make serious documentary films?"

"Gee, that's too bad. You should have thought about the publicity angle before you started sleeping with Rosalee."

"I never slept with Rosalee Lambert! I don't even know her!" Sam put the palms of his hands on Nora's desk and leaned into her face. "Do you know what you're acting like?"

"I haven't a clue."

"You're acting like a jealous woman."

"I am not!"

"Oh, yes, you are. I'd be flattered, except you're totally wrecking my life."

"Jealous of you and Rosalee? Ha!"

"Didn't you hear what I just said? There is no *me* and Rosalee."

"You expect me to believe that? The deputies showed me a snapshot of the two of you competing in the World Cup Footsie Playoffs."

"That photo was faked!"

"Sure, right."

"Listen to me, Nora. You never listen!"

"I spent six months listening to you, Sam, and where did it get me?" Nora suddenly realized she was yelling. Taking another deep breath, she attempted to speak in a more moderate tone.

"Look, our marriage wasn't all bad. I admit that. We had fantastic sex, and when we weren't fighting, you could be very sweet. I often thought you were quite wonderful in a horrible sort of way; but we could never communicate, we still can't communicate, and you were hell to live with."

"Hell, huh?"

Nora nodded.

"So, you think you were easy, do you? Well, for your information, there aren't many men who could make love while listening to Yanni. Not to mention that you forced me to eat tofu on Thanksgiving because you said baking a turkey was too much hassle. And remember how you went on for hours at a time about how your stomach pooched out like a beach ball?"

"That's not fair! I had undiagnosed PMS!"

"It doesn't matter. The point is, I never cared about your damn stomach! I always thought you were beautiful!"

She gasped, blindsided by the compliment.

Sam's face suddenly turned bright red. "Scratch that."

Nora stared at him in amazement. "I'm not going to scratch it. That was, uh, very, uh . . . nice of you."

"I didn't come here to be nice. Forget what I just said about your stomach. It doesn't matter. It's over between us, and a good thing too. I hate fighting with you, Nora. It drives me crazy."

Nora felt as if he'd slapped her in the face. She straightened up and folded her arms across her chest. Only an idiot would let herself be vulnerable around Sam, she thought. Well, she wouldn't let it happen again. "Of course it's over," she said coldly. "You ruined it. I wanted you to see me for who I was, but you never did."

"God knows, I tried."

"No, you didn't try, not really. You were hardly ever home. We never talked except to fight. And it didn't help that you cut our honeymoon three days short to take me to an oil spill."

"Don't start in on that. If I hadn't gone, my boss would have fired me. We needed two salaries to survive."

"Okay, granted. But all I wanted was one week of romance. Was that too much to ask? Why did we have to have all the romance *before* the wedding and almost none *after?* What happened?"

"Nora, for God's sake let it go."

"How, Sam? Other women have honeymoon photos of themselves cavorting on the beach in bikinis; I have photos of myself washing oil off pelicans with organic solvents! And . . ."

"And what?"

"And I still don't see why you had to sleep with Rosalee! She was married to Dale when you were playing footsie with her!"

At that instant, the phone rang. Sam hit the *Answer*

button. Unfortunately, the speaker was on. "This is Vendettas to Go," Sam said loudly. "How may I direct your call?"

Nora dived for the speaker to shut it off, but Sam blocked her with one of his old basketball moves.

"Hello?" said a familiar voice on the other end of the line. "This is Deputy Johnson. I'd like to speak to Ms. Wynn."

"Ms. Wynn is out on an eight-state bank-robbing spree," Sam said. "Can I take a message?"

"Hello?" Nora yelled. "Deputy Johnson? This is Nora Wynn. My ex-husband, Sam, is here, and he's just making a stupid joke." Again she lunged for the speaker. Again Sam blocked her.

"Mr. Gallo, are you really there?"

"Yes," Sam said. "Nora and I were just talking over old times. I was helping her recall an occasion when she used tofu in the commission of a felony."

"Don't pay any attention to him!" Nora yelled.

"She's been on her knees begging me to marry her again so I won't be forced to testify against her."

"I have not!"

"No testifying is going to be necessary, Mr. Gallo. That's what I was calling about. The crime lab has finished going over that photograph of you and Mrs. Lambert. Turns out, it's fake."

"Of course it's a fake. I told you and your buddy that this afternoon."

"Yes, well, we apologize for not believing you, but Deputy Rodriguez and I just collect statements, we don't evaluate them. And that photo was very convincing. The crime lab suspects it may have been done by a professional photographer: the skin tones, background, and shadows were nearly perfect. It used to be, when we had a photo of two suspects having lunch together, we had evidence that they knew each other; but not these days. In any event, Mr. Gallo, since there's no indication whatsoever that you and Mrs. Lambert were having any kind of relationship prior to Mr. Lambert's disappearance, you're no longer a suspect in this case."

"Glad to hear it. You don't happen to have any idea who faked that photo, do you?"

"No, but we're looking into it. Can you think of anyone who might want to involve you in the Lambert case? Someone who owes you money? A disgruntled employee? An old girlfriend?"

Sam stared straight at Nora. "No. Every woman who knows me thinks I'm the nicest guy she's ever met."

"Well, if you come up with the name of anyone who might have it in for you, give us a call."

"I'll do that." Sam switched off the speaker. There was a moment of silence. Nora looked down, fiddled with the papers on her desk, and then looked up. Sam was staring at her with *I told you so* written all over his face.

"I'm really sorry," she said meekly.

"Apology accepted."

"Is there anything I can do to make up for not believing you?"

"No, except maybe not calling me anymore to accuse me of plotting against you."

"I'm sorry about that too."

"Forget it. Let's just—"

"Part friends and promise never to speak to each other again?"

"Right. Maybe this time we can actually make it stick. As my mom always says: the road to hell may be paved with good intentions, but at least it's paved."

"I miss Lucia." Nora suddenly found herself on the verge of tears. "She doesn't come by anymore." She swallowed a lump in her throat and looked down at her desktop without seeing it. Everything in her life was so messed up, and now she'd been nasty to Sam, who had

once been a pretty good friend when they weren't fighting.

"Mom says she misses you too."

"Give her my love, will you?"

"I'll do that."

"Sam . . ."

"What?"

"Do you ever wonder if maybe if we'd tried harder,
we could have made it work?"

"No. I think we did the best we could. We just can't
help rubbing each other the wrong way. We're like fire
and . . ."

"Gasoline," Nora supplied. "You're right. We never
really had a chance even before you got that gig in South
America." She cleared her throat and became business-
like again. "Look, I have to leave pretty soon. I have
some pool guys coming to my house to clean my pool."

"In the middle of the night?"

"Someone threw purple dye in it. Kids probably.
Who knows? It just keeps happening. Anyway, it's not
your problem, but I do have to go. I'm paying the pool
repair guys by the hour, and they're probably already at
my house waiting for me."

Sam picked up Nora's sweater and held it out to her.
"Come on," he said. "Put that on, and I'll walk you to
your car. I'm parked in your lot."

Nora froze. "Walk me to my car? Why do you say
that?"

"Because it's dark out."

"It gets dark every night, Sam. If I want to get walked
to my car, I'll buy myself a German shepherd."

Sam tossed the sweater down on her desk and started
toward the door. "Fine. Walk yourself to your own damn
car then. Good-bye, Nora. It's been big fun as usual."

"Wait a minute!" Nora grabbed her purse and sweater
and ran after him. "Sam!"

He said nothing.

"Sam, speak to me. This is totally childish. I'm sorry. I didn't mean to provoke you again. Please don't be so sensitive. I've always had a thing about being independent. It's like a reflex or something."

They walked out of the building in silence, crossed the street, and entered the parking lot. Sam got into his car, shut the door, and rolled down the window. But instead of saying anything or starting his engine and leaving, he just sat there staring straight ahead with his lips clamped together.

Nora stuck her head in the window. "Come on. Please. At least say you forgive me for flying off the handle." Sam remained silent.

Nora gave an exasperated sigh. "You aren't going to talk to me, are you? You know, I've always hated it when you act this way. You may think you're being the strong silent type, but you look pretty silly sitting there like a stuffed owl. Oh, why do I keep trying to talk to you? What's the point!"

She straightened up, turned around, and stomped across the parking lot without a backward glance. Slamming her car door shut, she started the engine, shifted into reverse, and smashed into Sam's back bumper with a crash so loud it made her ears ring.

Sam was out of his car and standing by her window before she fully realized what had happened. "Look what you did to my car!" he yelled. "Damn it, Nora! How many times have I told you to look over your shoulder before you back up!"

Nora put her head down on the steering wheel and stared at her knees. She wished she were thousands of miles away on some Pacific island where everyone ran around in sarongs and no one ever yelled at anyone and the word *revenge* didn't exist.

Sam looked at her more closely. "Whoa," he said. "Wait a minute. Are you okay?"

She shook her head no.

"Are you hurt?"

Again she shook her head.

"Look, Nora, I'm really sorry I yelled at you like that."

Nora lifted her head, stared at him, and then put her head back down on the steering wheel. "Just go away," she commanded in a shaky voice.

"I'm not going anywhere until we figure out if you're hurt." Sam opened the door on the driver's side. "Come on." He took Nora by the arm and gently drew her out of the car. She caught hold of the side mirror to steady herself. Her legs felt like rubber.

"You're really shook-up. You aren't going to go into shock, are you?"

Nora shook her head.

"Please," he insisted, "talk to me, Nora. This isn't like you. So you put a dent in my bumper. It's not the end of the world."

"The brakes," she said weakly.

"What about the brakes?"

"Weren't any."

"Are you saying your brakes failed?"

She nodded. "I have to look under my car, Sam."

"Why?"

"I think someone may have cut my brake cables. It's one of the scenarios from the Revenge Fantasy Seminars. I think I have a flashlight in the glove compartment." She started to walk around to the other side of the car, but Sam caught her by the shoulder.

"Wait a minute. In the first place, your brakes are hydraulic. The only cable is on the emergency brake. In the second place, you aren't in any condition to crawl under your car. Let me do it."

"I'm perfectly capable—"

"I know you're 'perfectly capable.' That's not the point."

"What is the point?"

"The point is: if you pass out and fall down on the asphalt and bash your head open, I'm going to have to scoop up your brains and rush you to the hospital, and I'm not in the mood."

Nora smiled weakly. "You wouldn't by any chance be trying to be nice, would you?"

"Please, Nora. Sit down before you fall down."

"Okay." Nora took two wobbling steps back to her car, slid into the driver's seat, put her head back down on the steering wheel again, and closed her eyes. She heard Sam come around to the passenger's side, open the glove compartment, and get the flashlight. While he rummaged around under the car, she tried to remember the names of people who had taken her revenge fantasy seminars recently. Were any of them capable of attempted murder? The answer was no, unless, of course, you counted Rosalee. But maybe the motive for tampering with her brakes hadn't been murder. A real murderer would have fixed it so her brakes failed when she was going around a curve, not when she was safely parked. At least that's the way it was done in mystery novels. So maybe whoever it was had only wanted to scare her.

That thought made her feel a little calmer. Sitting up, she opened the door and slowly got out of the car. Sam's feet were still poking out from the rear end.

"So what's the verdict?"

Sam wiggled out and stood up. There was a smudge of oil on his nose. "Hung jury. Your seals are ruptured. There's brake fluid all over the place."

"Are you saying this is an ordinary mechanical problem?"

"Looks like it."

"Damn. Just when I thought I had everything all figured out. Thanks, Sam."

"Any time." There was an awkward pause. Sam cleared his throat. "Look, Nora, you can't drive your car without brakes, so how about I give you a ride home?"

"What is this? A declaration of peace?"

"Are you kidding? I'm only volunteering to give you a lift if you agree to fight with me every mile between here and Pasadena. Plus I still expect you to pay for my bumper."

Nora smiled weakly. "You're out of luck. My car insurance's been canceled."

"What did you do, sideswipe the Oscar Myer Weinermobile?"

"Damn it, Sam! I'm a *superb* driver!"

Sam grinned. "Don't worry about the insurance," he said, as he shepherded her toward his car. "I'll take a personal check."

14

When Nora and Sam arrived at Nora's place, they found a large blue van blocking the driveway. The pool repairmen were out on the back deck, lolling around in recliners, drinking Bud Lites, and stubbing cigarettes out on the tiles Nora used as coasters. They were both in their early twenties, with bleached-white hair and skin so tanned it looked like potato peels. Both had tattoos on their upper arms and large stainless steel rings in their noses. One also had a metal bar embedded in his lower lip. The last time Nora had called them for emergency repairs, she had determined that the bar made it possible to tell them apart.

"Water in your pool's purple, dude," the bar-lipped one informed Sam as soon as he caught sight of him.

Nora smiled graciously and reminded herself that no other pool service in town made emergency visits in the middle of the night. "It's *my* pool, and I know the water's purple. That's why I called you."

"What'd you spill in her, ma'am?" asked the one who came minus the bar.

Ma'am? Had he just called her *ma'am?* Nora didn't

know whether to be impressed by his manners or depressed by the idea that a kid who couldn't be more than eight years younger than she was had her classified as ma'am material. "I didn't spill anything in it. Someone threw in dye."

"Purple?" inquired the barred one, crumpling his beer can and looking around for somewhere to toss it.

"No," Sam said. "Awesomely bright orange."

The kid grinned. "Alf and I have been here for hours. Drained the sucker, cleaned her, refilled her, and what do you get?"

"She's still way purple," said Alf. "Or maybe kinda violet."

Nora went over and inspected the water. It looked a little less purple, but not a whole lot less. She thought about their claim that they'd been working for hours. Then she thought about the fact that she was paying them overtime.

Sam walked up and stood so close that his arm nearly touched hers. He peered at the water and then at the outlet hole where it was pumped into the pool. "What's the problem?"

"The filter, dude," said Bar-lip. "We can't get the dye out of the sucker."

"Don't tell me you're going to have to replace it?" Nora moaned.

"Afraid so, ma'am."

Sam bent down, cupped his hand, scooped up some water, and looked at it thoughtfully. "I'm not sure you need to replace that filter." He turned to Nora. "Do you have any idea what kind of dye this is?"

"Not a clue. Someone could have stomped grapes in here for all I know." She was surprised he was taking an interest in her pool.

Sam frowned and scooped out another handful of water. "Could be organic. Probably isn't, but what the heck?" He turned to the pool repairmen, who were staring at him as if their brains had frozen. Apparently nothing he was saying was in their manual.

"Have you tried vinegar?"

"Vinegar?" said Alf. "No way."

"Well, sometimes organic dyes turn white if you mix vinegar with them. You know, like when you put a vinegar dressing on purple cabbage. It's got to do with the pH."

The pool repair boy stared at him blankly. Clearly neither of them had ever taken chemistry.

Sam let the water drain through his hand. Nora noticed it left a faint violet stain on his palm. "Do you have any white vinegar?" he asked Nora.

"Sure. What do you plan to do?"

"Well, first I'm going to perform a simple experiment. If it works, I'm going to send Alf on a midnight run to the nearest supermarket to buy ten quarts of white vinegar while his partner and I pull your pool filter. When Alf gets back with the vinegar, we'll use it to clean out the dye."

Nora was practically speechless. "Thanks."

Sam grinned. "Don't thank me, Nora. It makes me nervous."

Five minutes later, they were all gathered around Nora's patio table staring at a highball glass filled with pool water. The water, which had been purple, had turned colorless the instant Sam poured in a few drops of vinegar.

"Awesome," cried the kid with the bar in his lip. "Totally awesome." He slapped Sam on the back. "Hey, dude, let's pull that filter!"

The vinegar was a great success. The filter turned white just as Sam had predicted, and the water that passed through it came out looking like pool water should.

After the repairmen left, Nora and Sam stood next to the pool watching it refill. There was a full moon and the water was so clean it was nearly invisible.

"That was really nice of you," Nora said.

"No problem." Sam put his hand in front of one of the jets, and the water suddenly trembled, scattering moonlight from one side of the pool to the other. Nora looked at the dancing lines of light, and then at Sam. She felt a number of complicated feelings, none of which she could quite get a handle on. There had been other evenings like this: times when they had stood together quietly in the darkness without saying much, and then gone back inside and . . . Against her will, she was assailed by memories of their lovemaking: the arch of his spine, the vulnerable spot at the base of his neck, the heat of his hands.

"A penny for your thoughts?" he asked.

She blushed to the roots of her hair. *I was just undressing you in my mind,* she thought. But what she said was "Nothing much."

She stuffed their past back in the part of her mind where she stored old memories and turned to face him. That was then, this was now; and now—on this particular evening in this particular place—she didn't like feeling indebted to him. *What would I do,* she asked herself, *if some friend—and not too close a friend at that—had cleaned my pool filter at this hour?* The answer was obvious.

"Why don't you stay for dinner?"

Sam stood up and dried his hands on his jeans. "You're joking, right?"

Nora stiffened. So much for nostalgia and moonlight. "Why should I be joking?"

"Because you can't boil water."

"That's so untrue! Who once baked a cherry pie so long we ended up using it as a doorstop? Who melted the teakettle? Who baked a chicken without taking out the paper package of giblets?"

"And who made macaroni and cheese without cheese, milk, or butter because she was too lazy to go to the store? Who insisted we eat microwaved Mexican dinners five nights a week and . . . ?" Sam stopped. "You know, for some reason, my heart's just not in this tonight. In fact, if you'll just admit that I make great breakfasts, I'll surrender."

"I'm not admitting anything," Nora said, but she took the sting out of the comment with a smile.

Sam saw the smile and was encouraged. "Tell you what: let's perform an experiment. I'll take *you* out to dinner, and we'll see how long we can go without fighting."

"Thanks, but I don't think that's a good idea."

"Why not?"

"Because it would be too much like a date."

Sam shuddered. "Nora, I wouldn't date you if you were the last woman on earth."

The tension broke. They laughed, and Nora found herself warming to him again. What a roller-coaster ride. If a client had ever described a relationship like this, Nora would have advised her to run and not look back.

"Wow. That's a relief. I'm glad we've finally found something we can agree on. Okay, Sam, I accept your dinner invitation. And if we're really not going to fight, I suggest we talk about some neutral subject. . . ."

"Like what?"

"The weather."

"The weather? Give me a break, Nora. What's there to talk about? Day after day, it's the same."

"It is not! There are microclimates in L.A., Sam. Definite microclimates."

"Bullshit," Sam said as they opened the back gate

and headed down the driveway toward his car. "When did you become a meteorologist?"

They continued to walk toward the car, arguing every step of the way, but as Sam had pointed out, their hearts weren't really in it. Against her will, Nora was remembering how funny and witty Sam was; and he was remembering how he'd always liked the way her hair looked in the moonlight. Bits of their past kept coming up and ambushing them: long walks they'd taken together; good times when they'd gone dancing with friends or stayed home and watched TV, sitting side by side and eating microwaved popcorn.

This is not a good idea, Nora told herself sternly. *I shouldn't be going to dinner with Sam. It will only mean trouble.*

I should tell her I've changed my mind, Sam thought. *Uninvite her. What am I doing?* He paused beside his car with the intention of saying that he'd just remembered he couldn't take her out to dinner because he had to get up early, but instead he said:

"So what are you eating these days? Are you actually cooking yourself meals, or are you still standing over the sink slurping Top Ramen?"

Nora chuckled and climbed in. "Don't start, Sam. Just don't start." As she settled into the passenger's seat, she felt as if she'd been transported back to an earlier era. The interior of Sam's car smelled exactly the same: fumes from a faulty muffler mixed with Sam's aftershave, plus the aroma of stale coffee. It looked the same too: enough sand on the floor to make a small beach, empty Starbucks cups, old copies of *Variety,* battered boxes of Kleenex. He had even failed to remove a teardrop-shaped crystal she had hung from the rearview mirror a couple of weeks before they split up. As they started down the driveway, Nora leaned forward to give the crystal a little spin for old times' sake. Suddenly, she realized that there was something sitting on the dashboard. It was big, black, and the size of her fist.

"Oh, my God!" she screamed.

Sam braked to a stop so suddenly, they would have hit the windshield if they hadn't had their seat belts buckled. He turned to Nora, who continued to scream.

"What is it? What's wrong?"

"That!" Nora yelled as she fought to release the catch on her seat belt. "That! That!"

"What!"

Still screaming, she pointed. Sam looked, and then he screamed too. A large black tarantula was perched exactly halfway between them. Throwing open the doors, they bailed out, ran around to the front of the car, and clutched each other.

"Spider!" cried Nora.

"Really big spider!" Sam agreed.

Nora threw her arms around Sam's neck and he drew her closer. Somehow the hug turned into a long, hot, breathless, oh-my-God, this-is-totally-fantastic kiss that left them both senseless for the better part of fifteen seconds. Nora was the first to get her brain booted up and working again. With great reluctance, she stepped back, seized Sam's hands, and removed them from her waist.

"Nora . . ." he murmured.

She clapped a finger over his lips. "Don't say anything. Listen, Sam, that was totally wonderful and totally horrible. Promise me we'll never do it again."

"I can't promise."

"You know it would be a total disaster for us to get involved again."

"Right. A total disaster."

"We can't ever kiss again. We can't so much as touch each other."

"Nuclear reaction kind of thing?"

"Exactly, Sam. Nuclear reaction. Always has been. Sex was our strong point. One kiss. Boom."

"You're right. We're sensible adults. We know better. No kissing. Seems a pity though." He cleared his throat. "Okay, so now that we've got that settled, suppose we go back to the car and get rid of that spider? Do you have any Raid?"

"No, how about a flyswatter?"

"Not unless it has a six-foot handle. That thing is as big as a teacup; it can probably jump at least three feet, and it's poisonous."

Nora turned pale. Approaching the car warily, she pressed her nose to the windshield. Sam followed her example. The spider was still on the dashboard.

"What are we going to do?"

"Wait until it dies of old age."

"Very funny."

They circled the car peering in all the windows. If the spider noticed, it wasn't intimidated. It just lay there like it was waiting for a chance to attack.

"Maybe we should call the zoo," Sam suggested. "Get someone out here with a tranquilizer dart."

Nora, who had always been the more practical of the two, had a better idea. "Forget the zoo," she said. "Let's call an exterminator."

Time passed. The pool finished filling, the automatic jets shut off with a quiet gurgle, and the moon rose high in the sky, shifting from silver to smoggy blue. Out in front of Nora's house, two exterminators in green uniforms and red baseball caps surrounded Sam's car, doing things best not thought about.

Inside the house everything was bathed in a golden glow. Sam sat at the kitchen table tearing off hunks of burned diet toast and scooping up scrambled egg replacer enhanced with canned salsa. He looked like he was having fun, as if the food on his plate were prime rib, as if he couldn't get enough of it; but Nora wasn't fooled.

She leaned forward and inspected his plate. Although she'd been too tired to fix herself anything but half a block of raw tofu doused in cayenne and sesame oil, she had insisted on making him something more substantial while they waited for the exterminators to send the spider on to a better reincarnation. Unfortunately, the egg replacer hadn't turned out quite as well as she'd hoped it would.

"How's it taste?" she asked.

"Wonderful." Sam crunched down on the toast, sending a shower of charred crumbs into his beard.

Nora knew he was lying, but she was pleased to see him make an effort to be nice about her cooking. She'd spent too many evenings listening to him rave about Lucia's fabulous ziti.

Sam picked up his fork and made a show of enjoying the spinach salad. Actually the salad would have been quite tasty if it hadn't contained sand. Nora made a mental note to herself to try to remember to wash spinach before she served it. She watched him chew carefully so as not to make crunching noises.

"It's really great," he insisted.

"Glad you like it."

They were being extraordinarily polite to each other. The memory of that kiss still hovered over them. They hadn't fought for the better part of an hour. Nora was just thinking that, nice as this was, it couldn't last, when the front doorbell rang.

She got up to answer it. Sam heard mumbled conversation, then an exclamation of surprise, then her footsteps as she made her way back to the kitchen. When she entered the room, there was a strange look in her eyes he couldn't decode.

"Is everything okay?"

"No. The exterminators just told me that they couldn't kill the spider."

"Why not?"

"Because it was already dead, damn it!" Nora approached the table and slapped a huge black tarantula down in front of him with a whack that rattled the china. "It's rubber, Sam! A rubber spider! Who's doing this to me? Why? Is it some wacko psychotic killer, or have I been designated a national testing range for mail order practical jokes?"

She picked up the spider by one leg and dangled it in front of him. "By the way, this is a variation on revenge fantasy scenario number 123, otherwise known as 'Confront them with their worst fear.' I'm totally terrified of spiders. This has to be an ex-client. But who? Maybe it's someone I matched up with the wrong person; or someone who heard me on the radio and hates my guts. Maybe it's even Rosalee. Maybe feeding Dale to the sharks was just a dry run for driving me nuts! No, scratch that. Rosalee's in jail. It has to be some other maniac!"

"Calm down."

"That's easy for you to say now, but wait until you see your car."

"What's wrong with my car?"

"Revenge fantasy seminar scenario number fifty-six. Really elementary, perfectly harmless, and highly effective."

Sam's car was right where he had left it, which wasn't surprising since all four tires were flat. Nora sat down on the gravel, folded her legs into a half lotus, and glared at the tires. The joker who had done this was probably lurking in the shadows right now, waiting for her to turn her back. Should she call Johnson and Rodriguez on the unlikely chance that all this vandalism was somehow connected to Dale?

Oh, right. And tell them what? *Hi, I know you're really busy trying to figure out exactly how Rosalee Lambert murdered her husband, but I wonder if you could spare a moment to come over to my place. You might like to bring the press with you. You see, my little chickens of revenge are coming home to roost. I've just been attacked by a rubber spider, and given who I am and what I do for a living, FOX or CNN would probably love to get me on camera.*

She watched Sam circle around his car, inspecting each tire for slash marks. She felt bad about dragging him into this mess. He came back to where she was sitting and stood over her.

"At least the tires aren't punctured. Someone just let the air out. Do you have any idea who's doing this?"

"Not by name, no, but it has to be one of my clients. When the harassment first started, I suspected my next-door neighbor, an old guy named Jenkins. He and I argued for weeks about the roses that line my driveway. He claimed they were over his property line."

"Roses?" Sam gave the bare edge of her driveway a puzzled look. "What roses?"

"Don't ask. Anyway, I didn't believe Jenkins when he denied everything, but he's been away for the last couple of days. I think his no-good son went with him, because it's been really quiet over there. They drove to Las Vegas to gamble—or at least that's the rumor in the neighborhood. Personally, I suspect they're secretly attending a lawn ornament convention in Sun City. In any event they appear to be gone, and meanwhile the fun continues."

"Did you say 'lawn ornament convention'?"

"Once again, don't ask. I expect them to come back

with a couple of those plywood lawn butts and a dozen motion-detector-equipped plastic frogs that scream 'ribbet!' every time a stray cat walks across their yard."

"So you have no suspects?"

"Wrong. Caroline and I have been running our client profiles through the computer trying to figure out who's out to get me. At present, I have hundreds of suspects, not including the tens of thousands of people who've read my column or listened to me on the radio."

"Sounds like marketing revenge wasn't such a great idea."

"Tell me about it. Look, Sam, I'm really sorry about your tires. This totally sucks."

"Totally," Sam agreed. "But fortunately a guy who buys retreads learns to be prepared." He went back to his car, opened the trunk, pulled out a small electric pump, plugged it into his cigarette lighter, started the engine, and began to reinflate his tires. Nora watched him, impressed. She probably didn't even have a tire iron in her trunk. Of course, by the time she got back to the parking lot to reclaim her car, that wouldn't matter, because no doubt it would have been stolen, disassembled, crushed, and compacted.

When Sam finished inflating the last tire, he disconnected the pump and stepped back. "Done," he proclaimed. He stowed the pump back in the trunk, walked over to where Nora was sitting, and sat down beside her. Picking up a piece of gravel, he skipped it across the driveway, and looked off into the darkness. "I imagine that whoever did this is watching us right now."

"Probably."

"Have you ever thought that it might be one of your old boyfriends?"

"Yes, but that's not likely. I'm on good terms with every guy I dated before you and I got married, and every guy I dated after our divorce. Jason's the one exception, and he's out of the picture for two reasons. First, *he* left *me;* and second, he's on some kind of round-the-world adventure with Felicity. Right now I believe they're in Nepal preparing to hang-glide off Mount Everest or something of the sort. Picturing Felicity in a maternity hang-gliding harness gives me the willies, so I try not to think about it. As for the other men I've gone out with, I've lost track of some of them, but in each case we parted in a friendly fashion. I can't imagine why any of them would be out for revenge."

"You actually got along with *all* of them?"

"Don't sound so shocked. For your information, I'm generally considered to be sweet-tempered, considerate, and easygoing. You have the distinction of being the only man I ever fought with. Believe me, I've spent years trying to figure out why."

"Did you?"

"Did I what?"

"Figure out why."

"Sort of."

"Care to elaborate?"

Nora looked down at her knees and tried to decide if she should be honest with him.

"Come on," Sam urged. "Tell me."

"Frankly with other guys, the emotions just didn't . . ."

"Didn't what? Come on, Nora. What are we playing here, charades?"

"The emotions just didn't run deep enough, damn it!"

There was an awkward silence. Sam picked up a piece of gravel and skipped it toward the place where Nora's roses had once been. Half a dozen pieces of gravel later, he spoke.

"Nora, I think I should sleep at your place tonight."

Nora started and looked at him as if she had forgotten he was there. "Bad idea, Sam. *Very* bad."

"Don't get the wrong idea. I'm not coming on to you; but I am worried about you. I could stay in your spare bedroom."

For a moment, she was tempted to say yes. Then she came to her senses. She was unnerved by what had happened in the last couple of hours, but she couldn't possibly spend a night under the same roof with him. "Thanks," she said gently, "but I'm a big girl, and I have this thing about independence, remember?"

"Do you have a gun?"

"What kind of question is that? Of course not. I couldn't possibly shoot at another human being. When I kill ants, I feel so guilty, I give them a funeral."

"But you're scared, right?"

"Yes. Okay. I admit it. I'm scared. But it's not your job to look after me."

"Has anyone ever told you that you're pigheadedly stubborn?"

"Yes. You. About a hundred times."

"I could sleep out here in my car if it would make you feel better."

She was touched by his concern, but accepting his offer was still out of the question. "No, Sam. Thanks. Really, I'll be fine. I'll call the Pasadena police and tell them that I thought I saw a prowler. I'll ask them to send a patrol car by to check on things."

"Are you sure that will do it?"

"I'm sure." She started to take his hand and then thought better of it. They sat in another awkward silence listening to the distant sound of traffic and not looking at each other. Finally they rose to their feet.

"Well, then, good night, Nora."

"Good night, Sam."

She turned and walked back toward the house. As she approached her front door, she heard him start his engine. His car began to roll down the driveway, its newly inflated tires making a soft, crunching sound on the gravel. Suddenly there was a squeal of brakes.

"Nora!" Sam yelled. "Come here! Now!"

Startled by the anger in his voice, she froze. Then she turned and ran back to his car, where she found him sitting behind the steering wheel looking furious. With his left hand, he was pounding on the dashboard. With his right, he was . . .

Well, actually Sam couldn't do anything with his right hand, because it was glued to the gearshift.

15

Nora opened the door on the passenger's side and stuck her head in. She could see at once that Sam wasn't seriously injured, but it freaked her out to think that someone had managed to get into the car and smear glue on the gearshift in the brief interval between the time the exterminators left and the time she and Sam went back outside to pump up the tires.

"Stop struggling," she said gently. "You're going to tear off your skin."

"Back off!" Sam snarled. "I don't need your advice!"

Nora backed off and waited for him to come to his senses. She didn't mind that he'd yelled at her. If her hand had been glued to a gearshift, she would have yelled too.

Once, back in the days before she became allergic to cats, she'd tried to Krazy-Glue the ends of her kitty's collar together so it wouldn't lose its ID tags. Unfortunately she'd forgotten that cats constantly lick themselves. In the end, she'd been forced to tackle her cat and rush him to a vet, who had applied something that made his tongue come unstuck from his collar. As Sam thrashed around in the car trying to remove his hand from the gearshift, she tried to remember what the vet had used.

Sam gave a final bellow and stopped struggling. Again she approached the car.

"How's it going?"

He glared at her and made another futile attempt to tear his hand off the gearshift.

"Don't panic, Sam. These things always hurt more when you panic."

"I'm not panicking," he said through clenched teeth. "I'm perfectly calm. I just have this one small problem: *my hand is stuck to the damn gearshift!*" He gave her a stony glare. "When you're through watching, maybe you could help me."

"Sure." She got a flashlight out of the glove compartment, leaned over, and inspected his hand from all angles, but there wasn't much to see. "Do you think this rates a 911 call?"

"No!" Sam snapped.

"Okay, then. How about I go inside, boot up my computer, Google 'Krazy Glue,' and see if there's a way to remove the stuff without taking off your skin?"

"Do it," Sam said, "unless, of course, you want me to spend the rest of my life in your driveway."

After checking to make sure no one was lurking in the bushes, Nora hurried back to the house while Sam sat in the car, glaring at the squashed bugs on the windshield. He wanted to turn on the radio, but he was to afraid to touch anything else without checking it out first.

After a while Nora reappeared carrying a bottle of nail polish remover. Climbing in beside him, she poured the nail polish remover on a rag and soaked his hand in it.

"Count to twenty."

Sam counted to twenty.

"Now take a deep breath and exhale."

Sam exhaled, and Nora carefully rolled the palm of his hand off the gearshift. Sam lifted it to eye level and checked it out. The skin on his palm was bright red and smelled like acetone, but there didn't seem to be any flesh missing. "Nice job. Thanks."

"My pleasure."

"Sorry I yelled at you. That's twice tonight."

"More than twice, but no problem." Nora flipped on the overhead light and gave everything a quick wipe-down with nail polish remover. When she finished, she shoved the rag into a plastic sandwich bag and sealed it.

"Did you know that the smell of nail polish remover can get you high?"

"I'd rather have a martini."

"Come inside and I'll make you one."

When they got back into the house, Nora headed straight for the kitchen. She took a bottle of vodka out of the freezer and a bottle of Cointreau from the liquor cabinet over the sink. Putting them down on the counter, she went to another cabinet and pulled out bottles of cranberry and lime juice.

"What are you doing?"

"Making you a cosmopolitan. It's something Caroline did for me once when I was really upset. Works wonders."

"A cosmopolitan isn't my idea of a real martini. Do you have any gin and vermouth?"

"Sam, hardly anybody drinks classic martinis these days."

"I still do. Look, if you don't have gin, forget the sweet stuff and just pour me a shot of straight vodka."

Nora poured Sam a shot of vodka over ice, and then began to make herself a cosmopolitan, but the smell of the cranberry juice made her gag. It was truly amazing low long the memory of a bad hangover persisted.

Grabbing a lemon from the fruit basket on the kitchen table, she squeezed it and added the juice to some vodka along with sugar, ice, and a little water. She and Sam sat across from each other, sipping their drinks.

"So," he said after a long pause, "I suppose the glue on the gearshift was another of your revenge fantasy seminar scenarios?"

"I'm afraid so. But you were lucky. The glue was supposed to be applied to a toilet seat."

"What other surprises can we expect?"

"It's hard to say. There's scenario 216: poodle poop in the air-conditioning system, a fiendish little fantasy created by a client of mine who breeds poodles. Then there's scenario 72: sowing the front lawn with radish seed, which is harmless and takes a long time to get results, so we'll scratch that one for the moment. Scenario 153 is epoxy in the ignition of a car, lots of potential trouble there; plus it seems like a good possibility. Scenario 210 involves smearing bacon grease on a garbage can to attract raccoons; scenario—"

"Stop. I get the picture. How many revenge scenarios are there altogether?"

Nora frowned and thought this over. "I'm not sure. Caroline and I came up with several hundred without even trying. Seminar participants spontaneously came up with a couple hundred more. None of them were intended to be carried out. They were all just supposed to be fantasies. We treated them like film scripts: you chose one and got emotional release, and that helped you get rid of your anger. Most of them weren't a tenth as violent as a lot of the stuff you see on TV. I believed I was performing a public service."

"Do you still?"

"No, I think I was a total idiot. My lawyer warned me, but I didn't listen. I saw myself as a kind of secular Mother Teresa, bringing peace and forgiveness to a troubled world. The truth was: I was more like—"

"A combination of the Corleones and the Sopranos, although that's a little unfair to both families."

Nora's frown deepened. "Watch it."

"Okay. Sorry. Point well taken. Actually, you were more like a kid who mistakes a real gun for a toy. Nevertheless, I have to be frank here. I've had it with being on the receiving end of these revenge scenarios of yours. I don't know who the hell is out to get you, but whoever it is has included me, and I don't intend to hang around waiting for someone to sprinkle cyanide on my pizza or send a more convincing photo of me and Rosalee to the cops."

He picked up his glass and took a sip of his drink. "Here's the bottom line: whether you want me involved in this or not, I'm going to find out who's out to get us. This is no longer just a question of rubber spiders. I'm rattled by what's happened tonight, and if you aren't scared, you should be. Have you called the police and reported any of this?"

"No."

"Why not?"

"Because if one of my clients is behind this harassment, it would be terrible for business if anyone found out about it. The press would have a field day. I can just see the headlines. Once the word got out, every time someone who had listened to my radio program or read my column or taken one of my seminars dented a fender or accidentally sprayed pesticide on a neighbor's lawn, I'd be sued. Also, if I make any kind of official report, it might get Rosalee Lambert the death penalty. According to the *L.A. Times*, one of her lines of defense is likely to be that other people who took my revenge seminars openly expressed anger, but none of them carried out their fantasies."

Sam frowned, plucked a lemon out of the fruit basket, and gave it a spin. He sat silently for a moment, watching it. "Okay," he said. "I understand what you're saying. So, I'm going to give you two choices: either you forget about the bad publicity, let Rosalee take her chances, and call the police right now, or else I sleep in your spare bedroom, and in the morning we put our heads together and start figuring out who wants you— and possibly me—dead."

"Dead?" Nora stared at him, shocked. "Do you really think someone wants to *kill* us?"

Sam nodded, seized the lemon in midspin, and brought it to an abrupt halt. "Yes, and here's why: I didn't want to tell you this, but I wasn't totally convinced that your brakes failed by accident tonight. That's why I offered to drive you home, and that's why I stuck around. I couldn't be sure. I kept thinking, maybe I'm on the wrong track. Maybe she just has a rotten mechanic. I even thought— and you'll have to forgive me for this one—I know for a fact that Nora once blew the head gaskets on her car because she forgot to check the oil, so maybe she did something like put something caustic in the brake fluid reservoir, and it ate out the seals.

"But we've had four attacks in a row here: the dye, the spider, the tires, and the glue. None of them were all that bad in themselves, but each was a little more serious than the last; and each indicates that someone is lurking outside this house watching our every move. This has convinced me beyond a reasonable doubt that your brakes failed because somebody wanted you to get hurt. So which is it? Do you want me to call the police, or do you want to make up a spare bed?"

Nora felt as if all the blood had drained out of her

body. The word *dead* stopped rolling around in her head and took on substance. "Don't call the police. I really don't want to go public with this. Please stay here tonight. And . . . thanks, Sam."

He reached out, patted her hand, and smiled. "Yo, dude," he said in a perfect imitation of Alf, the pool guy, "like, no problem."

It took Nora a long time to fall asleep. Just before dawn, she woke to the familiar sound of Sam's snoring. She lay for a while, listening to the rhythmic snorts, trying to figure out if they were annoying or comforting.

Comforting, she decided and, turning over, she fell back into a long, dreamless slumber.

The first thing she saw when she came into the kitchen the next morning was Sam sitting at the table eating actual scrambled eggs. Beside him sat a cup of freshly made coffee, a plate of brioche, and a stick of real butter.

"Help yourself," he said. "Your refrigerator only contained egg replacer, peanut butter, and club soda, so I made a quick trip to the store."

Nora gave him a weak smile. "Thanks, but could you please save the conversation until I've had some coffee?"

"I remember you as being a morning person."

"And I remember you not being able to open your eyes until you poured half a pot of unadulterated caffeine down your throat, so I guess we've both changed."

"Did you notice I put the toilet seat down?"

"Yes. I was in raptures until I noticed that you still leave little hairs all over the sink. Also I have a strong suspicion that you used my toothbrush."

Nora sat down at the table and poured herself a cup

of coffee. It smelled wonderful and tasted even better. Sam had always had a talent for making great breakfasts, but this was his best pot ever. Obviously four years of bachelor life had tuned up his cooking skills.

Sam finished his eggs, scraped the leftovers into the garbage disposal, rinsed his plate, and deposited it in the dishwasher. Returning to the table, he pushed a notepad and a pen toward her. "When you get your brain up and running again, I'd like you to make a chronological list of everything bad that's happened to you since you started running Payback Time."

Nora nodded and finished her coffee. Then she poured herself another cup, drank it slowly, savoring every sip, ate a buttered brioche, wiped her lips on a napkin, picked up the pen, and produced the following:

1. *Car insurance canceled due to traffic violations I never committed*
2. *Purse stolen*
3. *Roses cut down*
4. *IRS audit*
5. *Rosalee arrested for murdering Dale in a way she thought up in one of my seminars*
6. *Koi poisoned*
7. *Newspaper column canceled*
8. *Radio show canceled*
9. *Identity stolen; credit cards applied for in my name. Purchases made total over $7,000*
10. *Letter claiming Sam is having an affair with Rosalee sent to sheriff's department along with fake photo*
11. *Brakes fail*
12. *Purple dye thrown in swimming pool*
13. *Rubber tarantula*
14. *Air let out of Sam's tires*
15. *Krazy-Gluing of Sam's hand*

Sam took the list from her and reviewed it. "Whew."

Nora took back the list, reread it, and began to hyperventilate. Until now, she hadn't realized exactly how many bad things had happened to her in the last four days. She put her head down on the table and tried to control her panic, but all she could think of was that something much worse was bound to happen, something so terrible that just thinking about it made her want to start running and never stop.

"Are you okay?"

"No, I'm having an anxiety attack."

The next thing she knew, Sam had pulled his chair close to hers and had his arm around her. "Listen, I know you're upset, but I promise we'll find out who's doing this. Come on, sweetheart, calm down."

Nora rested her head against his shoulder. Gradually her heartbeat slowed, and she began to breathe normally. After a while, she sat up. Sam withdrew his arm. She felt embarrassed and oddly sad. It had been nice to hear him call her "sweetheart" again after all these years.

She cleared her throat, picked up the list, and read it for a third time. The number of bad things that had happened to her was still impressively terrible. "So, how are we going to find whoever's doing all this?"

"Logic." Sam moved his chair back to the other side of the table. He looked embarrassed too. The moment had been too intimate. "You have to figure out the habits of the man or woman you're looking for," Sam continued. "You have to be able to see what detectives like to call "the invisible details"—clues right in plain sight that most people would overlook."

"How do you know all this?"

"I sometimes read scripts for friends who want to direct features. A lot of the plots hinge on unsolved murders."

Nora groaned. Not appreciating the difference between fact and fiction was what had gotten her into this mess in the first place. If Sam heard the groan, he ignored it. Picking up the list, he studied it intently.

"Notice how I start out as a bit player and then take on a more central role? Maybe that means something."

"Like what?"

"I have no idea." Sam picked up the pen and crossed out 7 and 8 on the grounds that they were fallout from Dale's murder and Rosalee's arrest. Then he studied the list again. "You say you and Caroline ran every fact you could think of through your client database and came up with how many suspects?"

"About eight hundred probables and several thousand possibles," Nora said gloomily. "And there are probably thousands more who heard my radio show or read my column."

"Don't get discouraged. Your database is a great place to start looking for suspects. So, when did you run the last search?"

"Day before yesterday."

"Aha! Just as I thought! We have a new piece of information!" He pounced on the list, underlined number 10, and drew a circle around it. "Up until last night, no one, including the sheriff's department, knew that whoever was after you was capable of professionally faking a photo."

"But why would someone who was trying to get revenge on me drag you into this? What's the point? You and I have been divorced for years."

"Who knows, but at least it's a start." Sam folded up the list and stuck it in his pocket. "Finish your coffee and get dressed. We need to go your office and see if you've been offending any professional photographers."

* * *

An hour later, they stood in Nora's office staring at her computer screen. Instead of eight hundred names, they now had the names of 457 of her former clients who were involved in some way with photography. Most had listed the word under *Hobbies,* and were probably amateurs; but there were still over a hundred professionals—which was not surprising since L.A. was a movie town crawling with actors and would-be actors who needed head shots.

Nora printed up two copies of the list, took one, and handed the other to Sam. She read her copy and tossed it down on her desk. "Well, we've really narrowed down the range of suspects. Instead of taking half a year to check everyone out, it should only take us about three months."

Sam didn't seem discouraged. He studied his copy of the list eagerly. "Let's run the professional photographers' names again and see if any of them moonlight selling car insurance, working for the IRS, or selling novelty items like rubber spiders."

Nora gave an inward sigh. This was hopeless. She ran the new combination. This time the computer spat out only one name: a man in Long Beach who supplied props to studios.

"Forget him," she advised. "I remember the guy well. The only props he supplies are antique cars and trucks. He owns a 1957 Chevrolet Cameo, a 1966 Chevrolet pickup, and a Cadillac from the late seventies. He was one of my oldest clients, bought the '57 Chevy new when he was still in high school. Several women were interested in dating him, and he married one his own age, which is a little unusual. Anyway, he can't possibly be a suspect because he'd no more put glue on a gearshift than sacrifice his firstborn."

She picked up the original list it and examined it glumly. "There are still too many names." Suddenly

she was struck by an idea so obvious, she was amazed
she hadn't thought of it earlier. "Let's try running 'photography' against the DC file!"

"The what?"

"The file of my difficult clients, the real nuts, the people in the Love Finds a Way database who are so neurotic they make everyone else look appealing. Caroline
and I ran their names to see if they might have charged
stuff to my credit cards and they all came up clean; but
now, as you pointed out, we have a new clue." She sat
down at the computer and began to type in commands.
A name popped up on the screen.

"Enid Barker. No, she moved to Mexico back in
August to study with a Yaqui shaman."

She typed some more.

"Henry Canton. No way. This guy's 'photography'
involves several thousand out-of-focus slides of Tippy,
his pet ferret."

Suddenly she gave a triumphant whoop. "Ashley
Clay!" She pointed to the name on the screen. "This
could be the one, Sam! I fixed Ashley up with Dale!
She's allergic to everything. Dale put her in the hospital with his aftershave. I gave Ashley's name to the
sheriff's department deputies, but I'd forgotten she was
a professional photographer. After the disaster with
Dale, she came back to Love Finds a Way for more
dates, so I didn't think she had any hard feelings. I gave
her more matches on the house. It only seemed fair."

"Why did you give Ashley's name to the cops? Did
you suspect her of murdering Dale?"

"No, no. Nothing that terrible. Rodriguez and Johnson
asked me if I knew of anyone else who might have a
motive for murdering Dale. They seemed to be pretty
sure Rosalee had done it, but I guess they always check
all the angles. So anyway, I figured any woman Dale
had gone out with might have wanted to kill him, so I

gave them a list of all the women he'd dated. Ashley was on it, and I know for a fact she came out clean.

"She had a perfect alibi for the day Dale died. She was so sick she couldn't get up out of bed. The hospital had a tape of her calling the advice nurse. She told the nurse she'd eaten a salad that had been sliced by a knife that had sat next to a knife that had sliced an onion that had touched a piece of raw fish. Ashley wanted them to send an ambulance, but the nurse told her to take Pepto-Bismol and stay put. Ashley sued the hospital and the restaurant for ten million dollars and lost. The suit made the newspapers, which is how I knew exactly where she was the day Dale got dumped over the side of his yacht."

"Great work, Nora!"

"Wait! That's not all! I think Ashley is an eight on the Enneagram! Oh, this is too perfect!"

Sam gave her a blank look.

"The Enneagram," Nora continued excitedly. "Don't tell me you've never heard of it? It's a New Age way of classifying people into eight different personality types. It's a gold mine for figuring out if you're going to be compatible with someone. I classify all my clients into Enneagram types. You, for example, are a perfect three: a workaholic who is energetic, self-propelled, self-centered . . ."

Sam glared at her.

"Whoops," she said hastily, "let's not go there. The point is—and I'll have to call up Ashley's profile to confirm this—I'm nearly sure she's an eight. Eights are great when they're in good shape: loyal, protect the weak, have tons of self-confidence; but when they go bad, they can get scary. They're capable of physical violence and are one of the strongest revenge points on the Enneagram. Eights don't know the meaning of forgiveness. Think Mafia vendetta or southern feud."

"In other words," Sam said grimly, "eights are perfectly capable of killing a pond full of fish; rupturing brake seals; and maybe even faking a call to the hospital, renting scuba gear, swimming out to a yacht, and feeding a guy they didn't much like to the sharks."

That was a sobering thought. Nora had never really seriously considered that anyone besides Rosalee might have murdered Dale. She stopped smiling and quickly called up Ashley's profile on the computer. Her memory had served her well. Ashley was indeed an eight, but checking her out wasn't going to be easy since she had recently moved to Nevada and was now living in the desert in what she described as a "completely pollutant-free geodesic dome." Not only did she have no phone, her address was so vague and her property so remote, they'd be lucky to find it.

If you were running from the law, Nora thought, *you couldn't have found a better place to hide out.*

16

The ground was barren, the sun a cold orange ball, the air so dry you could have set it on fire with a carelessly tossed match. There was nothing green in sight for miles in any direction but evil green copper tailings, thorn bushes, and cactuses; and Nora and Sam were fighting again.

"Right! Turn right!" she cried.

"It's a left turn. Look at the map, Nora!"

"I am looking at the map!"

Sam screeched to a halt, sending a cloud of dust drifting out behind the car like a drag chute. Reaching into the backseat, he retrieved a bottle of mineral water and took a swig. He wiped his mouth on the back of his hand, pushed his hair out of his eyes, and looked at Nora irritably. "Do you want to drive or do you want to let me do it?"

"Don't get so defensive. I was just trying to keep you from making a wrong turn."

"Nora, how would you know if the turn was wrong or not? Remember the time you tried to drive to Santa Barbara by way of San Diego?"

"Look who's talking." Nora took the water bottle from him, drank, and made a face. The stuff was tepid and tasted like plastic. "Who once got both of us lost in the woods because he believed that moss only grew on the north side of trees? Face it, Sam. You're always 180 degrees off. If you were a migrating bird, you'd fly *north* for the winter." She tossed the bottle into the backseat and spread the map out on the dashboard. "Look. You can see right here that the road to Ashley's place turns off to the right."

Sam leaned over, traced out the road with his finger, and sat back with a smug smile. "Nora, you'd be right, except we aren't on this road." He poked at another part of the map. "We're on this one."

"No, we aren't."

"Yes, I'm afraid we are."

"How do you know? There aren't any road signs in this godforsaken wasteland."

"I have an excellent internal compass."

"Your compass is demagnetized, Sam. It's pointing in the wrong direction again."

"Fine. Have it your way. In fact, here." Sam opened the door, got out, and walked around to her side of the car. "You drive while I try to remember landmarks so we don't end up as a pile of bleached bones when we have to turn around and find our way back."

"Great." Nora changed places with him, put the car into gear, and turned right.

"You are going to be so sorry you did that."

"Don't backseat drive."

They bumped along in silence for another half an hour as the sun sank closer to the horizon. Long purple shadows began to stream across the desert like strips of ribbon. The sky turned from pale blue to pale yellow, and then to a fiery, gold-laced crimson that made the peaks of the distant mountains look like the teeth of a black whipsaw. As the sun set, the wind rose and a piercing cold poured through every crack in the car. Nora reached for the heater and the knob came off in her hand.

"It's broken," Sam informed her.

"Why am I not surprised?" Nora wondered how many other things in Sam's car were broken. She imagined the fan belt snapping, the two of them marooned for days without water, dying in each other's arms like the heroine of *The English Patient*. But of course, she and Sam wouldn't die peacefully in each other's arms. They'd fight to the last breath.

She jerked the wheel sharply to avoid a large pothole. The road was growing narrower, but that wasn't the main problem. They'd passed at least half a dozen dirt tracks since they made that right turn, any one of which could have been the road to Ashley's property. In short, they were terribly, completely—perhaps even hopelessly—lost; but she wasn't ready yet to admit that Sam had been right.

She drove for another mile or two as a cold darkness settled over the desert. Suddenly, she slammed on the brakes. The road had abruptly come to an end, and they were facing a gully, perhaps fifty yards across, filled with sand.

Sam cleared his throat.

"Don't you dare say anything," Nora snapped.

He stared out the window as if he had never had any intention of speaking, while she put the car into reverse and backed up until she could turn around. As she drove back toward the original intersection, she became increasingly certain that she wasn't going to be able to recognize it. Gradually she realized Sam was humming "I Left My Heart in San Francisco" with emphasis on the word "left."

Okay, two could play this game. Nora turned on the headlights and drove on a bit farther, watching the beams lurch with each bump in the road. Then she began to hum Aretha Franklin's "Do Right Woman, Do Right Man" with emphasis on the word "right."

Sam laughed. "Okay, you win. We're not lost."

"Yes we are." As much as Nora hated giving Sam the satisfaction of being right, it was no longer possible to go on pretending she knew where they were. At the next fork in the road, she braked to a stop. "So, the ball's in your court again. Which way do we turn now: left or right?"

"You're actually asking me?"

"Yes."

"Okay then, right."

"Thanks." Nora put the car into motion, gave Sam a wicked grin, and took the left-hand fork. Within minutes, they came to another dead end. Putting the car into park, she pulled the keys out of the ignition and handed them to Sam. "I surrender. You drive."

Sam accepted the keys with a look of smug satisfaction and climbed into the driver's seat. For the better part of an hour he drove as if he had a GPS system implanted in his brain, turning with total confidence from one dirt track to another. At first, Nora was impressed. Then, gradually, it began to dawn on her that he also had no idea where he was going.

The desert night grew colder. Overhead the stars were brilliant. Beneath them, two humans in a battered, brown, unheated Toyota Corolla kept driving in circles like hamsters trapped on an exercise wheel.

Around eleven, they finally bumped out onto a stretch of blacktop. In the distance, an orange and pink neon sign blinked in the darkness.

"Civilization!" Nora cried.

Sam headed for the sign. As they approached, it grew until it seemed to fill half the sky. Mounted on a tall metal pole, it consisted of a gigantic, flashing orange arrow and the outline of a twenty-foot-tall woman done in pink neon tubing. As the tubing blinked, the woman did a hula wearing only a pair of blue neon six-guns strapped to her waist. Under her was a set of letters that spelled out the words BANG BANG GIRLS FANTASY PALACE.

Nora and Sam pulled up in front of the sign and sat for a moment checking it out.

"Is this what I think it is?" Nora asked.

"My experience is pretty limited," Sam said, "but yeah. I think it is."

"I don't suppose it could be a local Holiday Inn run by a country-western band called the Bang Bang Girls?"

"I doubt it. So, do you want to drive on?"

"Yes. I strongly suspect the Bang Bang Girls only rent rooms by the hour."

They drove on. Forty miles down the road, they came to a run-down motel that looked like a set from *Psycho*. The only vacant room had a king-sized bed, but they were in no condition to continue searching. Renting it on the spot, they kicked off their shoes, put the chain on the door, stretched out as far apart as possible, and fell asleep.

Outside, the desert dreamed silently beneath the stars. Nora dreamed too. Her dreams were as cold and empty as closets in a new house, each resting in the next like a nest of boxes. Toward morning, the eastern sky began to turn gray. After a while, the sun appeared and the sand took on the color of dried rose petals.

As the desert warmed, Nora's dream warmed with it. She imagined herself lying in bed, kissing a handsome, red-bearded stranger. Slowly their breaths merged and their mouths melted together. The stranger slid over her naked body, and she cried out in passion. The heat of his skin burned and excited her. She raked her nails down his back, and pulled him closer. She wanted his tongue, his hands, his . . .

Suddenly she snapped wide-awake and gave a horrified shriek. Sam's face was half an inch from hers, and they had their arms around each other. Her cry woke Sam, who took one look at her and scuttled away so fast he almost fell off the far side of the bed.

"What are you doing!" he yelled.

"What do you mean what am *I* doing!"

"You crept up on me while I was asleep!"

"No, you crept up on me!"

"I did not."

"You did too."

"Back off, Nora!"

"With pleasure, you sleep molester!" Nora fled to the bathroom, locked the door, turned on the shower, and sat down on the edge of the tub. She stared at the bath mat, unable to think coherently. Had Sam been trying to seduce her? Given the way he'd reacted, it didn't seem likely. Maybe they'd rolled together by accident in the middle of the night. She imagined the dark motel room, their bodies inching toward each other like brainless jellyfish. How many hours had they held each other? She suddenly remembered how turned on she'd been; and then she remembered that the stranger in her dream had had a red beard.

She must have been dreaming of Sam! Okay, that was it! As soon as she got back to her office, she'd put together a list of men she was compatible with and go out on a date every night until she found someone who turned her on; someone who wasn't her ex-husband, someone she could talk to without arguing like a two-year-old. Meanwhile . . .

She turned off the warm water, removed her clothes, and stepped into a shower so cold it made her teeth chatter. She stood under the icy water for a long time

trying to wash all thoughts of sex out of her mind; but
no matter how hard she tried, she could still remember
the taste of the stranger's kisses. Cursing softly, she got
out, toweled off her hair, and got dressed. When she
emerged from the bathroom, Sam was standing by the
door with his coat on.

"Looks like it's going to be sunny again," he said,
not meeting her eyes.

Nora pretended to look out the window. "Most days
are sunny around here."

"Maybe we can find a place to eat breakfast and
someone who's heard of Ashley."

Nora nodded, and they continued chatting in the
same casual vein as they walked out and got into the
car. But they were too embarrassed to look at each
other, and there was nothing casual about the way they
took their seats and stared straight ahead.

They had breakfast in a roadside diner where a pet-
rified lemon meringue pie sat under a plastic dome, the
hash browns were fried into clumps of black grease, and
the coffee was so strong you could stand a spoon
in it.

"Ashley Clay, huh?" The owner of the diner leaned
over the Formica counter. He was a big man who wore
a spotted white apron and smoked a cigar. In L.A. he
would have received the death penalty for this, but here
cigar smoke was part of the ambience.

"Ashley Clay," he repeated as if gnawing on the word.
"Yeah, I know Ashley. We call her the Bubble Girl on
account of her allergies and on account of her living in
a plastic bubble. What kind of crazy woman lives in a
transparent dome in the desert? There's no use waiting
around here, hoping she'll show up. The Bubble Girl
never eats out. She never even buys a box of salt at the

Park-and-Save. She orders all her food in special from some organic outfit in Oregon."

"Do you know how to get to her place?" Nora was relieved that they had finally found someone who had actually heard of Ashley. She'd begun to think she was a mirage.

The owner nodded. "Her property's not far from here."

"Could you draw us a map?"

He chewed on his cigar and thought this over. "Yep, I can draw you a map, but my advice is don't go there. Woman's armed and dangerous. Nearly put buckshot in a UPS driver a few months ago. Poor guy had gotten sweet on her and was taking her some flowers along with her regular delivery of freeze-dried seaweed. The Bubble Girl claimed he was trying to murder her in cold blood. Said flowers made her stop breathing. Now she has to drive into town once a month to pick up her food. Always wears a respirator. Looks like a giant grasshopper."

Sam handed him a pen and a piece of paper. "We'd really appreciate it if you'd draw us a map to her place."

The owner picked up the pen, squinted at the paper, and drew a rough map. When he finished, he handed it to Sam. "Mind telling me why you're so hot to see her?"

"We need to ask her a few questions."

"Asking the Bubble Girl questions is like line-dancing with a rattlesnake. Plus the woman's got herself a new boyfriend just about as crazy as she is. Short guy with a mean look to him. The kind of sawed-off little bantam rooster you don't want to pick a fight with in a bar. Like I said, you're making a big mistake driving out to her place." He removed his cigar from his mouth and looked at them sadly. "In fact, you folks probably should be leaving me the names of your next of kin."

17

Apparently when people who lived in the Nevada desert told you something was "close," they meant "you will travel many miles." It took Nora and Sam nearly two hours to drive to Ashley's, even though the diner owner had drawn them a map accurate enough to launch an invasion. Except for moments when they had to decide which way to turn, they spent the entire trip in silence, wrapping themselves in a peace that was oddly comfortable.

As the cactuses and creosote bushes streamed by, Nora found herself thinking what a pity it was they hadn't been able to act this way more often when they were married. No one could make her feel more relaxed than Sam; and no one could make her feel more defensive. That was the problem, of course. Life with him had been a wild ride that often made other men seem tame in comparison. Which, she reminded herself, was exactly why she had to stay as far away from him as possible as soon as they got this whole Dale murder/revenge thing straightened out.

The moment she reconfirmed her decision never to

see Sam again, she was hit by a powerful wave of nostalgia. Against her will, she found herself remembering the first time they met. She had been eighteen, a senior at Davis High: pretty, popular, cheerleader, star of the varsity girls' field hockey team. Sam had been the new boy in town, a sophomore and a geek: not the computer-game-obsessed type with the white shirt and the horn-rimmed glasses; but the ripped jeans, baggy T-shirt, dirty tennis shoes, social outcast variety who looked like a doper but wasn't. Everywhere he went that fall, he carried a video camera. That was how she'd first seen him: on the other end of his camera aiming the lens at her as she tried to eat a peanut butter and banana sandwich on a slice of her mother's whole wheat bread.

"Please, no pictures," she'd told him in her best starlet drawl; but he'd gone on taping her. "Did you hear what I just said?" Sam had moved in closer. Annoyed, she thrust her face so near the camera she nearly left a nose print on the lens.

"Turn that damn thing off!"

"No. You're too interesting."

"What do you mean 'interesting'?"

"You're beautiful and lonely."

Nora had laughed. "I am not lonely." She pulled the other half of her sandwich out of the plastic bag with a flourish and began to eat it, pointedly ignoring him. After a few seconds, he gave up and wandered off to find another victim.

She had watched his butt as he walked away. He was pretty good looking even then; but since he was a sophomore and a social outcast who, under ordinary circumstances, couldn't have gotten a date with a senior cheerleader unless he'd won the lottery, that should have been the end of it. But it wasn't. After that first encounter, she had found herself thinking about him at odd moments, wondering who he was and what he was about.

His words lingered in her mind: "beautiful and lonely."
She didn't know about the beautiful part—that was for
other people to decide—but the lonely had always been
her own private secret.

As Sam braked to a stop, Nora snapped out of her
reverie and saw that they had come to another fork in
the road. The wind was beginning to pick up and what
little vegetation there was was dipping up and down
with each gust. To the west, the sky had taken on an
odd brownish white shade, like talcum powder mixed
with instant coffee.

"Which way?" Sam asked.

Nora shook the nostalgia out of her brain and consulted the map. "Left, I think."

"Sure?"

"I'd give it a probability of nine on a scale of one to
ten."

Sam shrugged and turned left. Fifteen minutes later,
they were rewarded with the sight of Ashley's dome
perched on the horizon like a giant soap bubble. As
they approached, it became clear that Ashley was heav-
ily into bleak. Her driveway was barren and perfectly
straight, bordered on either side by long rows of white
stones. For hundreds of yards in either direction, the
sand had been raked in complicated patterns that might
have been crop circles if there had been any crops. This
Zen-like atmosphere was completed by a small spring
that bubbled into a ceramic basin so white it made
Nora want to put on her sunglasses and the stumps of
what appeared to have once been cottonwood trees.

"I wonder why Ashley cut down the trees," Sam said
as they started up the driveway.

"Pollen, I imagine."

"Do cactuses have pollen too?"

"I don't know. Why?"

"Because either she's hacked all them down too, or

she's rented out her land as a nuclear waste storage facility. There isn't a living thing within half a mile of
this place."

They pulled up in front of the dome and got out.
Nora was relieved to see that it wasn't transparent. Each
section had been painted silver to reflect heat, which
meant that, despite what the diner owner had said, Ashley
didn't spend her days frying insanely like an ant under
a magnifying glass. The dome rested on a cement platform that served as a deck. Under the platform were
what appeared to be water and sewage pipes, and several large metal recycling bins. On the ground, to the
left of the deck was a bank of high-tech solar panels
that implied air-conditioning or perhaps at least some
kind of filtration system. Primitive maybe, and really
odd, but perfectly livable. Maybe this was what you
were reduced to when your allergy tests indicated you
hadn't been designed for this planet.

Nora and Sam climbed up a flight of cement steps
and began to circle the dome warily looking for a door,
but the place was sealed as tightly as a beach ball. The
thought that Ashley might have it in for them made
Nora move with extreme caution. Was Ashley really as
wacky as the owner of the diner had claimed? Was she
lurking inside that dome with a gun, waiting for the
right moment to send Nora and Sam off to join Nora's
koi? If she'd killed Dale, she probably wouldn't hesi-
tate to kill two more people, particularly out here in the
middle of nowhere. She could plausibly claim that
she'd thought Sam and Nora were trespassers.

Nora suddenly realized that she was holding her
breath. This was ridiculous. There was absolutely no
sign of danger. She had to quit acting as if she'd come
to pay a call on Freddy Krueger. She was scaring herself silly. Ashley didn't even appear to be home. The

only things in sight were a neatly folded white blanket, a Japanese pillow filled with buckwheat hulls, a straw mat, a white meditation cushion, an extra-large bottle of Dr. Bonner's Peppermint soap, and a string of Tibetan prayer flags flapping in the wind like multicolored handkerchiefs. What were the chances of having a fatal confrontation with an environmentally sensitive, Buddhist, yoga-doing, peppermint-soap-sudsing psycho killer?

"Hello," Nora called. "Ashley? Are you home? It's Nora Wynn from Love Finds a Way."

There was no response.

"Hey, Ashley!" Sam yelled. He knocked on one of the struts, and the dome quivered like a mound of aspic. Still no answer.

"Do you think she's hiding in there?" Nora asked, not because she still thought it was likely, but because she wanted Sam to confirm that they were in no real danger.

Sam obliged her. "I doubt it. Her pickup isn't in the driveway."

"Where do you think she's gone?"

"Probably off eliminating all life forms within a twenty-mile radius."

"Then I guess we'll just have to wait until she finishes purifying the planet."

They walked back to the car only to discover that they had managed to lock themselves out. As they were staring at the keys dangling from the ignition and wondering where to find a coat hanger in the middle of the desert, the sky grew dark and the wind suddenly tripled in force. Within seconds the air became a mixture of white grit and tiny pebbles. Nora gasped and began to cough. Beside her she could hear Sam coughing too, but every time she tried to look at him she felt as if someone had poured detergent in her eyes.

"What now?" she yelled over the howling wind. Sam reached out and grabbed her hand. He said something, but the wind blew his words away.

"Dome!" he yelled again. Nora squinted her eyes open a crack and nodded. Clinging to each other's hands, they fought their way through the dust to the dome and took shelter under the platform behind the recycling bins. It was bitterly cold as if all the heat had suddenly gone out of the sun. Nora shivered, hacked a few times to get the dust out of her lungs, and looked at Sam, who appeared to have been sprinkled with powdered sugar. He had dust in his hair, dust in his eyebrows, dust in his beard, dust in every fold and crevice of his clothing. One look at her blouse told her she was in the same state.

She folded her arms across her chest and clutched her elbows, trying to preserve what little warmth she had left. "I'm totally freezing," she yelled.

"Hang on," Sam shouted and threw himself back out into the storm. She saw him dash past the cement pillars like a blurred ghost, and then he was gone. A few moments later, he reappeared carrying the white blanket that they had seen on the deck. Unfurling the blanket, he handed it to Nora and sat back while she wrapped it around herself. It was wonderfully warm and snuggly. She settled down on the ground, tucked the loose ends under her legs, and made herself as comfortable as possible under the circumstances.

"Thanks," she yelled.

"No problem," Sam yelled in returned. He crouched down beside her, sheltering behind the bins as the wind knifed around them on both sides like a pair of dusty walls. His lips were blue, his teeth were chattering, and he had goose bumps all up and down his arms. Nora realized that unless she wanted him to die of hypothermia, she was going to have to share the blanket with him. Reluctantly, she opened it up and was immediately struck by a blast of air so frigid it made her gasp.

"Here," she yelled. "Crawl in."

Sam looked at her warily.

"Come on! You're obviously freezing. Damn it, Sam! This is no time to be stubborn. Get under this blanket before you go into cryonic suspension!"

Sam probably hadn't heard more than one word in ten, but he must have understood the general drift of what she'd said, because he sat down next to her. Nora rearranged the blanket so it draped over both of them. They had no choice but to touch each other, but they did so warily like strangers traveling economy class who are forced to share adjacent seats on a long flight. The wind made conversation almost impossible. They sat silently, listening to it howl, and gradually they grew warmer.

Nora closed her eyes and tried to pretend that she was sitting alone under the blanket, but it was impossible to blot out his presence. No matter which way he turned his head, his beard brushed her cheek; and she could feel the pulse of his heart where his chest touched her arm.

Again, she was seized by nostalgia and uninvited memories. A few weeks after they first met, Sam had asked her over to his house to see the video he'd made of her, and she had surprised herself and all her friends by saying yes. That had been the start of a friendship that lasted until Nora went away to college. They hung out together after school, eating burritos, drinking Mountain Dew, and arguing incessantly. She tore apart his videos like a film critic; he mocked the popular crowd she hung out with and taught her to play chess so well she soon started beating him. Everyone thought she was out of her mind to spend her afternoons with a sophomore two years younger than she was.

"Please tell me you aren't sleeping with this *child*," her friends had begged.

"Sam is totally awesome in bed," Nora had informed them with a smile meant to imply the boy had hidden depths. That had been a lie, or at least only a lucky guess, since at that point they hadn't done anything more than hold hands; but by then she was already feeling a loyalty to him that made her want the popular crowd to treat him with respect.

After she went off to college at U.C. Santa Cruz, they e-mailed each other for a while. Sam sent her accounts of his success on the varsity basketball team and his growing popularity, but Sam in writing had not been half as interesting as Sam in person. Gradually Nora found she had less and less to say to a boy who was still in high school. By the time she went to Rome for a quarter to follow in her mother's footsteps by studying art history, he only rated a postcard of the Colosseum; by the time she graduated, she had lost track of him altogether.

Then, years later, she ran into him at a party in L.A., and they had taken up where they left off with a few important changes. Nora was on the rebound, having just broken up with a philandering cameraman. Sam was available, interesting, a whole lot better looking than he'd been at sixteen, and yes—as she soon learned— truly awesome in bed. They had spent the better part of six weeks making love with such enthusiasm that they left handprints on the walls and gave each other rug burn; so much in love that they couldn't bear to be out of each other's sight.

It had been an extraordinary kind of love, a dizzy, mutual intoxication that made their differences seem unimportant. Sam had been as smart as ever, but with a maturity that now made him her equal. He was all she had remembered: kind, funny, honest to a fault, with a deep sweetness in their most intimate moments that made her feel as if, after years of hanging out with strangers, she'd finally come home.

At the beginning of their seventh week together, Nora had become convinced she was pregnant. She told Sam and, being a good Catholic boy, he suggested that they get married immediately. He hadn't just proposed marriage out of a sense of duty either. He loved her. He made that clear. He was willing to—wanted to—live with her and raise their child.

The pregnancy had turned out to be a false alarm, and now, five years down the line, Nora knew what a colossal mistake their marriage had been; but at the time it had seemed like a good idea.

The next day, they had packed their camping gear in the back of Sam's Toyota, driven to Las Vegas, set up their tent in the local KOA, had another wonderful afternoon of lovemaking, crawled out rubber-kneed and happy, driven into town, bought a marriage license, and treated themselves to a thirty-five-dollar, five-minute civil ceremony at the courthouse. Then they went back to the parking lot, climbed into Sam's car, and had the first nasty, no-holds-barred fight of their married life.

What had gone wrong between the time they walked into the courthouse single and the time they walked out of it married? Nora sighed and pulled her edge of the blanket closer. She had never been able to figure it out, although she had come up with quite a few theories including the possibility that marriage itself was a cosmic joke perpetuated on the human race by aliens who were conducting some kind of psychological experiment on hope and disillusionment.

Gradually her thoughts grew less coherent, and she drifted off to sleep, lulled by the howl of the wind. Without meaning to, she leaned closer to Sam and rested her head on his shoulder.

Sam sat quietly for a long time, lost in his own thoughts. After a while, he turned to Nora, arranged her head in a more comfortable position, and moved a few errant strands of hair out of her eyes.

Nora slept on, not feeling his touch. Soon Sam slept too.

They woke about half an hour later stretched out side by side with their arms around each other. Around them, the wind howled and the air was still white with dust, but neither Sam nor Nora noticed.

This time they didn't pull apart. Instead, spontaneously, they moved toward each other's lips. Their kiss was sweet, long, tender, wordless, and lovely. Nora felt the breath leave her body, enter Sam, and then reenter her body again as if he were breathing for her and she were breathing for him. She felt the warmth of his chest against the tips of her breasts and inhaled the familiar scent of his mouth: a combination of spice and fresh bread and something intoxicating that had always belonged only to him.

That first kiss was followed by another, sweeter and more passionate; then another. Nora closed her eyes and saw wavelike motions, invisible and clear, behind her eyelids. She wanted Sam again with the same overwhelming intensity she had felt the first time they made love so many years ago. For an instant she thought: *I shouldn't be doing this.* And then she remembered all the things she loved about him. They came back to her, not in parts, but whole; not as memory, but alive and present, as if someone had pulled dark glasses off her eyes and let her see him again the way she'd seen him on the first afternoon of the first day they met. She looked in Sam's face and saw herself reflected in his eyes. She saw that, despite everything, he still loved her.

What happened next was not a matter of words. They shed their clothes quickly without speaking, pulled the blanket back over themselves; and they lay naked and warm, making long, slow love with such sweetness and passion that Nora felt as if they'd risen up and were flying through the air together.

Stroking each other's bodies and whispering endearments, they called each other by the old, secret names no one else knew, the tender names of lovers who had slept side by side. And once again, after years of pretending to be strangers, they opened their hearts to each other and climaxed with cries that were drowned out by the howling wind. Then they fell back, kissed, and began again.

After a while they lost track of time. They became the only inhabitants of a private world: this Nora who loved and wanted Sam, and this Sam who loved and wanted Nora. Their lovemaking burned away years of flight and denial, so there was no longer any use trying to pretend it didn't exist. Against all sense, against all experience, against the advice of their friends, and their best attempts to forget they'd ever met, they were still hopelessly in love and always had been.

Finally they lay quietly, side by side. "I never stopped loving you," Sam whispered in Nora's ear.

"And I never stopped loving you," she whispered back. She smiled and pulled him close again. "Our divorce doesn't seem to be worth the paper it was written on."

They kissed one more time, a long, slow kiss that answered all remaining questions. Then, winding their arms around each other, they fell back to sleep, so tangled together that it would have been hard for anyone coming on them at that moment to sort them out.

18

When Sam and Nora woke for the second time, the wind had stopped blowing, the dust had settled, and the desert sky was the color of skimmed milk. Silently, they got up, brushed the grit out of their hair, and put on their clothes. For a moment they stood side by side, buttoning their shirts and looking everywhere but at each other. Then Nora began to laugh.

"Look at us, Sam! It's hopeless. We're like magnets. You know what this means, don't you?"

Sam grinned, turned to Nora, seized her by the hands, and drew her close. "Yeah. It means, like it or not, we're going to have to try harder to get along. Not that there's a chance in hell we'll be able to. How did we get so stuck on each other?"

"We didn't have a choice. We were doomed."

"Maybe we could flee to different continents."

"Fine, I get Australia."

"Wait a minute, I want Australia."

"My point exactly."

Sam took her in his arms and gave her a kiss. "I can see there's no use trying to fight this any longer. Okay,

I surrender. I'm clearly out of my mind to love you so much, but I can't help it." He suddenly became serious. "Nora, I mean it. I love you and I'm here for you if you want me."

Nora didn't know whether to laugh or cry. There was no way out of this. Someone had slipped them a powerful love potion, and they were just going to have to try to make the best of it. She remembered Jason, who had been so easy to talk to because he had lied. Life with Sam would never be that easy, but at least whatever he said to her would be honest. They'd fight; but Sam wouldn't lie to her—at least not about anything that mattered. Oh, maybe every once in a while he'd tell her she didn't look fat in a pair of slacks that made her look like a walrus, but he'd never cheat on her with her best friend, and if he said he'd be there as long as she wanted him, he'd be there.

How long will *I want him?* she asked herself. She honestly didn't know, but given the way she felt about Sam right now, the only reasonable thing to do was love him and see what happened.

"Sam," she whispered softly.

He started to kiss her again, then stiffened and drew back. "Turn around very slowly," he whispered. "There's a man standing behind you, and he's holding a gun."

Nora turned around and found herself staring down the barrel of a shotgun. The man holding it was a few inches shorter than Sam, with severely clipped brown hair and muscles like ropes. He looked like a miniature marine, but instead of camouflage, he was wearing blue plastic sandals, gray meditation pants, and a cotton T-shirt that said ARM THE WHALES. For an instant, all Nora could see was the barrel of the shotgun pointed at her chest. Then she looked up and realized that the woman standing to the man's left was Ashley Clay.

"Ashley . . ." she stuttered.

At the sound of Nora's voice, the man lifted the shotgun and pointed it straight at her head as if he'd happily blow it off at the slightest provocation. "Who the fuck are you?" he demanded. "And what the fuck are you doing on our land?"

"Brian!" Ashley cried. "Stop cursing and don't shoot! It's Nora Wynn!"

"You have the right to remain silent," Brian intoned, still aiming the gun directly at Nora's forehead. "Anything you say can and will be used against you in a court of law. You have the right to talk to an attorney before—"

"Brian, lose the cop act! That's Nora Wynn of *Love Finds a Way! Nora Wynn,* remember? The wonderful woman who brought us together!"

Brian lowered the shotgun until it was only capable of blowing off Nora's feet. Suddenly he became all smiles. "Are you really Nora Wynn?"

"Yes," Nora said cautiously, keeping an eye on the shotgun. She wondered when he was going to put the safety catch back on. Maybe shotguns didn't have safety catches. She felt rubbery in the knees and slightly sick. No one had ever pointed a real gun at her before.

"Sorry about threatening you with a deadly weapon." Brian's smile widened, and he gave her an apologetic shrug. "I thought I'd apprehended you in the process of committing of a felony."

"No problem," Nora said, still staring at the gun.

"Brian is so silly sometimes," Ashley said as if threatening to kill people was a cute little trait that she found totally endearing. "You have to forgive him. We'd never hurt you. You're our cupid." Ashley walked up to Brian and gave him a little nuzzle on the neck with the tip of her nose. She was in a lot better shape than the last time Nora had seen her: lean, tanned, and so cheerful she almost seemed manic. Nora noticed that she had cut her hair and removed her navel ring. Also, as unlikely as it seemed, she was wearing a lip gloss, undoubtedly organic and hypoallergenic.

"Brian's also environmentally sensitive," Ashley continued, giving Brian another little nose/neck rub, "but of course you knew that when you fixed us up."

"Right." Nora had no memory of having fixed up Ashley up with Brian, but if Ashley wanted to believe Nora was their "cupid," who was she to argue with a shotgun?

"Thanks to your matchmaking genius, we're making a new life together here in the pure desert air," Ashley continued, gesturing to the wasteland she'd created around her dome. "Brian used to serve with the L.A. County Sheriff's Department, but the smog was killing him. He has the most terrible allergies, which are totally due to irresponsible vehicular pollution and biotechnology, which is putting peanut genes in *everything*." Ashley pulled away from Brian and suddenly became quite fierce. "Did you know that most potatoes grown by nonorganic methods have chicken genes in them!"

"Uh, no. I hadn't heard." Nora was becoming increasingly convinced Ashley was wacked out enough to do anything, and the continued presence of the shotgun was nerve-racking even though it was no longer threatening anything but her pedicure.

"It's a scandal! What will next fall victim to corporate greed? Tofu?"

"That would really be rough for vegetarians." Nora tried her best to sound sympathetic. Actually the idea of chicken genes in potatoes was creepy; but Ashley's fanatical gaze of hatred when she said "chicken" was even creepier.

"Exactly!" Ashley gave Nora a triumphant smile. "I knew you'd understand." She suddenly seemed to see Sam for the first time. Her faced darkened, and she glared at him with the same expression she'd used when she spoke about the biotech potatoes. "Aren't you Nora's ex-husband, Sam Gallo?" The word "ex-husband" came out of Ashley's mouth in a snarl like the word "chicken." Nora silently willed Sam to deny who he was.

"That's me," Sam admitted.

Ashley whirled on Brian. "Give me that gun!" When Brian hesitated, she lunged forward, jerked it out of his hands, and aimed it at Sam.

"Wait a minute!" Sam protested.

"You wait a minute, you lying, thieving slime!" Ashley moved in on him, forcing him against one of the cement pillars of the platform. "You dolphin-eating, hunk of nonrecyclable plastic! You condor-killing, rain-forest-burning, low-life son of a bitch!"

Nora was awed by the originality of Ashley's curses. She wanted to yell to Sam to kick Ashley's legs out from under her before she shot his head off, but she didn't dare open her mouth.

Ashley raved for a few more seconds covering every possible aspect of Sam's family life, personal history, gender, and presumed environmental irresponsibility. Then she took a few steps back and turned to Nora. "You want me to kneecap the son of a bitch, Nora?"

"No! Are you crazy!" Definitely the wrong question. Nora tried again. "Don't hurt him, Ashley! Point that gun somewhere else! Please!"

Ashley lowered the gun and stared at Nora uncertainly. "You sure you don't want him kneecapped?"

"Yes!"

"But he stole your land. He's a rotten, thieving rat!"

"No, no! Sam never stole anything from me."

"But Sue said he bullied you into signing over a valuable piece of property."

"Sue?"

"You know, your friend Sue. Or maybe she was one of your clients. I mean, Sue adores you, Nora. She said you changed her life just like you changed mine."

Nora stared at Ashley blankly. Then, all at once she got it. One of her clients had deliberately sicked Ashley on Sam. This was the clue they'd been looking for!

"What's Sue's last name?" she asked eagerly.

"Rossett."

Nora's face fell. *"Susan* Rossett? You're telling me the woman who spoke to you introduced herself as 'Susan Rossett'?"

"Yes. You remember her now, right?"

"Oh, yes," Nora said grimly. "I remember her well. You might say I grew up with her. 'Susan Rossett' is my mother's maiden name."

Amber stared at her blankly. "She didn't look old enough to be your mother."

"I'm happy to hear that. I'd hate to think Mom was the one out to get me. What did she look like?"

"Well, fortunately she was scent-free." Ashley frowned, "But she'd used toxic chemicals on her hair. Also she was totally obsessed by patriarchal stereotypes and obviously had a thyroid deficiency. Plus, she's going to have back problems as she ages."

"Are you saying 'Susan' was a thin, good-looking blonde with big eyes who was wearing a short, tight dress and high heels?"

"Yes. I tried to warn her about the heels, but she couldn't stay. I think she had an appointment."

Nora bet "Sue" had run from Ashley like a greyhound once she'd delivered that lie about Sam. So who was this blond bombshell who had it in for her? Someone else from the DC file? Bliss Bronstad, maybe? At least now she knew the gender of her persecutor. She looked up and realized that Ashley was starting to glare murderously at Sam again.

"Ashley, let's get something straight. 'Susan' lied. She wasn't my friend, and her name wasn't Susan. Sam has *never* harassed me about anything. He's a wonderful guy."

"Really?"

"Really. He didn't force me to sign over that worthless piece of land. I was the one who wanted to get rid of it. I insisted on giving it to him, and as a favor to me, he took it."

Ashley lowered the gun and gave Nora an embarrassed smile. "Woops. Looks like I screwed up." She turned to Sam. "I'm sorry, Mr. Gallo. I shouldn't have threatened to kneecap you, but I meant it in the best possible way."

"No need to apologize," Sam said with near-surreal politeness. "But would you mind putting that gun down? It's making me nervous."

Ashley promptly put the shotgun on the blanket, sat down beside it, and gave Nora a wistful look. "This is such a big disappointment to me, Nora. I was so grateful to you for bringing Brian and me together that I wanted to give you a thank-you present. Not just some material thing, but something that would last a lifetime."

Kneecapping, Nora thought, *the gift that keeps on giving.* "I don't mean to sound ungrateful, Ashley, and I'm delighted that you're happy with Brian, but I don't consider kneecapping anyone a present. Maybe you could keep that in mind in the future."

Ashley's face turned bright red. She stared at her plastic sandals, which were twins of Brian's, picked up the hem of the blanket, and began to fiddle with it. "Uh, well, actually, Nora, that's not the present I meant." She looked up and pressed her lips together as if reluctant to go on. "Actually, I gave you . . . uh, well, I didn't give it to you really. I gave it to the . . ." She stopped in midsentence and looked at Nora as if she hoped Nora would fill in the blanks.

Nora had filled in the blanks long ago when she figured out Ashley was a photographer and an eight, but nevertheless, hearing the confession come out of Ashley's own mouth was chilling. She edged closer to the shotgun so she could stomp on Ashley's hands if Ashley tried to pick up it up.

"That 'thank-you present' wasn't, by any chance, an anonymous note to the L.A. County Sheriff's Department claiming that Sam was having an affair with Rosalee Lambert, was it? With a photo, maybe?"

Ashley nodded. "It was a really good photo, wasn't it?" There was a hint of childish pride in her voice.

"Fabulous," Nora said through gritted teeth. "How did you fake it so well?"

"I'm a professional."

"Ah, well, then, that explains it." Nora sat down next to Ashley and gave her a look of total sympathy. Then she grabbed the gun. The thing was a lot heavier than she thought it would be. She aimed the barrel at Ashley but kept her finger off the trigger. She'd never shot a human being and had no intention of starting now, but she figured she could fake it.

"Did you kill Dale Lambert?"

Ashley blinked her eyes repeatedly and leaned back against the recycling bins like she was about to pass out. "No," she whispered.

"Do you know who did?"

"Rosalee Lambert, his wife. It was in all the papers."

"Rosalee has pleaded not guilty. Is she lying or are you? Did you steal my purse, set up fake credit accounts in my name, buy snorkeling gear, swim out to Dale's yacht, and murder him with a winch handle? Did you turn me in to the IRS? Throw dye in my pool? Rupture my brake seals, and make up that bullshit about 'Sue Rossett' to throw me off the track?"

"I don't know what you're talking about."

Nora shoved the barrel of the gun into Ashley's chest. "Start talking, Ashley."

"I didn't," Ashley stuttered. "I don't. I never. I—"

"Nora!" Sam yelled. "Look out!"

Nora turned just in time to see Brian lunging toward her. Leaping to her feet, she put her back against one of the pillars and pointed the shotgun at him.

Brian froze. "I could take you down," he said softly.

"Try it."

"You wouldn't shoot me. You don't have the guts."

"Want to bet?" Nora waved him over to Ashley and made him sit down on the blanket beside her. "Now," said Nora, "where were we? Oh, right: I was asking Ashley if she killed Dale Lambert."

"No," Ashley said in a weak voice. "I didn't kill him."

"How do I know you're not lying?"

"The cops checked my story out and decided I couldn't have done it. A deputy from the sheriff's department named Johnson told me he was taking me off the list of potential suspects. I asked him if Brian and I could move out of town, and he said no problem."

"That's not good enough. Johnson never figured out that you were the one who faked that photo of Sam and Rosalee. He didn't know you were an eight on the Enneagram. Tell me the truth, Ashley. You were angry with Dale because his aftershave put you in the hospital, right? So you called the advice nurse to establish an alibi, and then snorkeled out to his boat, killed him, and framed his wife. Or wait. I have another thought. Maybe you and Rosalee were in this together."

"I'm a vegan, Nora. I couldn't kill anyone. I can't even touch snorkels. I'm allergic to rubber."

"That's still not good enough."

"Then try this," Brian snarled. "I was with Ashley for fifteen hours before Lambert disappeared and four hours after. It was our first date, the one *you* fixed us up on. I took Ashley to that damn restaurant where they poisoned her with raw fish, and I paid for the dinner with my MasterCard, leaving behind my signature; then I took her home and held her hand while she tried to get the advice nurse to admit her to the emergency ward. When that didn't work, I drove her to a private hospital and paid to have her admitted.

"There are about twenty witnesses to all of the above, plus hospital records, and a whopping bill that I'm still paying off. Also, I'm a former deputy with a ten-year reputation for telling the truth, which is why Johnson and Rodriguez—who have known me for years—concluded that Ashley had an ironclad alibi. Now put down that gun and stop acting like a bad actor on *NYPD Blue*."

Nora did a quick calculation and realized that, if Ashley had been in the hospital, there was no way she could have snorkeled out to the yacht and killed Dale. Sheepishly, she put down the gun.

"Okay," she said, "I'm convinced. I'm sorry, Ashley. When you admitted you faked that photo of Sam and Rosalee, I thought you might have killed Dale and then come after me. Clearly, I was way off base."

"You don't know anything about questioning a suspect," Brian said. "You're a total amateur. Lucky for you that you brought Ashley and me together. Otherwise, I'd run you in for criminal trespass, theft, and brandishing a deadly weapon."

He picked up the shotgun and shucked the shell out of the chamber. There was an awkward silence.

Sam cleared his throat. "So," he said to Brian, "what kind of truck do you drive?"

Nora stared at Sam in disbelief. What was this? Some kind of attempt at a male bonding ritual?

Brian gave Sam a cold look as if trying to decide whether or not to put the shell back in the shotgun. Then he softened a little. "Chevy Suburban." He shot Ashley an apologetic glance. "Of course, I'd rather have an electric truck, but it's not practical out here."

"Not yet," Ashley agreed, surveying the desert as if mulling over plans to spread solar panels over every square inch.

"Get into town often?" Sam asked. Suddenly Nora realized the brilliance of Sam's line of questioning.

"Not too often. We had to drive in yesterday to pick up some supplies. Ashley used to get her food UPS, but now the driver won't come out here. We got to the post office just before it closed."

"Those Chevy Suburbans are a great ride." Sam sounded as if he loved nothing better than sliding under a Chevy Suburban on a Sunday afternoon and getting oil all over his shirt.

"You can say that again." Brian was getting less hostile by the minute. Nora wondered if he knew the whole story of the UPS driver. Once again she counted up the hours and realized that Ashley and Brian couldn't possibly have been in L.A. rupturing her brake seals, throwing dye in her pool, putting a rubber spider on Sam's dashboard, letting the air out of his tires, and gluing his hand to the gearshift if they'd been picking up packages at the local post office at five yesterday evening. Now all she needed was to find out was what role, if any, Ashley had played in poisoning her koi and chopping down her roses. But there didn't seem to be any way to insert that question into the conversation, and at this point it probably didn't matter.

Sam must have reached the same conclusion. Standing

up, he brushed the dust off the seat of his jeans. "We have to go," he announced.

"So soon?" Ashley looked disappointed.

"I have to get back to work," Nora lied. "I have a big event tomorrow with a bunch of single certified public accountants who are looking for love." She had never been good at hiding her emotions. Her eagerness to get away must have shown, because Ashley's face fell.

"You're still mad at me about that photo, aren't you?"

Nora looked at Brian and then darted a quick glance at the shotgun, which still lay beside him within easy reach. "No, of course not."

"I'm really sorry. Really." Ashley turned to Sam. "I hope I didn't get you into too much trouble with the police."

"No trouble at all. Forget about it."

"At least let me offer you a cup of tea for the road." Ashley smiled at Nora hopefully. "We have a solar stove."

Nora and Sam exchanged glances. Sam shrugged. "Great. Thanks."

That proved to be a mistake. The herbal mixture Ashley brought them was brown, but there all resemblance to tea ended. The stuff was thick, bitter, and so unbelievably foul that Nora couldn't help thinking that it would have made a good murder weapon.

19

A long day's drive had brought Nora and Sam back to Pasadena just after dark. Now on the redwood screen that surrounded Nora's pool, pink and yellow bougainvillea petals trembled like a rack of pale butterflies.

Nora floated on her back on an inflatable raft looking up at the sky. She wore a white bikini, and the water around her was a dark blue green, every ripple tipped with a little gold arc of moonlight. Because she had turned off all the pool lights except the one at the bottom of the deep end, she appeared to be resting on a dome of paler blue. Behind her, her hair drifted free in the water, leaving a dark comma every time she paddled her hands lazily, turning the raft in slow circles.

Sam sat on the side of the pool, dangling his legs in the water, eating strawberries, and watching her with appreciation. She'd filled out over the years in a good way, so she was now curved where she'd been all sharp angles. The Nora on the raft was even more beautiful than the Nora who had come to him in his dreams over the years since their divorce. Even now, he had a little trouble believing she was real.

Nora was having a similar problem. The encounter with Ashley and her ex-cop boyfriend had been weird and scary; and even though Ashley's confession about the photo had solved one mystery, it had failed to solve others. Nora still had no idea who was taking revenge on her or to what lengths they were likely to go, but as she lay on the raft looking up at the place the stars would have been if most of them hadn't been obscured by a light fog, she felt perfectly happy and not at all anxious. All of which proved what a powerful drug good sex could be, especially when you combined it with love for someone you'd known for a very long time.

Sam, she thought, *is better than Prozac any day.* And then she closed her eyes, smiled, and twirled herself around a few more times. After a while, she heard him splash into the pool and come swimming toward her. She opened her eyes, just in time to see his head bob up beside the raft.

"Open your mouth," he commanded. Nora opened her mouth, and he popped a strawberry in it.

"Mmm," she said. "Delicious."

"Want another?"

"Yeah."

"It'll cost you."

"What's the price?"

"This," Sam said and kissed her. It was a long kiss, finished off by another strawberry. Nora ate the berry slowly, savoring the sweetness.

"More," she demanded.

"I'm all out."

"Well, darn, then. I'm just going to have to kiss you for free." And with that, she rolled off the raft into his arms and they both went under.

They came up laughing, kissed each other treading water, and then swam to the shallow end of the pool, where they began to make love. The pool was heated, the water was warm, and it was lovely to float back and forth against each other as if there were no such thing as gravity. Sam picked her up, peeled off her bikini, and held her close so the tips of her breasts bobbed against his chest. Nora threw her arms around his neck and her legs around his waist. It was like a slow dance or water ballet, but it felt much better.

Nora closed her eyes and let herself drift against him. She imagined tropical coral reefs and brightly colored fish, the salty taste of the ocean. Before people walked on land, she thought, their ancestors must have made love like this in water.

Sam gently caught her hair in a wet coil and played with it, floating it out and catching it, and floating it again. He bent and kissed her forehead and cheeks and mouth. His own mouth was warmer than the water.

At the touch of his lips, Nora stopped thinking about the ocean. They moved around the shallow end of the pool in wide circles as she thrashed and moaned, floating away, being drawn back to him, pushing, pulling, drumming the water with the palms of her hands as she laughed and cried out with pleasure.

After they finished, Nora floated for a while, supported by Sam's arms, looking at the moon and thinking absolutely nothing. The moon was not as quite as full as it had been a few nights ago. It was farther away and whiter, and a small piece was missing from the right-hand side. But the wisps of fog drifting across it looked like scarves, and watching it circle overhead as Sam twirled her slowly in the water was hypnotic.

She closed her eyes, and when she opened them again, Sam was bending over her.

"You must be really relaxed." He grinned. "You just went to sleep in the water."

"I did not!"

"Then why were you snoring?"

"I do not snore!" Nora tried to put some indignation into her voice, but fighting with Sam was getting increasingly difficult. She swam out of his grip, stood up, and fished both pieces of her suit out of the water. "I was practicing my Tuvan throat-singing."

She hoisted herself out of the pool, and he followed her. It had gotten chillier while they were in the water, so they dried off, put on shorts and sweatshirts, and sat down to finish the barbecued ribs they'd grilled earlier. The ribs had grown cold, but were still tasty. Nora ate eagerly, sucking the bones and licking the sauce off her fingers.

"I like to see you enjoy real food." Sam gave her a sly grin. "You used eat like a python: you inhaled anything you could put your hands on without really tasting it. The only exception was my pancakes. You always ate them slowly and made cute little smacking noises. I found that flattering."

In the past, this conversation about what Nora did or didn't eat would have turned into a fight, but tonight there was no fight left in them. Nora ignored the python remark. Sam passed her another rib. She ate it. It was as simple as that.

When they'd finished off the ribs, they rinsed their fingers under the garden hose, dried them on one of the towels, and started back toward the house. It went without saying that Sam was spending the night.

"So," he asked as they crossed a patch of grass between Nora's pool and her back deck, "what next?"

Nora didn't reply right away. She slid her bare feet through the grass, enjoying the sensation. She inhaled the scent of the flowers and looked at the moonlight making tree shadows on the white stucco walls of her house. She didn't really want to think about who was trying to get her. Not now.

"Let's forget the whole mess for tonight," she suggested. "Let's just enjoy each other."

"Great idea."

"Do you realize that's the fifth or sixth time you've agreed with me in the last couple of hours?"

Sam took her hand and gave it a friendly squeeze. "You're right. You know, Nora, we're losing our edge. Either we'll have to go back into training or resign ourselves to getting along. We must be getting old."

"*You* may be getting old, but I'm not!"

"Ah." Sam smiled. "That's more like it."

"For your information, I intend to stay thirty forever."

"Don't you mean thirty-*two?*"

"I'm only thirty. You've lost track. Come on, I'll race you back to the house!" Letting go of his hand, Nora made a dash for the back door with Sam in hot pursuit. Suddenly, she pitched forward with a scream and a curse. Sam, who was following closely behind her, collided with her, and they fell in a heap, knocking heads.

Nora was the first to sit up. "Damn it!" she yelled. She grabbed at the ground and jerked up a strand of wire that had been strung at ankle height. "Look at this! I could have broken my neck! I've had it, Sam! I've totally had it! Someone's trying to kill us!"

"Nora, calm down. Are you okay?"

"No, I'm not okay. And don't tell me to calm down! I've skinned my knee, I've broken a fingernail, and I'm furious!" She leaped to her feet. "Come out where I can see you, you miserable coward! You can't get away with this! I'm going to find out who you are and get you arrested! You can't go around stringing wires where people can fall over them! Come out and show your face, damn it!"

But nothing moved, and no one emerged from the shadows.

"It's no use," Sam said. "Come inside, Nora. We'll check out the house to make sure no one's in it, lock the doors, turn on the security system, wash off the dirt and grass stains, and put a Band-Aid on your knee. Then, first thing tomorrow morning, we'll go back to your office and run that data list again."

Nora bent down, grabbed the wire with both hands, and jerked it loose. "This whole scene is giving more me sympathy for Rosalee," she snarled. "We'd better figure out who's out to get me soon, or I'm going to pay her a visit in jail and ask her if she can recommend a good hit man."

20

Sam and Nora weren't in the mood to sleep after the wire incident, so they spent most of the night sitting in Nora's living room talking. The result was that they arrived at Nora's office at nine the next morning armed with a number of carefully thought out plans for tracking down the woman who was harassing her. They'd read the notes Nora'd taken during client interviews; they'd run the data in her computer through every possible combination they could think of; they'd review the lists of women who had taken the revenge fantasy seminars, reexamine the DC file, and reread Nora's newspaper columns looking for letters that sounded threatening.

If necessary, they'd even listen to the tapes of her radio show to see if she could identify the voices of any of the female callers. They'd find out who'd owed her money and not paid it, who had complained in e-mail or writing about anything connected with Love Finds a Way or Payback Time, who had not liked the people they'd been matched with. Sam even came up with the idea of using the Reverse Phone Directory to see if any-

one on their list of suspects had recently moved within
dye-tossing range of Nora's swimming pool.

Encouraged by the possibility that all this would actually result in some new leads, they strode through the
wrought-iron gate of her building in a cautiously opti-
mistic mood, nodded to the lions in the fountain, pushed
open the front door, and nearly collided with a burly man
carrying a computer sealed in a clear plastic bag. The
man was wearing a blue jacket, and the second Nora
saw it, she felt the ground slip out from under her. On
his right arm was an official-looking black and yellow
patch; on the front, enclosed in an ominous-looking black
rectangle, were six large white letters no U.S. taxpayer
ever wants to see: IRS-CID.

"Excuse me," she asked, hoping against hope that
the letters didn't mean what she thought they did, "are
you really from the IRS?"

"Yes." The man paused and looked at Nora intently.
"Internal Revenue Service, Criminal Investigation Division. I can show you a badge and photo identification if
you like, but first I have to load this computer into the
van."

The combination of the words "Internal Revenue Service" and "criminal" rendered Nora momentarily speechless. She looked behind her and saw a white moving
van parked at the curb. She hadn't paid any attention to
the thing when she and Sam had walked past it on their
way to the office. There was no writing on the sides. It
could have been a bread truck.

"Please step out of the way," the IRS agent commanded.

Nora not only wanted to step out of the way, she
wanted to run; but somehow she found the presence of
mind to hold her ground. "Is that my secretary's computer you're carrying?"

"Are you Ms. Nora Wynn?" The agent looked annoyed that she hadn't stepped aside, and for the first time Nora noticed that he was wearing a gun. A holstered gun, but a gun nevertheless. She felt an intense wave of anxiety coupled with a renewed impulse to flee like a bank robber who'd been caught holding the loot.

"Yes, I'm Nora Wynn. And this"—she pointed to Sam—"is my . . ." She came to a halt, not knowing exactly how to introduce Sam. Ex-husband? Friend? Lover? Her mind seemed to have frozen.

"I'm Ms. Wynn's ex-husband," Sam supplied. "What's this about? Does this have something to do with Nora's tax audit?"

The agent ignored Sam as if he didn't exist. All his attention was focused on Nora. "Ms. Wynn, are you the legal owner of two business licenses, one for a commercial revenue-generating entity whose legal name is 'Love Finds a Way' and the other for a commercial revenue-generating entity whose legal name is 'Payback Time'?"

Nora swallowed hard. "Yes."

"Then you have a problem."

"What kind of problem?" Sam asked.

For the first time, the agent seemed to recognize that he was talking to two people. "Explanation's not in my job description, sir. Just go on upstairs and one of the other agents will fill you in."

"There are more of you upstairs?" Nora cried. "What is this? A raid?!"

"Yes, ma'am, although we prefer to call it a 'search and seizure operation.' Now please move out of the way. It's a felony to interfere with a federal treasury division employee engaged in the performance of his duties."

Stunned into silence, Nora moved out of the way. The man gave her and Sam a little nod of acknowledgment and walked past them carrying the computer. In the courtyard, he paused and turned. "Look," he said, "I'm not supposed to tell you this, but you seem like a nice lady, so I'm going to step outside the box here. Don't yell at the agents upstairs. They get very nervous when they make a seizure of assets, and they always come with heavy security."

"Seizure of assets," Nora whispered in horror.

The man nodded and shifted the computer to his other arm. "You don't want to make them think you're liable to do anything violent. Like I said, if you obstruct the investigation in any way, they'll arrest you so fast you won't know what hit you."

"Investigation?"

"Play it cool, Ms. Wynn. You're facing federal criminal charges." He turned and began to walk toward the gate.

"Wait," Nora cried. "Please. What charges? What crime am I supposed to have committed? What am I being investigated for? How can you just walk off with one of my computers like this?"

The man turned and gave her a pitying look. "That's the problem with you white-collar criminals. You don't do your homework. The IRS is one of the most powerful agencies in the federal government. We can seize your house, your car, your bank account, and anything else you own. Didn't you know that?"

"Yes, but surely not without a trial."

"A trial before confiscation? Dream on." The man turned and walked away with the computer.

Nora watched him until he disappeared. Then she turned back to Sam. She wanted to say something, but she was so shocked her tongue seemed to have frozen to the roof of her mouth. Sam put his arm around her.

"Come on," he said. "Let's go upstairs and find out what's going on." Nora didn't move. "It's probably a mistake. Maybe it's another incident like the one last night. We know someone's trying to take revenge on you. Only this time instead of stringing a trip wire, they've been lying about you to the IRS. It's a hassle, Nora, but you're innocent of felony tax evasion, right?"

Nora nodded.

"Fine. Then it will all work out. Now, come on. We don't want to keep the IRS waiting."

Upstairs, they found Nora's office in total chaos. A beefy agent stood beside the reception desk with his hand on his gun as if ready to draw it at any moment. Two grim-faced agents in suits were searching every inch of the place. Another agent stood to one side, directing three large men dressed in the blue IRS raid jackets. The men in the jackets were loading Nora's paper files into cardboard boxes and sealing them. Nora's computer already sat by the door, sealed in plastic and waiting to be carried out.

Nora stared at them, dumbstruck. This was a huge operation, for what? The IRS had claimed that, at most, she owed them two thousand dollars in unreported taxes, plus interest. She tried to figure out how much tax money it took to pay eight people to raid her office and carry everything out, but again her mind froze.

Caroline suddenly bolted out of one of the inner offices. Tears were streaming down her cheeks, her hair had come undone, and her mascara was smeared. "They're taking everything!" she cried as soon she caught sight of Nora. "I tried to tell them they couldn't, but they had a search warrant."

"It's okay," Nora said automatically, but it wasn't. Nora put out her arms and enfolded Caroline, who put her head on Nora's shoulder and broke down in sobs. Nora had never seen Caroline cry and had never expected to.

"I did my best, Nora," she said between gasps.

Nora patted her on the back. "I know you did." Over Caroline's shoulder, Nora could see one of the guys in the raid jackets carrying out a box containing her color-coded client files. "What's all this about?"

Caroline stepped back and dried her eyes on the sleeve of her blouse, smudging her mascara even more. "I don't know. They won't tell me." She suddenly spotted Sam. "What's *he* doing here? Did he turn you in to the IRS? Is he the one who's been poisoning your koi?"

"No, no, Caroline. It's okay. Sam's on our side. He and I are back together again."

It didn't seem possible for Caroline to look any more stunned, but she managed it. "Uh, good," she said weakly. "Congratulations." She seemed unable to put the good news together with the bad, and Nora couldn't blame her. She was having the same problem. One of the men in the blue jackets emerged from Nora's office lugging her potted fig tree.

"Put that down!" Caroline yelled. "You're not going to get any information off the hard drive of a ficus!" Nora saw the armed agent by the reception desk begin to move in Caroline's direction. Again she reached out and put her arms around Caroline.

"Easy, honey. It's not your job to defend our stuff. Let them have whatever they want." She turned to Sam. "Sam, could you please walk Caroline to her car and stay with her until she feels calmer? She held down the fort until we came; now she needs to get out of here."

Sam gave Nora a look that indicated he'd much rather stay and help *her*. Nora gestured toward the armed agent by the reception desk and rolled her eyes in warning. "Seriously, Sam. Caroline needs to leave."

Sam shrugged. "Come on, Caroline," he said gently. When Caroline didn't move, he took her by the arm and guided her out the door. Nora watched them disappear, leaving her alone with the IRS.

One of the men in the blue jackets picked up Nora's computer and started out the door with it. Nora closed her eyes and willed this nightmare to go away. Surely she, repeated to herself, *surely* she wasn't important or successful enough to be raided by a whole team of IRS agents. That only happened to big corporations. So this had to be a mistake. In a few seconds, they'd realize they'd come to the wrong office and all this would be over.

"Ms. Wynn?" a voice said.

Nora opened her eyes to find herself facing a female agent. The woman was short with curly brown hair. She wore a blue blazer with brass buttons, a white blouse, a blue skirt that modestly covered her knees, and high heels just like the ones Nora always recommended to her female clients. The agent looked young enough to be playing hooky from high school, but Nora could tell immediately that she was no one to mess with. Her posture was perfect, her face a well-trained blank.

"Yes," Nora said. "I'm Nora Wynn. Who are you?"

"I'm Agent Pamela Carson, Internal Revenue Service Criminal Investigation Division." The woman presented Nora with a badge and a photo ID. The badge had an eagle at the top with its wings spread around some kind of shield with words on it Nora was too upset to read. She stared at the photo, trying and failing to find some trace of softness in Agent Carson's face.

"Please, Ms. Carson," she said, "as one woman to another, I'm begging you: tell me what's going on here."

The woman-to-woman appeal was a mistake. Ms. Carson's face grew blanker than ever. "Ms. Wynn," she said with icy politeness, "your personal tax audit and our subsequent investigation has revealed major irregularities of a previously unanticipated magnitude."

"What irregularities? I reported every cent of income from my business."

"Ms. Wynn, I'm not in charge of prosecuting your case, but I need to advise you that it's against your best interests to lie to a federal agent."

"I'm not lying!" Nora fought to control herself. "Really," she said in a more reasonable voice. "I'm not." She suddenly realized Ms. Carson was holding a sheaf of papers out to her. "What are those?"

"These documents detail the charges that have been lodged against you. They also include a copy of the federal warrant to search your property and seize anything that might contain evidence of money laundering, mail fraud, and felony tax evasion."

"Felony! You mean as in go to federal prison for the rest of my life!" Nora accepted the documents but she was so rattled she couldn't read them. The type swam before her eyes. She pressed her lips together and reminded herself that, unlike Caroline, she couldn't afford the luxury of getting hysterical, even though under the circumstances hysteria seemed like the only logical reaction.

"What am I supposed to have done?"

"It's all there."

"Yes, but could you please summarize the charges for me, Ms. Carson?"

Ms. Carson shrugged. "If you wish. As I said, your tax audit and our subsequent investigation have revealed major irregularities." She stretched out her hand, and Nora gave the documents back to her. Ms. Carson pondered them for a moment. "To be specific: you're being investigated on suspicion of felony tax evasion, receiving stolen assets, mail fraud, and money laundering."

"Mail fraud? Money laundering? I don't understand. In fact, I'm not even sure what money laundering is except that drug dealers do it."

Nora was instantly sorry that she'd mentioned drugs.

Ms. Carson gave her an appraising glance as if the last pieces of a puzzle had just snapped together. "To continue to state the charges lodged against you, Ms. Wynn, as per your request: the IRS has found multiple bank accounts in your name, evidence that you failed to report the money in these accounts as taxable income, and no evidence that you earned this money legitimately. Furthermore, there is evidence that you used electric wire transfers and bulk shipping to move over three hundred million dollars from the above-mentioned accounts to offshore jurisdictions with bank secrecy laws, doing so in increments under three thousand dollars to avoid the mandatory federal record-keeping threshold."

"Three hundred million dollars!" Nora shrieked.

Ms. Carson glared at her sternly. "One more outburst like that, Ms. Wynn, and I will have to have you confined to one of your offices under armed guard until this operation is completed."

"Sorry," Nora said, meekly. "Please go on." Her mind was churning around in crazed circles. Millions. *Millions!* The only thing she'd ever had millions of were the ants who invaded her kitchen every fall. Millions? No way. As for multiple bank accounts, she only had two: one personal, one business, plus a couple of CDs, which she was probably going to have to empty to defend herself against all this.

Maybe someone was trying to frame her for Dale Lambert's murder. Dale had been doing illegal currency trading. Bretano Global had lost millions. If those millions had somehow made it into bank accounts with Nora's name on them, she was in big trouble. Should she mention the Dale possibility to Ms. Carson?

No. Bad idea. Very bad idea. Better to remain silent. If they sent her to prison, she'd never see the stars again, never drink a decent cup of coffee, eat another piece of cheesecake, take a walk on the beach, see a movie, make love to Sam . . .

"In addition . . ." Ms. Carson continued.

Oh, no! There was more.

". . . our agents have uncovered evidence that for some time you have been channeling smaller sums of money through fake matchmaking accounts in two of your business operations: Love Finds a Way, and"— Ms. Carson consulted the documents as if reassuring herself that she had the name right—"Payback Time." She paused and looked up. "By the way, during the course of this investigation, I've often wondered exactly what a business named Payback Time involves."

"Revenge," Nora said weakly, wishing she'd never heard the word.

"Ah." Ms. Carson whipped out her Palm and made a note of it.

"Write something else down," Nora said. "Write down that I'm innocent."

Ms. Carson closed her Palm with a snap. "That's not for me to decide, Ms. Wynn."

"I'm a victim of identity theft. Someone is stalking me. I've been subject to vandalism and personal attacks. This is all a malicious plot to destroy my businesses and my life. I wish I'd reported these problems to the police as soon as they started happening so there'd be a paper trail to prove what I'm telling you, but until last night I thought it was just some cranky neighbor or a disgruntled client out for petty revenge, and being in the revenge business myself, I didn't want the bad publicity."

"Are you telling me that you've been framed?"

"Right," Nora said eagerly.

"Ms. Wynn, do you have any idea how many people

arrested on charges of receiving stolen assets, money laundering, mail fraud, and felony tax evasion claim to have been framed? You might want to find a more convincing line of defense. Meanwhile, don't try to access either your personal or commercial bank accounts or sell stock, bonds, or any other investments. All your assets have been frozen pending the outcome of this investigation. Don't try to sell your house or your car. Also, you are hereby warned that if you make any attempt to flee the country, you will be detained and put in a federal facility. In fact, you aren't even permitted to leave Los Angeles County until this matter is resolved."

"What *can* I do?" Nora moaned.

"My advice: hire yourself a good lawyer."

"With what? You haven't left me with enough change to make a phone call."

"That's not my problem." Ms. Carson returned the documents to Nora. "Have a nice day."

After the IRS raiding party left, Nora wandered from office to office in shock, looking at bare desks where computers had been and filing cabinets standing empty and open. The agents had seized everything, including a copy of *Dating for Dummies,* the contents of four wastebaskets, and the trash in the snack room. The data files and backup tapes that had been the core of her business and the envy of every matchmaker in L.A. were in a moving van on their way to some unknown destination where they would be pored over by accountants who would look at every byte. Who had done this to her? Who had thought up such a demonic scenario?

When Sam came back from walking Caroline to her car, Nora went to him without a word and put her head on his shoulder. He put his arms around her and held her for a long time. There was some comfort in his embrace, but not enough.

"I'm totally ruined," she told him.

Sam stroked her hair and pulled her closer. "It'll be okay, sweetheart. You'll see."

"No, it won't, Sam. I'm out of business, out of money, maybe out of a house, and probably on my way to prison. If the cash in those fake bank accounts turns out to be the same cash Dale Lambert stole from Bretano Global, I may even be looking at life without parole."

"Don't borrow trouble. You're not going to prison. We'll find out who did this to you."

"How?"

Nora had hoped Sam would have an answer for that question, but he didn't say a word. He just pulled her closer.

"It's no use. Don't even try to comfort me." Suddenly, instead of feeling whipped, Nora felt as angry as she'd ever felt in her life. "This is war, Sam! I don't have any data files left, but the IRS didn't seize my brain. I still have a memory. I can reproduce the DC file almost in its entirety, and I remember all the female clients I rejected because they were unstable or showed inappropriate behavior. I may not be able to remember their phone numbers or addresses, but that's what telephone directories are for. The feds may have taken cyberspace away from me, but I'm not totally helpless. I'm going to find whoever did this and make her sorry she ever messed with Nora Wynn."

"Brave girl," Sam said. "What can I do to help?"

"Make me some coffee while I try to find some paper. I need to make a list."

Sam went off to make coffee, and Nora went into her office to find a tablet and a pen. Pens were easy, as were rubber bands, paper clips, and plastic rulers; but

the IRS had apparently cleaned out every scrap of paper
except a photo of Nora's parents, which now lay unframed
on her desk, blank side up. Reluctant to draw up a list
of suspects on it, Nora went searching for paper else-
where. In what had formerly been Amber's office, she
finally located a small memo pad the IRS had somehow overlooked.

She sat down at Amber's desk and began to draw up
a list of names. For a few minutes she was all energy
and determination. Then, gradually, she began to see
how futile it was. She had no way to cross-match, no
client profiles, no list of their hobbies and habits. This
was hopeless. Completely, utterly hopeless. Where had
she ever gotten the idea that she could fight the IRS
and win?

She put down the pen and stared at the list of names
she had created. Even if she had her entire database,
there was still no logical reason to believe that whoever
was persecuting her would be in it.

When Sam arrived with a mug, she was still staring.
"Here's your coffee," he said.

"Thanks." The IRS agents had left a ceramic coaster,
Amber's Mona Lisa mouse pad, and an empty in-out
basket. Nora gestured to Sam to put the mug down on
the coaster.

"Are you okay?"

"No." She continued to stare at the list. "I keep wishing Amber were still here. She handled all our computer files and financial records."

"I don't understand why you don't suspect her. She
was your bookkeeper."

"I did suspect her. After she quit, I checked her out.
Her computer was clean: no weird stuff in the recycle
bin, no record of any visits to suspicious Web sites. The
files she left for her successor were in perfect order:
both on her computer and in hard copy. The financial

records she'd been handling were impeccable. If she'd wanted revenge, she could have erased my entire database. Instead she apologized for quitting and made us all a fresh pot of coffee before she left.

"Believe me, I'd like to pin this on someone, but Amber isn't a credible suspect. She doesn't have the guts to do something this fiendish, and she doesn't fit the description of 'Sue' that Ashley gave us. 'Sue' is a sexy blonde. Amber's dull, dowdy, and so shy she can hardly cross the street without apologizing to the traffic. I suppose one of the temps I hired might be the guilty party, but from what Ms. Carson told me, it sounds as if the trouble started long before I hired the first temp; plus I ran background checks on all of them and they came up clean."

"Ever run a background check on Amber?"

"Cut it out, Sam! This isn't helping!"

"I'm sorry." He put his hand on her shoulder. "Still friends?"

"Umm," Nora said, noncommittally.

Sam drew up a chair and sat down beside her. There was a long silence. Nora could hear the emptiness of the building ringing around her. Everything seemed hollow including the pit of her stomach. *There's nothing good left in my life except Sam,* she thought, *and I'm being nasty to him because I'm upset. I wouldn't blame him if he decided I wasn't worth the trouble.*

Sam put his hand on her shoulder. She started at his touch. "Sam, I'm sorry I snapped at you just now."

"You don't have to apologize."

"Why not?"

"Waste of time. I know you're upset, sweetheart. I'd be upset too."

She rested her head on his shoulder, and they sat for a while longer. Little by little, things didn't seem quite so bleak. Finally Nora sat up and managed a weak smile. "What shall we do next?"

"You really want my advice?"

"I really do. You're the only person I trust, and right now with Caroline out of commission, you're my only real friend."

"Okay, here goes. But first promise me you won't get mad at me again."

"I promise."

"Call your lawyer, but first call Amber."

Nora wasn't angry, but she was disappointed. She'd hoped he'd come up with a new suggestion that would get them somewhere.

"I know you don't believe Amber's involved in this," Sam continued, giving her shoulder a quick massage, "but she's still worth calling. She handled your financial records. She knows who owed you money and who didn't pay up. Maybe she can give us a clue as to who might have been angry enough to turn you into the IRS and hack your matchmaking accounts."

Nora picked up the phone without a word and began to punch in Amber's number.

"You aren't fighting me on this?" Sam said in wonder.

"No. I'm a new woman."

Sam smiled. "Don't change too much. I liked the old Nora."

Nora put the receiver to her ear and waited for Amber to answer, but instead she got a recording from Pacific Bell informing her that Amber's number had been disconnected. She hung up and turned to Sam.

"That's odd. Amber didn't say anything about moving." Nora looked at Sam thoughtfully. "Where do you suppose she went?"

"I suppose she could have moved in with her boyfriend, or found a better apartment."

"She doesn't rent an apartment. She owns a house she inherited when her mother died. Amber loved that place. She'd never sell it."

"You have to admit that it's strange that she had her phone disconnected."

"Very strange."

They stared at the phone as if Amber might call and explain, but it just sat there and refused to ring.

"What now?" Sam said.

"I have no idea." Nora picked up her mug and took a sip of coffee. She stared at the coaster, which was one of the few things Amber had left behind when she quit. The coaster depicted a small red boat in full sail on a turquoise-blue ocean. It was pretty but bland. *A lot like Amber,* Nora thought. She took another sip of coffee and started to set the mug back down on the coaster.

Suddenly she froze. She had just had a burst of revelation so intense it made her feel as if her mind might explode. It was like one of those conversion experiences you read about: when tongues of fire rain down out of the sky and fill your head with light.

Sailboat! Amber! Boyfriend!

"Oh, my God!" she cried.

Sam jumped to his feet so fast he upset his chair. "Nora! What's wrong? Are you okay?"

"Yes! I'm fine. I'm more than okay! Sam, I owe you an apology. I've changed my mind. I think you might be totally right about Amber!"

"What are you talking about?"

"This!" And in a burst of nonstop inspiration, Nora told Sam her theory. She pointed to the coaster. Amber had talked about a boyfriend who had taken her sailing. Could that man have been Dale Lambert? Amber had been upset the day Rosalee came in for her client interview. Suppose Amber had overheard Rosalee's outburst, been dating Dale, and had not known until that moment that he was married? That would explain Amber's tears, wouldn't it? Not to mention Amber's abrupt announcement that she had "just broken up with her boyfriend," who was not, as Amber had claimed, a twenty-something librarian, but a middle-aged banker.

Dale had been doing illegal currency trading. The millions Dale embezzled could be the same three hundred million dollars that had shown up in fake bank accounts someone had opened in Nora's name. If so, maybe Dale and Amber had gotten back together. Maybe Dale had also been the "new boyfriend," the one Amber claimed owned cardboard box factories.

It would have been so simple for her to launder money for him. Amber, as Sam had pointed out, had access to the financial records of Love Finds a Way and Payback Time. Using her home computer so there'd be no records at the office, she might easily have created fake matchmaking accounts and channeled money through them, then moved on to the wire transfers and bulk currency shipping. And that wasn't all: to set up those fake bank accounts in Nora's name, all Amber would have had to do was steal Nora's purse!

Nora leaped to her feet and paced back and forth across the room growing more and more excited. "You know what this means?" she cried. "It means that, if Amber has the millions Dale stole from Bretano Global, she must be the one who killed Dale! Think about it, Sam: It makes sense. She could have read my notes on the revenge seminar Rosalee attended and found out about Rosalee's fantasy of hitting Dale over the head with a winch handle. She could have gone to a surf shop, bought herself a snorkel, fins, and one of those plastic kayaks with a credit card taken out in *my* name, paddled out to the Lamberts' yacht, and killed Dale while Rosalee was sleeping belowdecks.

"I don't know how she got hold of Rosalee's diary,

but I bet Dale had given her a key to his house, which would have made it easy for her to plant it in that can of flour where the cops would be sure to find it. That little mouse-faced *child* framed Rosalee for murder, Sam; just like she framed me for money laundering! It all makes sense!"

"Nora, hold on—"

"No! You hold on! There's more!"

"Aren't you jumping to a lot of conclusions?"

"Look who's being cautious now. Sure I'm jumping. I'm leaping. I'm on a roll! Think about it, Sam! All the time Amber was laundering the money for Dale, she must have been intending to do him in. Why else would she have taken those Spanish lessons and collected those travel brochures if she wasn't planning to flee the country? She only made one mistake, and it was a big one: She put on a blond wig and a tight dress, renamed herself 'Sue Rossett,' and told Ashley Clay you were harassing me about the land. Why did she do it? Who knows? Maybe she hated me and just wanted to add as much stress to my life as possible.

"Amber knew Ashley was in the DC file, but she never could have predicted that Ashley would react by sending that fake photo of you and Rosalee to the sheriff's department. When it showed up, linking me more closely to Dale's murder, Amber must have panicked. She must have known that she might be forced to show the cops the financial records of Love Finds a Way and Payback Time. So she quits her job, right? And then for good measure, she punctures my brake seals and throws dye in my pool to deflect suspicion from her and throw it on a disgruntled client."

Nora paused in front of Sam and looked at him breathlessly. "So what do you think?"

"It's a brilliant theory."

"Right."

"And all the pieces hang together."

"Right."

"Except for that ticket to Paraguay that Rosalee bought herself."

"I forgot about the ticket. Well, I'm sure it works in somehow."

"Also, there's no evidence Amber ever met Dale Lambert, much less had an affair with him and killed him."

"Then we'll get evidence. Look, Sam, I know I'm right. I can feel it in my bones."

"A few minutes ago you 'felt in your bones' that Amber couldn't possibly have had anything to do with this."

"So my bones are flexible. So sue me. Darn it, Sam, don't ruin a perfectly brilliant theory with something as trivial as logic. Come on. Help me out. We'll start by searching Amber's desk."

Sam opened the top drawer and peered inside. "Why bother? The IRS already cleaned it out."

Nora pulled out another empty drawer and scanned it eagerly. "I thought you were the guy who read mystery scripts. You should know there's always evidence if you look hard enough."

A few moments later Nora emerged triumphantly from the recesses of Amber's desk with a tube of lipstick, held it aloft, and gave Sam a victory sign. "Look at this! Revlon ColorStay Scarlet! I'm almost positive it's mine. Amber hardly ever wore lipstick, and when she did, it was always some variation on pink. Plus the color was always gone half an hour after she put it on because she had a habit of chewing her lips like a rabbit. I bet the day she stole my purse, she rummaged through it, found this, decided the color was wrong for her, threw it back in her desk, and forgot it."

Sam inspected the black plastic tube and then returned it to Nora.

"Why aren't you celebrating with me, Sam? We're definitely on the right track."

"Other people have used this desk since Amber left."

Nora's face fell. "Oh, right. I forgot about the temps."

"Also you can't be sure this lipstick is yours."

"No, I suppose not." She turned back to Amber's desk. "Come on, let's keep looking." They continued, but the rest of the search was over almost before it began. The IRS agents had been thorough. Except for a few paper clips, a pad of Post-Its, half a dozen ballpoint pens, and some stray rubber bands, the drawers were empty.

Nora picked up Amber's mouse pad and turned it over on the off chance something might be stuck to the underside, but all she found was an old coffee stain. "Okay, that's it for her desk. Now let's search her office."

Once again, the IRS hadn't left them much to go through. The filing cabinets were empty; the bookshelf behind Amber's desk had been stripped; the shredder had been cleaned out; and the contents of the wastebasket had been dumped into a carton, and carried off. Only a pile of phone books remained.

Nora inspected the cover and back of each directory in case Amber had scrawled down something incriminating; then she opened each book and shook it to make sure nothing was stuck between the pages. While she was doing that, Sam got down on his hands and knees and looked under the furniture. Net result: a coupon for dry cleaning, more paper clips, and a lot of dust.

Nora wasn't about to give up. She went back to Amber's desk and started pulling out the drawers. A few minutes later she gave another whoop of triumph. Stuck behind the bottom left-hand drawer was a crumpled postcard. Nora extracted the card, put it on the top of

Amber's desk, and smoothed out the wrinkles. One side featured a photo of waterfalls surrounded by dense tropical jungle. The other side was blank except for a printed caption that read *Iguazu Falls*.

Nora stared at the blank side, willing a message to appear. She felt disappointed. There wasn't even a stamp. Amber could have brought the card back from South America in her suitcase when she was checking out places to run to after she killed Dale, or she could have bought it in a gift shop here in L.A. It might even have belonged to one of the temps. She tossed the postcard back down on the desk and stared at it glumly.

"Maybe I'm on the wrong track, Sam. Maybe you were right. We still haven't found one shred of evidence that links Amber to Dale."

Sam picked up the postcard, turned it over, and contemplated the photo of the falls. "I directed a travel promo on Iguazu Falls when I was in South America."

Nora whirled around to face him. "You've been there!"

"Yes. The company flew me to Iguazu with a three-person crew and hooked us up with their on-site personnel. We got the full tourist treatment: a walk through the rain forest with a trained guide; a ride in a rubber boat that went under the falls. They even issued us bags of cashews to lure the coatis into camera range. Everyone was nervous because eleven Argentine tourists had just drowned a month before when two tour boats collided under the falls, so we were under strict orders to produce a video that would make the place look as tame as Disneyland, which wasn't easy. You can't imagine how much water pours over those cliffs and what terrifying force it has. Iguazu Falls is one of the most impressive things I've ever seen; it's beautiful beyond description; it makes Niagara look like a leaky faucet.

"But that's not what's so interesting about it." He

tapped the photo with his index finger. "Half of the falls are in Argentina and the other half are in Brazil. Paraguay's right next door. Because of the three borders—which anyone with enough bucks can cross, no questions asked—the whole region is an infamous nest of smugglers, aging ex-Nazis, terrorists, and people on the run from the law. If you'd just murdered your embezzling, currency-trading, married boyfriend, framed his wife, laundered millions of bucks in stolen money, and were looking for a great place to hang out beyond the reach of extradition, you couldn't buy a ticket to a more felon-friendly neighborhood than Iguazu."

Nora leaped out of the chair so fast she knocked it over. "You're brilliant!" she cried. She threw her arms around Sam's neck and gave him a kiss.

"Easy, Nora. Don't get your hopes up. It's just a theory. We have to be realistic. We still don't have any hard evidence. Maybe Amber's still living in her house. Maybe her phone was disconnected because she didn't pay her bill; or maybe she closed her old account and got a new number because too many telemarketers were calling her at dinnertime."

Nora turned and jabbed at the postcard. "And maybe she's right there in Iguazu."

21

Amber lived in Culver City not far from the Sony Studios. The house she had inherited from her mother turned out to be a small white stucco two-bedroom with a patch of front lawn about the size of a throw rug. The grass, which looked as if it could use watering, was that sturdy Bermuda variety that always made Nora think of rows of sharp green teeth.

Amber's car wasn't in the driveway and didn't look as if it had been for some time. A Joshua tree had littered the asphalt with brown, sickle-shaped fronds; there was an advertising circular stuck in the screen door, and two yellowed newspapers occupied a prominent place on the front steps.

Nora and Sam walked up to Amber's front door and rang the bell. Somewhere, deep inside the house, chimes sounded and then there was silence.

Nora rang again. The same eight notes were repeated with a hollow echo. They waited. No one opened the door, and there was no sound of anyone approaching.

"I'm putting my money on Iguazu," Nora said.

"Looking more likely all the time," Sam agreed.

Nora put her face to the picture window, shaded her eyes against the glare, pressed her nose against the glass, and peered through a crack in the drapes. Amber's living room was dark and apparently deserted.

"What do you see?" Sam asked.

"A red velvet sofa, a couple of chairs covered in zebra-striped material, a huge home entertainment center, and a white lamp that appears to represent a faun eating a bunch of grapes."

"Tell me you're kidding about the lamp."

"I wish I were. I had no idea Amber had such flamboyant taste in furniture. I'm pretty sure no one's home." Nora stepped back from the window. "Come on. Let's look in some other windows and see if we can spot any sign of what she's been up to."

"What if her neighbors see us poking around and call the cops?"

Nora looked up and down the street. All the houses in Amber's neighborhood appeared to have been made from the same kit: picture window in front, garage snout-out facing the driveway, small lawns—some with flowering trees, some covered with a patch of dead grass or those white pebbles people put down to save themselves the trouble and expense of watering. Except for the occasional bark of a dog, the street was almost eerily silent. There were children's toys on the front lawns, but no signs of children.

"Relax. We're in the land of two working parents or single moms. The kids are all in school or day care, and Grandma is probably off playing tennis in Sun City. In other words, what we have here is a typical suburban, witness-free zone. If Amber's been doing what we think she's been doing, she must have found living in this neighborhood very handy."

They walked around to the side of the house where they found a gate made of redwood, which looked for-

midable but yielded easily to a push. Letting themselves into Amber's backyard, they closed the gate and
began to check things out. The grass here was even
drier than it had been in front; some patches had even
gone to seed. There were a couple of large terra-cotta
pots of scraggly geraniums and lavender that also seemed
on the brink of expiring from thirst. The only plants
that looked as if they were going to make it were the
jade trees, the live-forever, and a few other succulents
Nora couldn't identify.

Amber's plants might have been slated for an early
death, but her patio furniture could have made the
cover of *Sunset* magazine. Every item was brand-new,
beautiful, and very expensive. The most impressive piece
was a large teak table from Smith & Hawken shaded by
a white umbrella and surrounded by eight teak chairs.
Nora calculated the entire setup must have cost well
over two thousand dollars. Amber also had one of those
expensive copper drink stands, several lounge chairs—
also teak—and a huge, shiny, two-burner iron-and-
stainless-steel gas barbecue grill that could easily have
cooked an ox.

Nora stared at the grill grimly. She had a pretty good
idea who had paid for that monstrosity. This must be
part of the loot that had shown up on her credit card
after her purse was stolen. Amber's beds were probably
made up with sheets Nora had paid for; there was probably Nora-paid-for china in Amber's cupboards, and
bill-it-to-Nora perfume dabbed behind Amber's treach-
erous little ears.

"Come on," she said to Sam. "Let's have a look inside."

They walked up on the deck and made their way to
the sliding glass doors that led to the kitchen, but there
wasn't much to see unless you counted a bowl of moldy
oranges on the table, which added to the evidence that

Amber was long gone. Except for a bathroom window made of glass slats, all the other windows at the back of the house were covered with iron bars wrought in a lacy pattern designed to keep out burglars while suggesting a hint of Spanish romance.

Nora pushed one of Amber's teak chairs up to the left-hand window while Sam took the right. They peered through the bars and dirty glass.

"I'm looking at a bedroom," Sam said. "Bed's made. No sign of anyone. Hey, Nora, you aren't going to believe her bedspread. It's purple velvet with tassels. Also the walls are black and silver. Are you sure Amber never worked for the Bang Bang Girls?"

But Nora wasn't listening. She was staring transfixed at Amber's study. There wasn't much to look at—only a desk chair and a large oak desk—but on the desk was one of those corny Mona Lisa mouse pads Amber favored. And what was that mouse pad holding down? Pink file folders, that's what! Folders that undoubtedly contained Nora's matchmaking profiles, which Amber must have made off with when she quit!

"Check this out!" Nora yelled to Sam. "Hard evidence! Amber's a thief at the very least!"

Sam joined her at the window, and for a moment they both stared at the incriminating pink folders.

"I'm going in," Nora announced.

"How? You'd need a blowtorch to get through this ironwork."

"Simple." Nora jumped off the chair, pushed it under the bathroom window, and tugged at one of the glass slats. When it didn't give, she took off one of her shoes, cracked the slat in half with a sharp blow, reached in gingerly, removed it, and opened the window from the inside. The rest of the slats came out easily, leaving a hole just large enough for a slender woman to wiggle through.

"I never knew you had such a talent for breaking and entering," Sam said as he stacked the discarded slats on top of the copper drink stand so they wouldn't step on them.

Nora shrugged. "Neither did I. But the sight of that monster barbecue grill I paid for was inspiring. Come on, give me a boost."

Sam laced his fingers together, and Nora stepped on them, put her hands on the ledge, and hoisted herself through the window. Unfortunately the window was over an open clothes hamper. She came down in it, and it toppled and tipped her into the bathtub. Giving a loud yell, she grabbed for the shower curtain, which ripped, sending plastic shower rings pinging down on the tile floor like hail.

"Are you okay?" Sam called.

Nora extracted herself from the hamper and rubbed the place where her head had struck the soap holder. "I'm fine." She limped back to the window. "But the bathroom is totally trashed. When—and if—Amber ever gets back from Iguazu, she's definitely going to know she had company. Come to the kitchen door, and I'll let you in."

A few moments later, they entered Amber's study. Nora made straight for the pink folders, which contained . . . nothing. Worse yet, there was a box of a hundred more folders in assorted colors in the side drawer of Amber's desk. The other drawers were empty except for boxes of paper clips, a bag of rubber bands, a brand-new tube of Chap Stick, a pile of quarters, self-sealing envelopes, mailing labels, reams of blank paper, and a sheaf of American-flag return address labels that Amber had apparently obtained by sending a donation to a disabled veterans group.

"This is bad," Nora said. "We just burglarized Amber's house, and all we've discovered is that she steals office supplies. Actually, maybe she doesn't even do that. She could have bought all this stuff from Staples. Come on, Sam. We have to get out of here. I think we may have made a really stupid mistake."

"Wait." Sam made a sweeping gesture that took in Amber's study. "What's wrong with this picture?"

"What's wrong is that we just committed a felony!"

"No, I mean what's wrong with this room? Look."

"The room's empty. Or nearly empty, anyway. Desk, chair, rug: what's to look at?"

Sam frowned as if trying to work something out. "Well," he said, "I was just thinking: if you were leaving your house forever, what would you do with it?"

"Rent it or put it up for sale."

"Exactly. And you'd move out all your furniture, wouldn't you? But Amber hasn't. So either she plans to come back, or she has so much money she can just walk away from everything she owns. However, there's one room in this house she didn't walk away from: this one. And if she plans to come back to it, she's done something really strange. I can see marks on the carpet where her computer stood, but I don't see any computer. I see a mouse pad, but no mouse. I see faded spots about the size of filing cabinets, but no filing cabinets. My bet is she took that stuff because she had something to hide."

"You mean, you think . . . she took it with her?"

Sam grinned. "No. It's way too heavy. I think she—"

"Stored it!" Nora cried. "You think Amber put her computer and all her files in storage!"

"I'd bet money on it," Sam said. "But the question is, where? Come on, let's have a look around."

For the next two hours, they searched the house looking for clues that might lead them to the storage space where Amber had stashed her computer, but Amber hadn't left behind a scrap of paper with anything printed on it: no old PG&E bills, no credit card statements, not even a receipt for groceries. Finally, they admitted defeat, gave up, and did their best to put things back the way they'd found them. As they let themselves out the back door, Nora stopped to take one last look at Amber's fancy patio furniture. She was positive it had been purchased with her money, but she hadn't been able to find any evidence of that, and probably never would. Amber was too smart and too thorough. No wonder she'd been such a great bookkeeper.

She gave the copper drink stand a kick of frustration and was just about to walk on when she noticed a small metal garden shed in the back corner of the yard.

"Hey," she called to Sam, who was just stepping out through the gate. "Come back. We're not finished." She pointed to the shed. "We should probably have a look in there."

They went over to the shed and tried the door. It wasn't locked, but there was nothing inside except a shovel, two rakes, a green plastic watering can, a plastic bag, a coil of garden hose, and a bunch of sticks that looked like garden trash. Sam opened the plastic bag and discovered that it contained potting soil.

"So," he said, "I guess that's that."

"Not quite." Nora peered into the coil of hose, moved the watering can, and looked between the tines of the rake. "I just realized that I've lost one of my gold earrings, which means we have to go back into Amber's house and find it."

She straightened up and looked at Sam grimly. "Oh, forget it. What's the point? We're totally screwed anyway. Our fingerprints are everywhere and—"

She suddenly stopped speaking and peered intently at the floor next to the garden trash. "Wait a minute. Good news. I see my earring. It's . . . What the hell!" A small furry creature had just darted out of the shadows, seized the earring, and scurried into the trash pile with it. "A mouse just stole my earring!"

"A mouse?"

"Maybe a rat. I don't know. How do you tell them apart? Anyway, whatever it was took it in there." She pointed to the pile of sticks. "I'm going after it. I love those earrings. My mom gave them to me last Christmas."

"That rat might bite if you corner it."

"Just prop open the door and stand back." Nora picked up a rake, walked over to the pile of sticks, and gave it a sharp slap. The pile was amazingly hard, as if it had been wrapped in plastic or something. She struck again, and a creature about the size of a lab rat came dashing out and made a panicked scramble for the open door. Nora only got a quick glance of whitish gray fur and big ears.

"Hit that pile of sticks some more," Sam suggested. "There may be another one in there."

Nora gave the pile a few more sharp whacks, but apparently it had been a bachelor pad. By now, she had managed to crack the nest—for that was obviously what it was—open. A musky odor rose from the remains. She held her breath and poked at it with the tines of the rake trying to locate her earring. There was a bunch of junk inside: aluminum tabs from soft drink cans, wads of newspaper, bones, pinecones, even a metal ring with a rusty key on it.

"Hey, Sam, come over here and bring the other rake. I think I've found a pack-rat nest."

Sam picked up the rake, went over to the nest, and helped her pull it apart. Inside, well toward the back, they found her earring sitting on a pile of shredded paper—not pack-rat-shredded paper, but paper shredded by a machine. Some of the strips were red. Nora examined them, hoping to find a name or an incriminating word, but they were blank.

Another dead end, she thought wearily. She disentangled her earring and put it in her pocket. No way it was going back in her ear until she'd soaked it in bleach. Using the rake, she pushed the key ring out onto the floor.

"Does that key look like it goes to a storage locker?"

Sam picked up the key and looked it over. "Afraid not. It's got a Toyota symbol on it."

"Damn, I knew it couldn't be that easy." Nora raked through what was left of the nest, crouched down, and pulled apart the sticks, trying to ignore the smell. But there was nothing else of interest: just more paper and some shiny scraps that looked like those strips of Mylar people sometimes hung on fruit trees to discourage birds.

She was in the process of calling it quits, when something strange caught her eye. It was her own name, staring at her from a wadded-up piece of yellow paper. Reaching out, she plucked the yellow ball from the surrounding mess, unfolded it, and smoothed out the wrinkles. As she read what was printed on it, a slow smile spread over her face.

"Sam," she said, "we've just struck gold. It appears I've been renting a climate-controlled storage unit here in Culver City. And that's not all. My access code is listed. The directions say I'm supposed to keep it in a safe place."

22

An hour later, Nora and Sam stood in a well-lit, carpeted, storage unit reading Amber's files. The unit was filled with everything they had ever hoped to find and more. Amber's computer, printer, and shredder were there; her files were neatly boxed and indexed; even the corny snowstorm paperweight she'd kept on her desk at Love Finds a Way sat on its own special little wooden rack. There was a metal desk, a chair, and a telephone in case whoever rented the unit was seized with an urge to make a call or use the Internet. In other words, this windowless, anonymous space was a working office. It even had a small refrigerator filled with mineral water, a hot plate, a tin of cookies, and a box of the green jasmine tea Amber had always favored.

Everything was color-coded and perfectly organized. In one cardboard file box, Nora had discovered receipts for the money transfers that had triggered the IRS raid. In another, she had found dozens of pink folders. This time the folders weren't empty. They contained matchmaking accounts from Love Finds a Way, but not ones Nora recognized.

Nora stared at the names and tried to summon up faces to go with them. Lee Halman? She'd never heard of him. Jordan Athanas? Man? Woman? Nora couldn't remember. Chinito Zumbo? She would never have forgotten a name like that in a million years, but apparently she had.

She read every file, searching without success for a familiar name. According to these records, she had not only interviewed these clients (and charged them top rates); she had fixed them up multiple times after providing them with extensive personal services like handwriting analysis, psychological testing, and professional image consulting. Each had paid Love Finds a Way a whopping seven thousand dollars or more for the privilege of being custom-matched. All of them hadn't been satisfied by the first round, and had come back as repeat customers, contracting for all the services they had had earlier, plus several that Nora had never offered.

When she finished the last folder, she tossed it down on the desk and looked at Sam triumphantly. "Every one of these accounts is phony and most of them are nearly a year old. I never met these clients; they never existed. Now I know what triggered my first tax audit. Amber was embezzling from me long before Dale came along."

"Right. It all holds together. So now that we have hard evidence, what do we do?"

"Some more snooping, that's what." Sitting down, she turned on Amber's computer. "How are your hacking skills?"

"Not good."

"Neither are mine." She studied the screen intently. The wallpaper on Amber's desktop was a tropical island surrounded by crystal-clear water. On the right-hand side of the screen, a large sailboat swept by, leaving a white wake. Suddenly she gave a groan. "Damn! We're being prompted to supply a password. I should have known Amber would think of everything. So what about it? Want to guess?"

"Try her birthday," Sam suggested.

"She's way too smart for that. I'll try mine."

Nora typed in 03/17/70. It didn't work. "Any other thoughts?"

"Name of favorite sports team? Year of graduation from high school."

"This is totally impossible!"

"Maybe she pasted a copy of her password on something, like that maybe." Sam pointed to the snowstorm paperweight. "I mean, look at that thing. It's totally out of place."

"You're right. Why else would she have a paperweight in here?" Nora reached out, picked up the paperweight, turned it over, and examined the bottom. Her face fell. "We lose. There's nothing. Amber's just guilty of terminal bad taste."

Sam frowned and stared at the computer. "Try 'Iguazu,' " he said.

"Amber couldn't have been that dumb."

But she had been. The password worked and with a yell of triumph Nora plunged in, clicked away, and within ten minutes they had enough additional proof of fraud and money laundering to put Amber away for a long time. Nora printed up the information and stared at it longingly.

"Darn," she said.

"What's the problem?"

"I just remembered: we illegally broke into Amber's house, which is how we found out about this storage unit." She pointed to the printouts. "Then we got all this information without a warrant. Talk about illegally obtained evidence! If we turn this over to the sheriff's department, Amber will probably go free. And if she murdered Dale, she may get away with that too. Meanwhile you and I will be lucky not to end up in prison for burglary. We can't use any of this." She gathered together the printouts, rose to her feet, and started for the shredder.

Sam stopped her. "Wait. There's no need to rush. Let's rummage through her computer a little more, and then let's imitate Ashley."

"Yes! Of course. What a great idea! The sheriff's department couldn't use any of this stuff as evidence if we took it to them, could they? But I bet they'd find a good reason to come out here with a warrant and look around if we sent them an anonymous letter telling them the access code to this unit and claiming we have a reason to believe Amber killed Dale. There's just one problem: *do* we have a reason? I'm more convinced than ever that she knocked him out with that winch handle and threw him overboard, but so far we still don't have a shred of proof that she even knew him."

"Let's see if we can find some." Sam leaned over and clicked on Amber's e-mail program. "You'd be surprised what people keep in their address books." He clicked again and the computer obligingly provided a name: *Dale Lambert, sailorboy@hotmail.com.*

" 'Sailorboy'?" Nora yelled. " 'Sailorboy'! Please, tell me Amber doesn't delete her old e-mail!"

But Amber had—every last piece of it. The juicy love letters they were hoping to read sent by crafty, murderous Amber to doomed, adulterous Dale were nowhere to be found. They spent another fifteen minutes or so looking everywhere they could think of, but either Amber had never written Dale, or she'd had the sense to cover her tracks. Finally they gave up. Nora printed out Amber's address book with the incriminating address, shoved the chair back from the desk, and got up. "Well, that's that."

She started to turn off Amber's computer, but once again Sam stopped her.

"I just had another idea."

"What?"

"This." He slid the mouse across the desktop and launched Amber's browser and connected it to the Internet. Then he clicked on a little arrow that produced a list of all the Web sites she'd recently visited. The third URL was the Web address of United Airlines.

Sam gave a whoop of victory and pointed to the screen. "Looks like someone was planning a trip!"

"Can we see where she was trying to go?"

"Not unless we can figure out her password."

"Can we cut and paste it from her browser?"

"Nope. It's hidden. But we can look at her temporary Internet files if she hasn't deleted them recently."

Amber hadn't, and a few seconds later they were staring at a screen that was displaying a proposed itinerary that included a flight to Buenos Aires, followed by a flight to a small town not far from the Argentine side of the Iguazu Falls.

Nora stared at the itinerary, and suddenly everything seemed much more serious and dangerous than it had been when her suspicions were just a theory. "Did she buy the ticket?"

"There's no indication she did, but that doesn't tell us anything. She could have called United and bought it by phone." Sam sat back. "I'd say Amber's long gone. But at least we know she's probably somewhere in Argentina."

"She must have murdered Dale."

"Yeah, poor sap. He might have been an embezzling, lying, cheating, slime ball, but he didn't deserve Amber."

"Do you think they'll ever be able to find Amber and bring her back to face trial?"

"I wouldn't bet on it. But this should help support

Rosalee's claim that she's innocent. Also, it should go a long way toward getting you out of the jam you're in with the IRS."

Nora stared at Amber's itinerary and tried to think of some way to track her down, but nothing came to mind. Argentina was huge, and if a person with three hundred million dollars wanted to disappear down there, it probably wouldn't be very hard. Maybe Amber would dye her hair and have plastic surgery. Or maybe she wouldn't even bother.

Suddenly Nora did a double take. "Sam! Look!" She rose to her feet and pointed at the screen. "Amber was trying to buy *two* one-way first-class adult tickets! We must be the most inept hackers who ever lived! Let's try to find the full itinerary. Maybe we can figure out who went with her."

The full itinerary was also in Amber's temporary Internet files folder, but "Charles Marinero," the name of her proposed traveling companion, meant nothing to either of them. They stared at it, disappointed.

"Are you sure it doesn't ring any bells?" Sam asked.

"Unfortunately, it doesn't. Maybe Marinero is one of my clients. Amber had all their addresses. She could have matched herself with him. If I still had my files, I could check for his name. But they're all sitting in an IRS warehouse somewhere."

"Amber requested a vegetarian meal for herself and a low-cholesterol meal for him. I'd say that probably eliminates any guy under forty unless he's a health nut."

"Maybe he's a rich older man like Dale."

"If he is, he should watch his back. No one with a fat bank account should set out on a trip with Amber without taking out extra life insurance."

Nora leaned closer to the screen. "Now that's odd,"

she said, frowning. "Amber and Marinero didn't travel together. His ticket is dated November sixth. Hers is for the seventh. That doesn't quite make sense, does it? Amber quit on the seventh—the day after Dale was murdered—so that means she must have known ahead of time when she was going to kill him and flee the country. She easily could have traveled with Marinero on the seventh. The real question is, why did Marinero leave a day earlier?"

"Maybe he was in on the murder. Maybe he was going down to Argentina to rent them a hideaway."

"Charles Marinero," Nora repeated. She stared at the screen and her frown deepened. "There's something about that name, but I just can't put my finger on it." Suddenly she realized why the name sounded familiar. No! It couldn't be! But there it was, right there in front of her, a possibility so mind-blowing that she could hardly breathe when she thought about it. She turned to Sam and tried not to get her hopes up. "Sam, do you speak Spanish?"

"A little, why?"

"I'm seeing the word 'marine' in 'Marinero.'"

"I'm not following you."

"Plus 'Charles' left for Argentina on the day Dale disappeared."

"Are you saying Marinero helped Amber murder Dale?"

"No." Nora took a deep breath. "I'm saying Marinero *is* Dale."

"But Dale's dead."

"Is he? They never found his body, did they?"

"No, but—"

"Sam it's been right here in front of us all along, only we've been too blind to see it! The first time Rosalee came in for an interview at Love Finds a Way, she told

me Dale's nickname was Chuck. Later she explained
that his family called him that when he was a kid because he had fat little cheeks like a woodchuck."

"And?"

"Don't you see? 'Chuck' may be short for 'woodchuck' but it can also be short for 'Charles.' 'Charles
Marinero' left for Argentina on the evening of November
sixth only a few hours after Dale disappeared. And I'd
be willing to bet serious money that if we look up
'Marinero' in a Spanish/English dictionary, it's going
to mean 'sailor.' "

"Sailorboy!" Sam cried.

"Chuck/Charles/Sailorboy/Marinero, otherwise known
as Dale Lambert. Not dead, not even missing. Dale Lambert, alive and well in Argentina, where he fled after he
and Amber faked his death and framed Rosalee so they
could spend those millions Dale embezzled from Bretano
Global. How did they do it? Who knows? Maybe those
surf shop charges on my credit card were for an inflatable boat. Maybe Dale smeared his blood on the winch
handle, slipped over the side of the yacht while Rosalee
was sleeping below, and had Amber row him to shore
and drive him to the airport. The details don't matter.
Let's print up this itinerary and get out of here. We've
got an anonymous letter to write."

They waited impatiently for Amber's printer to finish. When the pages were ready, Sam retrieved them
from the tray and Nora began to shut down the computer. She was just wondering if she should wipe their
fingerprints off the mouse and keyboard, when she
heard the sound of footsteps coming down the hall.

"Turn off the light," she hissed to Sam. "Someone's
coming." Sam ran for the switch, but before he could
reach it, the door of the unit swung open and they
found themselves face-to-face with the last person they
wanted to meet.

Amber had changed a lot since Nora last saw her. Her hair was white blond, her lips liquid red, her eyelashes coal-black. Instead of orthopedic shoes, a clunky beige sweater, and a white blouse with a Peter Pan collar, she wore gold and purple stiletto heels with toes long enough to kill spiders, half a dozen gold chains, and a low-cut, metallic gold dress so small, so short, and so tight that it clung to her curves like plastic wrap.

"Well, well," Amber said. "Aren't you two the busy little beavers?"

"Amber!" Nora cried. "I thought you were—"

"In Argentina? No. I didn't go on the seventh after all. You did look at my travel itinerary, right? Why else would you be here? By the way, you sure spent a long time searching my house. Benny thought you were never going to leave. You don't know Benny, but he lives across the street from me. I hired him to watch my place and call me if he saw anyone snooping around the place.

"I've been lying low for a while. I've had this weird intuition that Dale might try to bail on me, so I thought it would be good insurance to put together a little blackmail packet before I joined him. In fact a good friend of mine just suggested I remove the hard drive from my computer and store it separately, so when I got Benny's call I figured I'd come over here and kill two birds with one stone."

Amber raised her hand, and Nora saw with horror that she was holding a gun.

"Amber, for God's sake!"

"Don't bother trying to talk me out of taking care of this my way, Nora. You never understood anything about me. I'm not even sure you ever saw me, not really. I was just the dowdy little bookkeeper, wasn't I? The girl who did all the scut work for the famous matchmaker. Do you have any idea how much I hated you and Caroline? No? Well, at this point it doesn't matter. You and your ex broke and entered. I could shoot you for that and probably get away with it, but I'm way past the point of worrying about an alibi."

No, Nora thought. *This can't be happening. People only get shot in movies. Amber wouldn't . . .* Suddenly she knew, with chilling certainty, that Amber would.

"Look, Amber," Sam said. "There's no point in shooting us. Murder just stirs up trouble. Let's make a deal. You take me hostage, and Nora will sit down and reformat the hard drive of your computer so every file's erased. Then we'll get a drill and punch a hole in it just to make sure. We'll shred these folders and any other records you want to get rid of. When you're satisfied there's nothing left to incriminate you, you let Nora go, and I'll drive you to the airport—"

"Shut up," Amber said. "What kind of fool do you think I am? That plan has holes big enough to drive a truck through." She raised the gun and pointed it at Nora. "It's way too late for deals. You know too much."

Terrified, Nora took a step backward and collided with Amber's shredder, which toppled over with a loud crash. For a split second, Amber's gaze shifted away from Sam, who went for the only weapon at hand. Scooping up the paperweight, he hurled it straight at Amber's head. Sam had not been a varsity basketball star in high school for nothing. His aim was perfect. The paperweight flew across the room and hit Amber squarely between the eyes, knocking her off balance just as the gun went off, blowing a hole in the ceiling.

Before she could recover, Nora and Sam tackled her. Amber screeched and cursed and thrashed around and threatened, but now it was two against one. Sam sat on her back and Nora sat on her legs, and every time she lifted her head, they pushed her face into the rug.

At last Amber stopped struggling. "Listen," she said

in a muffled voice. "Let me go, and I'll make you a deal. I'll pay you ten million dollars. That's five apiece."

"No way," Nora said.

"Come on, Nora. Lighten up. I didn't kill anyone."

"You tried to kill us."

"I was bluffing."

"Tell that to the hole in the ceiling. Besides, you framed Rosalee. She might have gotten the death penalty."

"No way."

"Way."

"Look, you two. What do you want to let me go?"

"Well." Sam gave Amber's head a gentle push rugward. "For my part, I'd like to see justice done. How about you, Nora?"

"Justice works for me. Plus, to be frank, Amber, I'd like never to see shoes like these again." Nora pulled off one of Amber's purple and gold stiletto heels and examined it with disgust. "These pointy-toed horrors are an offense to true shoe-loving women everywhere."

"Are you saying you're going to send me to prison for wearing *bad shoes!*" Amber shrieked.

"Right. You're just lucky fashion crimes don't carry the death penalty." Nora tossed the offending shoe into one of the open file boxes, reached over, jerked the extension cord out of the wall, and passed the cord to Sam.

"Let's hog-tie her and call 911."

"Hog-tie?" Sam said.

Nora grinned. "An expression I learned when I was doing research on southern belles." She jerked another cord out of the wall and began to loop it around Amber's ankles. "Hold still," she commanded, "and stop yelling. We're not going to kill you."

23

Dale Lambert sat on the veranda of his hacienda in shorts and a tank top, rocking lazily in a wicker rocker, drinking a papaya daiquiri, reading a copy of the *International Herald Tribune,* and watching a flock of green and yellow parrots squabble over a pile of stale crackers that the cook had tossed on the lawn beside the swimming pool.

Crackers always went stale in the tropics before you had a chance to eat them, but still, Maria shouldn't have thrown them there. When he first arrived, Dale thought the parrots were exotic and beautiful, but now he found them annoying. Back in L.A., he never would have imagined that a flock of the little bastards could sound like a hundred doors all creaking at the same time. Their racket put his teeth on edge. If his Spanish had been good enough to tell the cook to throw garbage where garbage belonged, he'd have been able to solve this problem without getting up out of his rocker, but he'd have to wait for Amber. Fortunately, she was due to arrive any time now.

He tossed a coaster at the parrots, which sent them squawking up in the air for a few seconds before they

went back to the crackers. *Hopeless,* he thought. Doing
his best to ignore the racket, he went back to the *Tribune.*
He spent most mornings searching it for some mention
of Rosalee's trial, but for the last couple of weeks it
seemed to have dropped out of the national news. The
case was probably still being covered in the California
papers, but he had about as much chance of getting hold
of a copy of the *L.A. Times* in this part of Argentina as
building a snowman.

He had just turned to the financial page and started to
read an article on insider trading when he heard Amber's
plane coming in. Putting down the paper, he polished off
his daiquiri and headed toward the airstrip to meet her.

The plane was a small silver dot against a sky so
bright he immediately regretted stepping off the veranda without his fancy new Panama hat. He walked
slowly toward the airstrip, dripping sweat from every
pore. Planes usually circled once to signal that they were
about to land, but this one was coming in fast with no
preliminaries. Amber must be anxious to see him.

Dale leered at the plane and thought of the great
sack time he'd be having with her during the afternoon
siesta hour. He hoped she'd had brought the fancy underwear they'd bought on Nora's credit card a few days before he "died." Dale had enjoyed the idea of screwing
up Nora's credit as a payback for all the losers Nora
had fixed him up with, but he enjoyed the underwear
more. There was a cupless bra and one particular pair
of pink silk crotchless panties with red ribbons . . .

Dale's mind wandered off into an erotic fantasy. By
the time the plane landed, he was so lost in underwear
that, when the first passengers got out, it took him a
few seconds to realize something was wrong.

Amber was nowhere in sight. Instead, six men were
running toward him. With a start, Dale realized they

were wearing ski masks. For an instant he froze and stared at them in disbelief. What the hell? It was ninety-eight in the shade with a humidity of 95 percent and they were wearing *ski masks?* And carrying—

Guns! They had guns! Dale suddenly realized that this was not a party of friendly bankers who had arrived to convert his American dollars into gold bullion. Giving a scream of terror, he turned and bolted back toward the house where he too had a gun, but he was too slow, too tubby, and too out of shape to outrun six weight-lifting, superbly trained Brazilian *pistoleiros*.

Pistoleiros were men who made their living chasing down prey like Dale and killing them, nosily or quietly as the occasion demanded. In Brazil it was an old profession. Besides *pistoleiro,* there were a dozen words in Brazilian Portuguese for a man who could be hired to kill another man for a price. In some cities in the northeast, there were even open-air markets where they sat at tables wearing mirrored sunglasses, nursing beers, and waiting to be hired. The usual price was two hundred dollars, American, or a little more if the intended victim happened to be in Paraguay or Argentina like Dale. *Pistoleiros* never checked in with immigration, and near Iguazu Falls they moved back and forth across the three borders as silently and swiftly as eels.

Although Dale didn't know any of this, the sight of the men scared the hell out of him. He was so sure he was going to die that, as he stumbled screaming back toward the house, he wet his pants. He heard them drawing closer and closer, and then they were on him like a pack of dogs. Someone kicked his legs out from under him with a brutal boot to the shins, and he was down, groveling in the grass among the fire ants, writhing in pain and expecting to have his head blown off any moment. For a few seconds he just lay there with his eyes pinched shut, expecting to die and hoping it wouldn't hurt too much.

Nothing happened. Confused, Dale turned over and found himself looking up at six men who had pulled off their ski masks and were standing over him, staring at him with nasty grins. One bent down and extended a hand. He had a pocked face and a scar from one ear to the other as if someone had tried to slit his throat.

"Get up," the pock-faced man commanded in a thick accent.

Trembling, Dale took the hand and was pulled roughly to his feet.

"Don't kill me," he begged.

The men laughed. "Nobody gonna kill you," the pock-faced man said. "Bretano Global want you brought home alive, *rapaz*. This your lucky day."

Two hours later, a small plane carrying Dale Lambert landed at a military airport near Buenos Aires. The men inside shoved a handcuffed Dale out of the hatch and took off immediately.

Dale sat on the blazing-hot tarmac in his dirty shorts and began to cry. A group of officials were walking toward him. Five were armed soldiers; two wore the uniforms of the Argentinean police; and three were Americans in dark suits with F.B.I. written all over their faces.

The group paused in front of Dale, and the soldiers aimed their machine guns at him. There was a quick conversation in Spanish between the Americans and the Argentinean cops. Dale continued to sob, but except for the soldiers, who were threatening to riddle him with bullets if he tried to escape, everyone ignored him.

There was an exchange of papers. One of the feds turned to Dale and crouched down so they were at eye level.

"Dale Lambert," he said, "you are being extradited to the United States to face charges of mail fraud, illegal currency trading, embezzling, money laundering, identity theft, tax evasion, and conspiring to frame your wife, Rosalee Lambert, for murder."

24

It was a beautiful February morning, and Nora and Sam were sitting at Nora's kitchen table, eating Sam's famous waffles and watching two emerald-green hummingbirds feeding on the bougainvillea outside the sliding glass doors. Every time one of the birds turned, its feathers trapped a bit of sunlight, transforming it into an iridescent red flash.

"Seriously," Sam said as he slathered more butter on his waffle and topped it off with maple syrup, "what are we going to do with the reward money from Bretano Global?"

"How about taking a vacation somewhere with room service?" Nora reached for the syrup and butter and attacked her own waffles with enthusiasm.

"Sounds like a good idea. Where do you want to go?"

Nora paused with her fork in midair. Her hair hung loosely over the shoulders of her blue kimono, and she looked utterly relaxed. She frowned thoughtfully, and then gave Sam a mischievous smile. "Not Brazil or Argentina."

"Definitely not," Sam agreed. "Iguazu can wait."

"How does a few weeks in Tuscany sound? Italy's the land of your ancestors. Maybe we could track down the origins of your mom's lasagna recipe."

"Tuscany." Sam considered the possibility as he finished one waffle and started in on another. "What's it like?"

"I don't know. I've never been there. But I hear they have great wine, fabulous food, and cute little hill towns." Nora licked a bit of syrup out of the corner of her mouth and grew thoughtful. "Of course that would mean I couldn't wear high heels without getting them caught in the cobblestones. But I could solve that problem by buying a pair of low-heeled Cynthia Rowleys. I've always wanted to own a pair of Rowleys, but they're really expensive."

"Buy three pairs, sweetheart. Live it up."

"Great idea. Three pairs of Rowleys it is." Nora marveled at how much easier it was to get along with Sam these days. Ever since they'd turned Amber over to the cops, they'd hardly fought at all.

She took a sip of coffee, watched the hummingbirds dive in and out of the flowers, and thought about fidelity, betrayal, and love. She'd been betrayed by Jason and Felicity and Amber and seen Dale betray his wife, and yet despite that, she had found the courage to trust Sam. By some miracle, they were able to talk to each other these days in a direct way they had never managed when they were married. At night, lying side by side in bed, or on mornings like this, sitting across from each other at the breakfast table, they shared their feelings, thoughts, and dreams.

In the years they had been apart, Sam had changed. He didn't work all the time the way he used to, and, having promoted Carolyn to comanager of Love Finds a Way, Nora didn't pull such long hours either. As a result they had started to build a life together. A very sweet life.

Nora wanted to believe they could make it work this time, but she still wasn't sure. Would this harmony last or would they start squabbling again? Perhaps they were only getting along so well because everything was going their way. The murder charges against Rosalee had been dismissed; the IRS had decided Nora was innocent of tax fraud; Dale and Amber were about to go on trial—a deeply satisfying fact that made Nora feel extra cheerful every time she thought about it. And, as if all that weren't enough, Bretano Global had promised Sam and Nora a hefty reward—so hefty that trying to decide how to spend it had become one of their main topics of conversation.

Nora put down her coffee cup, carved off a bite of waffle, popped it into her mouth, and decided not to think too hard about the fights she and Sam weren't having. The real issue this morning should be shoes. Should she buy brown ones (practical) or red ones (flashy)? For a while she purchased phantom pairs of fantastic footwear and lined them up in her closet on imaginary shoe racks. Gradually her thoughts returned to Sam.

Maybe the fact that things are going well has nothing to do with catching Amber and Dale, she thought. *Maybe Sam and I are getting along because we've finally grown up.*

Now that was a pleasant thought. She looked at him sitting across from her in a terry cloth robe with his hair and beard flying in all directions, and regretted the years they'd wasted in foolish misunderstandings.

"A penny for your thoughts," he said.

"I was just thinking how wonderful it is to fall in love with your ex-husband all over again," she said. And leaning across the table, she gave him a kiss.

But there were still a few pieces of the puzzle missing, and it wasn't until several days after Amber's and Dale's trials began that everything fell into place.

That morning, Sam had left early to finally begin shooting the documentary on low-riders, financed by the reward money from Bretano Global. The film meant that Nora and Sam weren't going to Tuscany and Nora wasn't buying those three pairs of outrageously expensive shoes, but they had both agreed it was time for Sam to stop doing commercials and work on something he loved.

To be honest, Nora had a few regrets about all those Italian hill towns she wouldn't be tramping though this summer, but they tended to disappear every time she saw how happy and excited Sam was.

By the time she rolled out of bed, he had been gone for hours. Throwing on jeans and a T-shirt, she wandered down to the kitchen and made herself a strawberry protein shake with a couple of eggs and poured herself a cup of strong coffee. Then she went to the refrigerator, pulled out a jar of almonds, and dumped exactly six into the palm of her hand. The almonds and shake were part of a high-protein diet she'd adopted when she finally faced the fact that a girl couldn't keep eating buttered waffles every morning and expect to fit into her pants. It was the first real diet she'd ever been on, and the coffee, which was chock-full of blood-sugar-lowering caffeine, was seriously illegal, but Nora figured the diet police didn't patrol her neighborhood, so she drank it with guilty pleasure.

She was just staring at the last almond, wondering if she should eat it now or hoard it until lunchtime, when she heard someone rap on the glass sliding doors. Startled, she looked up and saw Mr. Jenkins standing on her back deck. Behind him was a young guy with bleached hair and a face like a ferret whom she recognized as his son, Ryan. Ryan was dressed in a white puka bead necklace and baggy paisley swimming trunks that hung down past his knees at one end and threatened to slip off at the other. As always, he had the spaced-out expression and blood-shot eyes of the frequently stoned. No, that was unfair, Nora thought. Maybe he just had allergies.

She popped the last almond into her mouth, washed it down with coffee, and got up to open the door. They'd already seen her, and there was no getting away.

"Good morning," she said with exemplary friendli-ness considering that Jenkins had recently added a flock of plaster penguins to his lawn ornament collection. She wondered where he bought them. Maybe Ryan brought them back from Tijuana on his dope runs. "What's up?"

"Ryan's got something to tell you." Jenkins looked at Nora with uncharacteristic nervousness. She noticed that he was dressed up. Not only was he wearing a long-sleeved white shirt with a few buttons missing and frayed cuffs; he had on a tie. The formal effect was somewhat spoiled by the fact that the rest of his outfit consisted of bright green sweatpants and pink rubber flip-flops. Nora decided that he probably had a mirror that only let him see the top half of his body. Still, what was the occasion? Had someone died? No, not even Jenkins would wear pink flip-flops to a funeral.

"Ryan has something to tell me?" she said, stalling for time so Jenkins could collect himself.

"Yeah." Jenkins turned to Ryan. "Tell her, you low-life, worthless excuse for a son."

Whoa, Nora thought.

"I . . ." Ryan looked at Nora with the oddest expres-sion she had ever seen: part anger, part terror, and part paranoia, combined with a proud foolish grin that made him look like a poster boy for slackers everywhere. He struggled to speak and then appeared to give up.

"Yes?" Nora prompted.

Instead of answering, Ryan produced a white, card-board box of what appeared to be Chinese takeout.

"What's this?"

"Tell her, damn it!" Jenkins snarled.

"For, like, you," Ryan stuttered. "For, like, sorry."

Nora had lived in southern California long enough to delete the word "like" from any sentence as completely as she deleted spam from her e-mail. She accepted the box, which was surprisingly heavy. When she moved it from side to side, it made a sloshing sound.

"What is it? Soup?"

"Open the damn thing," Jenkins snapped. And then he seemed to remember that he'd come over to be polite, because he immediately added a word Nora had never heard him say before. "Please."

Nora opened the lid of the box and peered inside to find five small goldfish in a plastic bag. Suddenly she understood. She wheeled on Ryan. "You poisoned my koi!"

"Koi?" Ryan backed away from her as if she'd gone nuts.

"Koi are fish. You killed my *fish!*"

"Well, yeah," he stuttered. "Like, sort of."

"No 'sort of' about it," Jenkins snapped. "Be a man, Ryan. Speak up."

"I'm only twenty-five," Ryan said, giving his father a hunted-rabbit look. "I'm not ready for the man thing."

Jenkins shoved his face into Ryan's, and for a moment Nora was afraid the two were going to come to blows. "Listen, you worthless leech, at nineteen I was fighting in the rice paddies of Vietnam."

"No, you weren't. Mom told me you were too flat-footed to get into the army."

"Shut up." Jenkins turned back to Nora. "You see what I gotta put up with? He drinks my beer and eats my Ball Park franks. He drives my car, dings it up, and doesn't buy gas. He's got no backbone. His mother spoiled him. Twenty-five: no job, no family, no ambition. He thinks he should be given a goddamn teddy bear and an allowance."

Ordinarily Nora would have been fascinated to learn what went on behind the closed blinds of Jenkins's house, but at the moment she was only interested in the fate of her fish. Or rather, her late fish, the ones she'd buried under the camellia bush because she couldn't bear to throw them in the garbage.

"Why did you do it?" she demanded, glaring at Ryan.

"Uh." Ryan looked at his father, who was also glaring at him and making "go on" motions. Either Ryan found this encouraging, or it terrified him into speech. "I had this girlfriend, Heather, and, like, we lived together, and, like, she read your newspaper column, and, like, she called in to your talk show, and, like, she was a fan, and, like, she cut the laces of my running shoes because you, like, told her to, and, like, she scratched all my coolest CDs and put starch in my underwear, and, like—"

"Shut up!" Jenkins yelled. He turned to Nora. "He can't even talk, so I'll tell you what happened. His live-in girlfriend got mad at him. She tried some of your dirty tricks, gave up, and threw him out on his ass. Did he blame himself? Did he ever think that maybe—just maybe—the woman was sick of supporting a twenty-five-year-old man who cheated on her, kept three skateboards in the living room, and couldn't even hold down a job delivering pizza? No. He blamed you. You were the Queen of Revenge, so Mr. Dimwit here decided to give you a taste of your own medicine, only he did sneaky like he does when he steals my cigarettes. So I made him come over here and confess like a man."

"You did not!" Ryan spoke with unexpected force. Nora was startled, and Jenkins clearly was too. Ryan squared his shoulders and drew himself up to his full height, which couldn't have been much over five six. "I was, like, coming over to, like, confess anyway. Because, like, I've had this spiritual awakening thing, and I wanted to, like, make amends."

"What sort of spiritual awakening?" Nora asked. "Did you find Jesus?"

Ryan shook his head. "N.A."

Nora interpreted this as "nay," a.k.a. "no," which was weirdly archaic but maybe the kid had a secret thing for Shakespeare. "So who did you find then?" Despite being furious about her koi, she was fascinated. "Buddha? Krishna? Mohammed?"

"N.A." Ryan repeated. "You know, like Narcotics Anomalous."

"Anonymous, you idiot!" Jenkins had finally found his tongue. "It's Narcotics Anonymous." He turned to Nora. "You know: A.A. for druggies."

Nora finally got it. Ryan, who had probably been smoking pot since he was old enough to strike a match, had been trying to tell her he had started going to N.A., otherwise known as Narcotics Anonymous. N.A. was a classic twelve-step program for drug addicts. Some of Nora's clients, who had been in it and who were now reliably sober, had told her they had to work on a step where they were required to find everyone they'd harmed, apologize, and make amends. Ryan must be working on his step.

Nora looked at him with more respect. Maybe if she'd had a father like Jenkins, she'd have been tempted to stay stoned twenty-four hours a day. It must take guts to stay sober in that house, not to mention to walk over to your neighbor's and confess that you'd poisoned her fish.

She looked down at the goldfish in the carton, which were small feeders that ran ten-for-a-dollar instead of thirty to seventy-five bucks apiece. Then she looked up at Ryan, who was staring at her nervously. "Thanks," she said.

Ryan relaxed, but she didn't intend to let him enjoy it for long.

"So while we're on the subject of confession, did

you also happen to throw purple dye in my swimming pool on a couple of occasions?"

Ryan winced. "Yeah," he said. "Like, sorry."

"And you let the air out of the tires of my friend's car, right?"

He nodded.

"Put Krazy Glue on his gearshift?"

"Uh-huh."

"Threw a rubber tarantula on his dashboard?"

Ryan looked blank.

"A tarantula's a kind of spider," Nora clarified. "In this case, a rubber spider. That was your work too, right?"

"Right," Ryan said, not meeting her eyes.

"Did you also slash my brake seals?"

Ryan brightened. "No way." He seemed to be relieved to have finally found something he could deny. Nora had been pretty sure the brake seals were either an accident or a good-bye present from Amber, but it never hurt to check.

"How about that wire I tripped over? Did you string it across my yard?"

Ryan's face once again took on a look of abject misery. Nora couldn't help thinking that he looked a lot like a puppy who'd missed the newspaper. "Yeah. Like, I hope you and your boyfriend weren't hurt or anything."

"I could sue you for that. In fact, I might even be able to get you arrested."

Both Ryan and Jenkins looked horrified. "Please—" Jenkins said for the second time in known history, but Nora didn't let him finish.

"But I'm not going to." Their relief was palatable. "If . . ." Father and son tensed up again. ". . . you honestly answer three more questions." She put the carton of goldfish down on the kitchen counter, folded her arms across her chest, and stared at Ryan sternly. "Did you get my auto insurance canceled?"

"Yeah."

"How?

"I, uh, like, used to work as a temp for your, like, insurance company and I kinda of, like, hacked into the computer . . ."

Nora couldn't help being impressed that Ryan could hack into anything. He didn't look like the kind of person who had computer skills. On the other hand, he did look like the kind of kid who had spent most of his teenage years blowing up aliens on a computer screen.

"I, like, gave you a lot of traffic tickets," Ryan concluded. "Like, sorry."

"What else did you do?"

"Nothing."

"If you're lying to me, Ryan, I'm going to see that you do jail time. There's no skateboarding in jail. Am I making myself totally clear here?"

Ryan nodded sheepishly.

"I'm asking you once again: what else did you do?"

"Nothing."

"Think, Ryan. Does the word 'roses' mean anything to you?"

"Like, no." Ryan stared at her with growing panic. "Like, I don't know anything about any roses."

Nora felt she had shown the patience of a saint, but this was too much. "Liar!" she snarled.

Jenkins cleared his throat. "Uh, that was me. I left that note for your yard guys."

Nora wasn't surprised that Jenkins had done it, but she was very surprised he'd admitted it. She stared at him, at a loss for words.

"Yo! This is so wack!" Ryan turned to his father. "Liar, liar, pants on fire!" he mocked. "Hey, Dad, who's the dumb dude now?"

Jenkins ignored Ryan as if he were a small, yipping dog. "I'm sorry," he told Nora. "I'll pay you for the damn things. Look, I know you could sue my ass and get Ryan thrown in jail, but the kid's troubled." Jenkins's face suddenly seemed to collapse in on itself. "I'm getting old. I live on a disability pension. I got a heart condition."

"Like, he doesn't have a heart," Ryan cried gleefully. "Like, they cut him open and looked inside, and it was, like, all empty."

Nora looked at the old man who clearly loved his son despite everything, and the son who clearly hated him. She felt a sudden sorrow for both of them that erased her anger. No revenge she'd ever imagined could possibly be worse than their family life.

"Forget it," she said gently. "I'm not going to sue you or have either one of you arrested, and you don't have to pay me for the damage. It's all okay."

"Okay?" Jenkins looked stunned. He couldn't understand, but why should he? There probably hadn't been many people in his life willing to cut him any slack.

"I'm saying that I'm willing to forget that any of this ever happened."

"But don't you want *anything?*"

"All I want is for the three of us to try to live next door to each other in peace."

"No money?"

"Not a cent."

"You gotta want something. Everybody wants something."

Nora suddenly realized that there was indeed something she wanted, and that if she didn't ask now, she'd never get it. "Your lawn ornaments," she said. "Could you . . . ?"

Jenkins gave her the saddest look she'd ever been given. "Get rid of them? Yeah, I could."

Nora saw that he loved those ugly ornaments, loved them more, perhaps, than he loved his own son. She couldn't bear to finish that sentence, so she changed it;

and that was the moment she gave up revenge, finally and forever. *Life is too short for paybacks,* she thought. *They're bad karma. I should have realized that long ago, but I've always had to learn things the hard way. In the future, I'm going to try to be a woman who doesn't hold grudges, a woman who does her best to forgive everyone, even if they don't deserve forgiveness.*

"No, not get rid of the ornaments," she said. "Repaint them. Mickey's ears are peeling, and the Seven Dwarfs need new pants."

"Paint them?" Jenkins said with a grateful smile. "Sure. I'll get right on it."

"Also, I can't help noticing that the flamingos' Hawaiian shirts are getting a little threadbare. Did you know you can buy them new ones in the children's department at Sears?"

Jenkins looked at her as if she had just handed him his life back. "Great. Thanks for the tip."

"And one more thing: I think it's time we knew each other's first names. Mine's Nora. And yours is . . . ?"

"Otto," Jenkins said. He stuck out his hand. "Howdy."

Nora took his hand and shook it. "Howdy, Otto," she said.

She talked to Otto and Ryan for a few more minutes, then said good-bye and closed the door. After they left, she went to the front window and looked at the ugly statues that were going to be part of her view for as long as she owned this house.

She stared at Mickey's peeling ears and the penguins' plastic beaks, then gave a small sigh and pulled the drapes. Being a good neighbor wasn't easy, but you had to start somewhere.

25

Loose ends

On the day Dale Lambert was sentenced, the media was full of stories about corporate corruption, money laundering, and rich people who were cheating on their taxes. Two days earlier the stock market had taken another bad plunge due to reports of illegal currency trading, a man in Ohio had tried to frame his wife for murder; and only a week before that, there had been a spectacular shoot-out between a millionaire drug dealer's army of *pistoleiros* and the Argentine military near Iguazu Falls. Add to all this the fact that the judge was in a foul mood, and the result was predictable: Dale got twenty-two years in federal prison.

Not long afterward, Amber got ten years for aiding and abetting him. Then, thanks to a hole in the ceiling of the storage unit that supported two charges of attempted murder, she got two additional consecutive life sentences.

Long before Amber and Dale started eating prison food, Felicity and Jason's baby had been born. It had been a girl but, since Jason and Felicity hadn't sent Nora an announcement and since none of Nora's friends told her, Nora didn't find out about the child until much later.

By the time Nora learned there was one more Messier in the world, she had gone out of the revenge business, shut down Payback Time, and was far too busy and happy to begrudge Jason and Felicity whatever married bliss they could manage. In fact, on the rare occasions when she thought of them, she was tempted to send them a thank-you note. After all, if they hadn't betrayed her, she might never have gotten back together with Sam. Worse yet, she might actually be married to Jason.

Instead, that summer, she married Sam again. This time, they didn't run off to Nevada in blue jeans, and Nora didn't buy an expensive wedding dress or hire a caterer to sculpt ice swans. She and Sam simply invited her parents, Aldo and Lucia, Caroline, and a few other close friends to join them in Nora's backyard for a simple ceremony. It was July and the new rosebushes along the driveway were in full bloom. The roses were Sam's wedding gift to Nora. Nora's wedding gifts to Sam were a gold ring to replace the silver one he'd chucked in the ocean when they split up, a promise to try not to fight with him, and, of course, her heart.

Nora had learned an important lesson in the past year, one she treasured. Even before Jason dumped her at the altar, she had known that, no matter how many computer programs and psychological profiles told you a man was right for you, you could never be absolutely sure he'd love you and you'd love him. Now she knew the other half of the equation: that you could love someone passionately for years, perhaps even forever, without knowing why. She often thought that no computer in the world would have matched her and Sam, and yet they were very happy together.

"I'm offering a new service," she told clients who came to Love Finds a Way. "I'm calling it the 'Cupid's Arrow Option.' It works like this: I fix you up with ten people chosen at random from our database. Cupid's arrows were random. One of them might strike you. Interested?"

Most people looked at Nora as if she were out of her mind. After all, what were they paying a matchmaker for if not to supply them with a perfect match? But some took her up on the offer.

"Love," one single woman told her, "is a gamble. Let's roll the dice."

Nora, who couldn't have said it better herself, adopted this as the motto of the Cupid's Arrow Division of Love Finds a Way, and gradually this part of the business began to show a modest profit and even grew popular, although it always remained small.

Acknowledgments

I would like to thank the Virginia Center for the Creative Arts for awarding me a fellowship that allowed me three peaceful, distraction-free weeks to work on *Payback Time* during the spring of 2002. I would also like to thank novelist Sheldon Greene, who read every draft; novelist and short-story-writer Janice Eidus for her invaluable editorial suggestions; filmmaker Renée De Palma for her superb observations about life in Los Angeles; attorney Marilee Marshall for tips on how the legal system works; the Southern California Conference of the Well for helping me track down information on birds, weather, pack rats, and a whole host of other things I never could have found in any other region of cyberspace, and Angus Wright for his continuing understanding, support, and love.

Without the generosity of these people and many others, this novel would not have been what it is. Any mistakes or inaccuraces that remain are entirely my own.